RUSTLERS AND WIDOWS

THE SETTLERS
BOOK ONE

REG QUIST

CKN Christian Publishing
An Imprint of Wolfpack Publishing
9850 S. Maryland Parkway, Suite A-5 #323
Las Vegas, Nevada 89183

cknchristianpublishing.com

Paperback ISBN 978-1-63977-604-7
eBook ISBN 978-1-63977-501-9
LCCN 2022945901

ALSO BY REG QUIST

Novels

The Church at Third and Main

Hamilton Robb

Noah Gates

Terry of the Double C

Just John

Just John: The Complete Journey

Just John

Northward to Home

Reluctant Redemption

Reluctant Redemption: The Complete Series

Reluctant Redemption (Book 1)

A Winding Trail to Justice (Book 2)

Rough Road to Redemption (Book 3)

Mac's Way

Mac's Way: The Complete Series

Mac's Way

Mac's Land

Mac's Law

Danny

The Truth of The Matter (Book 1)

The Truth Through The Storm (Book 2)

RUSTLERS AND WIDOWS

"Well, looky what we got here, Travis. I don't know as I've ever seen such a wearisome sight in all my born days. Scraggly bearded kid, wear'n noth'n but rags. Cast-offs from the poor house, more 'n likely, judging by looks. Ain't hardly got enough meat on his bones to be counted as human. Rid'n a wore-out nag what oughta be put out of its misery. Should oughta be a law against allowing such destitution to be in the presence of us genteel folks. But there he sits on a wore-out saddle, jest a-studying on you and me."

None of that description was accurate, but Rory let it go. For now.

From one of the chairs set along the boardwalk in front of the saloon, Beamer allowed his wandering eyes to scan the kid from top to bottom, with a bully's arrogant grin on his face. From the dusty town road to the crown of his rain-and work-destroyed hat, and then back down again, Beamer's critical eyes judged the young man. Travis, with a blank grin on his face, was doing the same, as if the two of them were in a competition for the title of town fool.

The kid returned the stare, his face expressionless. Beamer grinned more widely and said, "What-sha look'n at kid, jest a-sett'n there? Don't know as how I care for ya staring at me that way."

The kid had ridden up sideways to the hitch rail, his horse's nose almost touching the nose of a big bay gelding tied to the railing. The two animals nudged each other in familiarity. The position put him close to the boardwalk, and the chairs shaded from the early summer sun by the roof of the overhang. And it put him sideways to the men, rather than face to face. After a long pause, the kid answered.

"I'm looking at two cowardly, worthless, murdering thieves, sitting lazy on a sunny morning."

"Whoa up there now. That there's strong talk, kid. You watch your mouth. Talk like that could make me believe you've got evil thoughts in your mind toward me and Travis. I don't care for that at all. I don't know who you think me and Travis might be, but you got the wrong gents."

Being a smarter than average hanger-on, the man sitting in the third chair quietly rose to his feet and stepped out of the line of fire, fearing what was to come.

"No. I got the right murderers. There's no doubt about that at all. I'm Rory Jamison. My father, the man you murdered and stole gold from, was Jacob Jamison. Of course, I don't expect you took any notice of the man's name, nor much cared, for that matter, who he was. A man worth a thousand of the both of you put together. I'm guessing you might not know his name. Nor mine either. No, you didn't take notice of the man working hard at his gold claim back there in Idaho. An honest and hard-working man. A man kneeling by the stream, with his back to you. And his son, that would be me, working alongside him. But it seems right and proper that you know his name before you die.

"There were three of you. Where's your cowardly friend? The one with the half-strangled voice. The one that hid in the bushes behind the tent until your dirty work was about done. The one I watched shooting into that good, old man as the three of you laughed and tore the camp apart looking for our stash of gold."

Rory was talking, telling his story, for the benefit of the listeners standing by. He wanted them to know why he had ridden to their windblown and fly-infested excuse for a town.

"Oh, I know. You thought your first shot at my head had killed me right off. Well, it come pretty near close enough, at that. But I was in no way dead. I was sure enough shot, with my blood staining the creek water red. I couldn't move, or I'd probably be full of lead, just as my father was. Head hurt something fierce, but I managed to hold one eye cracked open, watching you do your dirty work. And I could hear well enough. I been some long weeks nursing myself back to where I can ride and follow a trail. And that trail leads right to this here boardwalk and the two murderers sett'n on it."

Several men and a couple of women, ever curious in a sleepy town where little ever happened, stopped to listen, joining those who were already there. A few heads poked out of adjoining store doorways. Moment by moment, the silent crowd grew.

"But, oh, I surely do remember that day. You tore our camp apart, dumping flour, coffee, and beans out of the cans we stored them in, hoping to find our gold. When you found no more than the cleanup from that morning's panning, you screamed, ran out of the tent and shot Pa again. But you had already killed that honest man, and near enough killed me, and all for maybe twenty dollars in dust and a few small nuggets.

"Now, rightly, it ain't my job, this law-keeping thing, but since neither the county sheriff nor any other law-dog cares to earn his keep, seems I have it to do. I've come to take my piece of rightness from you. And to take back my horses you got tied here, to that railing. Outright stupid of you to keep these stolen horses. Two good rides branded *JJ*. Double J. Jacob Jamison. That was my father's name and that was his brand. With him now murdered and dead, those are my horses."

Several people who had watched and listened as this dialogue went along glanced at the brands on the horses. Grim, accusing faces turned toward the two seated men.

Pierre, Montana, was known far and wide as a rough-and-tumble settlement. A town with little law, and that bit only coming from whatever local sheriff had survived his election. But even in Pierre, back shooting and horse stealing was frowned on.

As Travis and Beamer squirmed uncomfortably in their seats, glancing from the kid to the crowd and back again, Rory asked once more, "Hate to kill just the two of you, knowing your strangle-voiced friend don't deserve to live either, but I guess I'll just have to take what I can get for now. You're both wearing handguns. Can't hardly get them out, sitting in those half-barrel chairs like you are. You might just as well stand up and do your best. You're going to die this morning, but you'd best give it a try. Won't do you no good. But at least these folks will know I didn't shoot you down the way you shot Pa and me down."

Beamer, unable to take more talk, or to accept the

knowing looks of the townsfolk, came boiling up out of his chair with a growl of rage, reaching for the Colt strapped high on his right hip. Travis, always the follower, was just a second or two behind him, coming to his feet. Rory had no weapon in sight except the carbine that was still snuggled down in the scabbard on the right side of the saddle. He slid his hand off the saddle horn and under the left flap of his jacket, and reached for his own cross-draw holstered Colt. The weapon, now securely held in the kid's big, work-hardened hand, was spitting fire and lead almost the instant he had first moved his hand off the horn. The first shot burned through Rory's denim jacket before burrowing its way into Beamer's chest. The kid's second shot took Travis at the base of his nose. Travis was smashed backward, his gun still in his hand and his head hitting the saloon window, breaking it and showering anyone close by with shattered glass. Beamer was down but still alive.

A roaring shout arose from the interior of the saloon and a man wearing a star on his shirt burst through the swinging doors, holding a six-shooter before him. His growling shout and the rasping words, "What's going on here?" told Rory that this was the third man. As the sheriff turned toward him, Rory could see clearly that this was the man who had hidden in the bush, back at the gold camp. The man he had watched shooting into his already dead father.

Rory squeezed the trigger again, missing the quickly moving lawman. A shot from the sheriff stung across the knuckles of Rory's gun hand, missing bone but tearing off a strip of skin. Blood welled up and flowed like a fountain. He dropped the Colt and was reaching for the carbine when the seriously wounded Beamer managed to get off another shot. That lead took the faithful blood-red bay Double J Ranch gelding in the side of the head, killing him instantly. As the horse dropped to the road, Rory kicked his feet from the stirrups and swung his legs wide, straddling the dead animal, lifting the carbine from its scabbard as he dropped. The soles of his boots were now firmly planted in the dust of the road.

Rory took a two-hand grip on the carbine, holding it hip high, ready for whatever might need doing. The sheriff had gotten off one more shot which whined off harmlessly into the air. Rory swung the carbine and squeezed the trigger, knocking the sheriff off his feet but not killing him. Fearing another shot from Beamer, who was still moving, Rory swung the carbine that direction and, firmly holding the carbine hip high, drove two shots into the man's chest, literally nailing him to the space where the boardwalk met the outside wall of the saloon. As the sheriff was rolling onto his side to bring his Colt back into line, Rory ended the matter with two more .44-40 slugs.

A bare ten seconds had gone past since the shooting began.

The powder smoke cleared, drifting off in the constant wind. The echo of shots quieted down. The street fell into silence. Men who had ducked away in fright slowly reemerged from their quickly chosen shelters. Rory never took his eyes off his three foes until someone stepped forward and looked down at the men.

"Well, son, I'm guessing you done what you came to town to do. And a good job you made of it too. But now I'm thinking you'd best take those two JJ horses and get yourself down the road to somewhere else. Might be best if we didn't see you around here again. We're live-and-let-live folks here in Pierre, but even so, you just might have worn out your welcome for this one day. We kind of like a quiet town, if you catch my drift. With you taking up residence somewhere down the line, I expect that quiet might return."

Without a word, Rory bent and picked up his Colt, reloading it with his left hand while he kept his eyes on the man who was speaking, and then snugging it back into the cross-draw holster. His right hand was covered in blood, big drops dripping from the ends of his fingers. Blood was running down the stock of the carbine and gathering around the trigger.

Ignoring the blood, Rory took the carbine in his left hand while he reached across the dead bay gelding, untying his bedroll and saddlebags. He then pulled the tie strings on the carbine scabbard. He stepped to the closest, saddled JJ horse and tied the gear in place, keeping his eyes on the men gathered about. He checked the cinch and loosed the reins of both animals from the hitch rail. Stepping aboard, he said to no one in particular, "There's a fine saddle on that bay. He was a good horse and a faithful companion, doing an honest day's work. If someone will drag him out of town, showing him the respect he deserves, the saddle is yours as payment. Sorry about your sheriff. Might be best if you were to choose a better man next time."

He turned away from the hitch rail and, leading the loose horse beside him, trotted just a short distance. He had scouted the place before confronting the murderers. A filth-strewn alley ran between two buildings. Rory turned the horses into the space, his shoulders feeling tension and his ears listening for the cocking of a weapon, fearing that as soon as his back was turned, someone in the crowd might decide to become a hero. At the back of the buildings, he turned south, out of town, raising the horses into a distance-eating lope. One mile south, he picked up the lightly tethered packhorse he had left there an hour before.

Rory Jamison had celebrated his eighteenth birthday, sitting alone and lonely on the trail, by a small coffee fire, just three weeks before.

2

As his horse plodded slowly south, toward the Double J and home, leaving Pierre Montana far behind, the events of the past many weeks were amazingly clear in his mind, considering the groove in his skull the bullet had left. And the fearful headaches that troubled him from time to time as a result.

Just a few days before, the murderers' trail had become clear. The noose was tightening. Rory had been following that sometimes dim trail, asking questions, risking deadly exposure, for the past hundreds of miles of his travels. And then it had all come to a head on the dusty street of Pierre. Justice, he refused to think of it as revenge, had been done. Justice the law should have dealt with but didn't.

It had begun, of course, with the raid on their small gold camp, where Rory's father had been murdered and

Rory himself had been grazed by a lead slug and left for dead.

The young man was several long weeks in recovery. He was a full day lying on the shallow bank of the gold stream before he could push himself to his knees and crawl into the tent. The river had supplied all the water a man could want, but now he needed food. In a tin beside the small sheet iron stove, he found some dried and molding biscuits. Ignoring the mold, he broke them into small pieces and held them, piece by piece, in his mouth until they softened. They tasted terrible, but they would provide nourishment of a sort anyway. He wished he could find the tin of molasses to use as a sweetening dip, but it was somewhere in the debris littering the floor of the tent. He choked down enough dried-out biscuits to satisfy, for the moment, and crawled to his bunk.

Another night and most of a day went past before Rory could balance himself and stand. Even then, the pain in his head came near to being unbearable. The bleeding began again. He didn't have the strength to tear a towel into pieces, so he wrapped the whole thing around his wounded head. It was only then that he noticed his bedding was red and ruined with blood. The temptation was to simply lie back down and let it all go. He didn't know how much blood a man could dribble onto the ground and still live, but he feared he might be close to the losing point. But his father still lay on the riverbank, dead, with at least five or six bullets in him. His head was still bobbing in the rippling stream. Rory had to do something. He couldn't leave him that way.

He took a few steps before he sank again to his knees. Pushing the pain aside as best he could, he crawled to the river. There he collapsed and wept, with his arm laying over his father's shoulder.

Somehow, although his memory was faded—he remembered the pain more than his actions—Rory had dragged his father's body away from the river and into the trees and brush. Judging his position to be well above the spring flood line of the river, he began to scoop out a grave. He wasn't strong enough to wield the heavy pick they had used in digging for gold, but he could manage the shovel. Night was full upon the forest before the last of the dirt was pushed into the grave and leveled down. In the morning, he would drag up enough rocks to protect the grave from predators. But for now, he needed sleep and food. There were three biscuits left in the tin. He would make them do for one more night. But he needed coffee. His father was a man who valued being prepared and had taught Rory to follow that route. Beside the sheet iron stove was a wooden box that had held blasting powder at one time, but now held kindling and a few larger pieces of wood. It would make enough fire for coffee.

Before he lay down again, Rory emptied his pockets of the things stripped from his father's body and clothing. The most precious item in his father's small accumulation was the tintype photo of the small family—father, mother, Rory, and a younger sister, just a baby. It had been taken in the flower garden on their small ranch home by a traveling photo-taking man.

Rory fingered his father's pocketknife fondly before setting it on the small table beside the photo. The rest of the accumulation didn't amount to much. A few coins, a folded piece of soiled paper where the weights of the gather from the digging and panning were kept daily. And for some unknown reason, a mystery that brought the first smile to Rory's face since the shooting, a button. Rory fondled the button and thought, *Never believed in throwing anything away. Might not know where he put an item, but for sure, he hadn't thrown it away.*

As the days dragged on, Rory slept, ate what was left in the larder and then, fortunately, was able to bring down a nice doe deer that came to the stream for water. He had given up on the search for gold, although the stream had proven its worth for the past two summers, and the early part of the current year. Rory had neither the heart nor the strength to search any further, to dig out the old streambed, or spend the hours panning out the sand and gravel from the digging. He was done. He wanted only to get out. To regain his strength and ride out. To home? Well, perhaps. His father had not sold the ranch or the herd, preferring instead to partner with his brother. The ranch, the Double J Ranch that would now be Rory's, or at least the half, might feel like home if he gave it a try.

But there were questions. Would he be welcomed by a family that didn't really know him? Did he want to be a cattleman? He didn't know. He really only knew he no longer wanted to live alone in a tent digging for gold in upper Idaho. He wanted to retrieve the well-hidden stash from their partial summer's digging, load up his two horses, and head out. The large deposit in the Boise bank from the previous two years' digging was safe enough where it was. He could deal with that later.

He loaded the canvas sacks he and his father had sewn during quiet evenings into the larger canvas pannier prepared for that purpose. He would then wrap the pannier inside his bedroll, hoping to disguise it somewhat, although it would make a lumpy package. Anyone paying close attention would be suspicious, but he would deal with that problem when it arose. If anyone challenged him for what was his, he would have an answer.

He had always been good with his hands. His father gifted him with a strong body, and after the years of digging for gold, his hands were the equal of any man. He had also always been good with a gun. And the one thing he had not forgotten while his head healed enough to allow for travel was the practice of drawing and shooting. Not wishing to attract attention from other miners up and down the river, he had not actually fired the weapon. But he knew that wouldn't be an issue if the occasion arose.

While he was resting and recovering, he had removed the holster from his father's gun belt. Carefully, he worked two holes into the leather with a nail left from the few they had brought to the claim. Although the tent was held together with rawhide strips tied around spruce sapling poles, the table, a couple of stools, and the cot frames were made of sawn wood. A small sack of nails had made their construction easier.

Smiling to himself, Rory remembered his father saying, *We're going to be here for a while son, we need to have a few comforts.*

Choosing the position carefully, Rory worked the nail through his own gun belt, leaving two holes on the left of the buckle to match the holes in the holster. Satisfied that the position of the holster would place his father's .44 for a fast cross draw with his right hand, Rory cut the nails to length and hammered them into rivets that would secure it all in place. Carrying two guns would be a load if he was walking, but on horseback, it wouldn't make any significant difference. And it would serve his purpose well, he hoped.

Although Rory didn't sense it at the time, the attack

on their camp and the murder of his father had turned him from a smiling and sometimes almost flippant seventeen-year-old into a serious and determined man, fully able and prepared to face whatever came his way. Whether he had the wisdom to go with the determination was yet to be proven.

He would saddle up in the morning. There was nothing left to do at the camp but load the horses. If he was challenged, he would find out if he could handle a carbine or a holstered .44 as well as he believed he could.

The gold had been dug out of the jumble of rocks he and his father had carefully hidden it in. Nearly thirty pounds of gold, a mix of nuggets and dust, all carefully tied in small canvas bags. The bedroll he wrapped it into was made from his father's blankets, carefully washed in the river. His own blood-stained bedding had been burned.

He would leave the tent and fixings. There was still gold to be retrieved from the sandy bottom of the river, as well as from the old streambed that wound its crooked path along the shoreline. It was still a good claim. If someone came along and wanted to take it over, that was fine with him. He had no intentions of coming back. He would leave a note for anyone happening along.

He was tying up the last of the load on his father's horse. His own was saddled and ready. He'd said his goodbyes at his father's grave. Rummaging through the tent one last time assured him there was nothing missed worth the taking. Most of the cooking utensils were to be left behind, but the coffee pot and one pan for frying, boiling, dipping water, or whatever other chore might arise, were in the canvas pannier.

The sound of men talking, and a wagon passing on the rough trail a dozen yards above the camp sent him into hiding. It was too late to move the horses and the white tent was easily seen from the trail. There was nothing he could do about that. But this was his third summer on the diggings. He knew every corner. Every nook and cranny. Every possible hiding space in the bush and among the rocks. He chose the one closest, a steep-sided, high bank, fifty feet downstream, covered with a solid growth of bush and riverside shrubbery. Holding his carbine in his hand, he waited.

"Whoa there, team. Merkle", the man shouted, "That's Jamison's tent down there and two saddled horses. Might be someone riding out wants to join up with us. How about you check that out."

Following a crashing through the bush by someone who hadn't bothered to notice the trail down to the claim site, a voice called out, "Hello the camp! Merkle here. And Proder. Couple of others. From upstream claims. Heading out. Room for one more to ride along if these saddled horses mean you're of that intention. Don't rightly remember your name, but we met just the once. Time's-a-wast'n. Make yourself known or we'll get on our way."

Rory remembered the man. Yes, Merkle was the name. He had come to the camp once. Visited. Had coffee and hadn't been seen since. Gold seekers weren't much on sharing information about their claims. There was little visiting along the stream. Cautiously, Rory had stepped into view. His carbine was held at arm's length, pointed to the ground.

"I remember you. Visited once last year. Perhaps it was the year before. Rory Jamison. I'd join up with you if the invitation holds."

"It holds. Get a move on, though. She's a long trail to Boise, and we plan to make it with as few night stops as possible. No time to waste around. We want to get there, get our supplies, and get back for as many more weeks of digging as this unpredictable country allows, before winter closes us in."

Keeping his eye ever on Merkle, Rory walked to his horse. He checked the cinch one more time and then felt the tie-down ropes on the bundle his father's saddle carried on the packhorse. He had left the packsaddle behind, figuring the valuable riding saddle would be of more benefit when he reached the outside. He swung aboard as Merkle turned and headed back toward the bush.

"Trail over here a bit. No need to blaze out a new one."

Merkle looked where Rory was pointing and headed that way. At the wagon, Merkle introduced the men.

Pointing, he said, "That's Proder on the wagon. Gunner and Handley."

Rory nodded without offering to shake.

Merkle asked, "What happened to your father? He not with you?"

"He's here. Right down there in that bush. Covered over with dirt and rocks."

The words shocked the other men. After a few moments of stunned silence, Merkle asked, "What happened? He have an accident?"

"It was no accident. He was bushwhacked. Shot in the back while he was panning the stream. Shot me, too, but I lived through it."

"Tell us about it, son."

"Not much I can tell you. Three men. Thieves, I'm guessing. Shot us both with no warning and no words. Tore the camp apart looking for gold. Only found that morning's cleanup. Rode off and I haven't seen them since. I was hurt pretty bad. It took a while to get any strength back, else I'd be long gone by now."

Merkle looked around at the other men before he spoke.

"Must be the same group that knocked over those two camps to the north of us. Sounds like them anyhow."

Being of a practical nature and wishing to get back on the trail south, Proder asked, "You hoping to come back? What about the tent and what all?"

"I'll not be coming back. Anyone comes along is welcome to the tent and the fixings. Left a note to that effect. I'm ready just as soon as you fellas are."

Proder's answer was a flip of the reins onto the backs of the team and a loud, "Hi-up you horses. Pull it up." The rattle of the wagon put a stop to any more inquiry.

The first day's travel was rough going on the poorly hacked-out bush-trail, with the iron-rimmed wagon wheels climbing over stumps left from the quick clearing job and constantly hitting embedded rocks. The camp that night was quiet as the tired men got their suppers put together, extinguished the fire before darkness settled in, and were soon in their bedrolls after setting the night guard rotation.

The trail improved as they moved south, avoiding the few thrown-together gold camp towns along the way. None of them wished to be noticed or be questioned. That they all had gold in their packs or secreted in the wagon was a solid probability. There was no discussion on the matter. But to enter a town along the way was to be noted by someone. They had enough supplies to see them to Boise, and there was nothing to be gained by drawing attention to themselves.

Being unaware of the growth in the gold fields, Rory knew nothing at all about the gold camps they passed.

He inquired, without naming out any one man, "Could you get your supplies at one of these camps? Might be a store in any one of them."

Proder answered, "Oh, there's stores enough alright. But for what they're charging, we can afford the extra time to go to Boise." He didn't mention a bank, but Rory thought that was the true reason for taking the long trail.

Midmorning on the third day of travel, four riders approached in a rush out of a small side trail into the bush. Without warning, one grabbed the halter of the nearside horse and pulled the team to a halt. Proder hollered out, but the man held firm. His three partners pulled up a few feet away with drawn guns.

What appeared to be the leader hollered out, "Hold up there and…"

It would never be known what he intended to say. He got out just the first few words before Rory's .44 was out and speaking. The shouting man dropped his gun to the ground, grabbed his belly, and slumped over the saddle before slowly sagging sideways and dropping to the ground. Two more saddles were emptied by Merkle and Handley. The rider who had halted the team spun his horse in a half circle and headed back into the bush. He was never seen again.

In the quiet of the trail, as the slight breeze was carrying the powder smoke away, Merkle and his partners studied Rory. Finally, Gunner, who had so far avoided conversation on the drive south, said, "You're quick on the shoot there, Jamison. And a good thing it is too. Those men weren't here to wish us a safe and happy trip."

Proder stepped on the wagon's brake handle and climbed down. Handley, sounding concerned, said, "We ain't got the time to bury these fellas, Proder. I'd as soon as not get some miles behind us. Leave these for the varmints."

"I got no intention of burying them, but there's little chance we were to be the first for them. Let's see what they've managed to gather up."

Rory sat in his saddle while the other three men went through pockets, saddlebags, and bedrolls. Proder stripped the gun belts and carbines from the men and dropped them into the wagon. He then turned back and loosed the saddles from the three riderless horses, dropping them onto the ground. No one asked, but he said anyway, "Hate to see a horse tied to a saddle and no one around. Poor brute could carry the thing for days.

"We don't want anything to tie us to these men, so we'll keep nothing but those small sacks of dust. Maybe the guns."

The gold sacks were gathered up and distributed evenly among the men. Gunner held out four small canvas sacks to Rory.

"You earned these, young man. Put them in your saddlebag."

"Thanks, Gunner, but you keep them. I'm not going to want anything to remind me of this matter."

The other three studied him with care. Gunner hunched his shoulders and passed one sack to each of the others, keeping one for himself. Each man stepped to the back of the wagon and moved their gear around enough to hide the sacks. Rory figured they had all their gold in the wagon, but he didn't ask, and didn't care.

Proder was back on the wagon seat.

"Let's get on down the trail here, fellas. 'Hi-up you horses, let's get 'er movin'.'"

3

THREE DAYS LATER, THE WAGON LED THE WAY INTO BOISE, with the four riders divided, two to each side. The first stop was the bank.

Proder pulled the wagon as close to the front of the bank as possible and set the wheel brake. Stiffly, he stepped to the ground and hunched his shoulders, swinging his arms through the air to get some movement back into them.

Without a word, the men tied their horses to the hitch rail. They stepped down and went directly to the wagon. Rory, his jacket removed on the warm afternoon, his dual pistols in plain sight, and his carbine hanging from his hand, was standing on the boardwalk keeping watch, a position he assigned to himself. His four riding mates dug out their stash of canvas bags. Rory would need a few minutes to retrieve his own when his turn came.

The men went directly into the bank, each man carrying several small sacks. Rory remained where he was, watching. In less than one-half-hour, the men were back.

"You not banking, Rory?"

"I figure to, but I need to spread out my bedroll. I was hoping we could lower the wagon tailgate for just a few minutes."

Proder pulled a couple of latch pins and lowered the boards to a level position, like a worktable. Rory lifted his bedroll down and spread it on the boards. The men stood in wonder as their young partner opened the canvas pannier and pulled out sack after sack, far more than any of them had managed to accumulate.

Gunner pulled in close to cover off the sight line for any curious onlooker.

"That's a sizable stash there, Rory. Good for you."

"Over half of this was the work of my father."

"Not much to say about that we ain't already said. It's yours now. Keep it in good health and happiness, young man."

Rory gathered several sacks into his hands, seeing well enough that he couldn't get it all in one trip. Gunner picked up three sacks while Merkle and Handley picked up the others. Together they walked into the small bank. A teller led Rory into a back room, as he had done for the others. Gunner, Merkle, and Handley followed, laying their sacks on the counting table.

"We'll be next door wetting our throats, Rory. Come join us when you're done here."

When the men were gone and the door closed, the clerk poured the contents of the sacks, one by one, into a weighing dish. He then weighed it carefully, gesturing for Rory to confirm the weights, and marked it clearly in a book, on a page with Rory's name at the top. When he completed the weighing and the calculating of weights to dollars, he looked at Rory and said, "This is a lot of money, young man. Too much to be traveling the country with. What do you want me to do? I can count out the cash for you if you wish, or whatever you want."

"I want some traveling money. Gold coin in small values and some bills I can hide away. I'm thinking three hundred dollars in all. The rest I want added to the account that's already in my name, mine and my father's."

"Right you are. Just let me get a deposit form and we'll be finished up here in no time at all."

While the man was doing the writing up, Rory told him briefly about his father. It wasn't something he cared to discuss, but he didn't want any problems with the account.

The clerk stopped writing long enough to look up, listening carefully. When Rory was done, the clerk said, "That's a terrible, shameful act. You have my sympathy. It doesn't really make a difference on the account, though. Either of you could sign so we can leave it as it is."

～

BACK ON THE STREET, Rory remembered the invite to the saloon. But first, he asked another rider who was just tying up his horse, "Any idea where there's a stable?"

With that information received, Rory took both animals and stalled them, carrying his saddles into the tack room and asking for the shoes to be checked over. The hostler moved in to brush down the animals after ladling out a liberal feed of corn for each one.

Rory came from the tack room with his bedroll over his shoulder.

"Can you direct me to a laundry?"

"No need to. Just lay your wash over your saddle in

there. Laundry runner comes by here often enough. He'll take whatever you leave out for him and bring it back when it's done."

Rory walked over to the saloon to join his fellow travelers.

"Step up here, Rory. I'll buy you the first round."

"Thanks for that offer, Gunner. But I have to be honest, I don't want or need a drink."

He smiled to cut off any hurt feeling from turning down the offer before he said, "But if you all wanted to join me for a meal, it would be my treat. I appreciate you letting me ride along on the trail down country. The hotel just along the street a piece has a dining room."

Gunner responded, "Well, I've had my drink and a couple more besides, and I'm ready for a bath, haircut, some new clothes, and a good meal. Looks like the meal might be first. Come on, you gold diggers, Rory's buying supper."

Before Rory turned back to the door, he called the bartender over.

"Looking for three fellas. Might have been through this way in recent weeks, maybe a month or two ago. One was tall and whisper-thin. One was tall but heavier. One had a raspy voice, as if he had been partly strangled at one time. Rough-looking fellas. Do you remember seeing the likes of that?"

The bartender gave him a serious look before calling over another barman. He nodded at the new man and spoke to Rory.

"Tell Sarge here who you're looking for."

Sarge wore an off-white shirt with the top three buttons open and the sleeves rolled up as far as possible on his thick, muscular arms. His face held no smile. Rory, not feeling as intimidated as the barman might have expected, repeated his question and description.

The two men behind the bar listened and then stood in silence, studying Rory. What they thought they saw was a young man not dry behind the ears yet. A misjudgment like that could lead to all kinds of complications, but Rory had no intention of causing trouble, so the moment passed.

"Tex, Easly, Griz. Griz, he's the one with the growl. You want some advice? Free, but valuable just the same. You let it go, whatever it is. It ain't worth the misery of finding them."

"I thank you for your concern, sir. But I still wish to find them."

Again, the men all waited. Rory's partners were now taking an interest.

Sarge studied Rory before he said, "Look, fella. I shouldn't care. And maybe I don't. Young fella like you. Too young to be in my saloon at all. Really should throw you out. Tell you to go home. Speak proper, like maybe you had a good upbringing. You'd stand just no chance at all against those men. You really don't want to find them. You hear me now?"

"You're a better man than you give yourself credit for, Sarge. And thanks for the advice. But my goal won't change. Whatever you tell me won't go any further than just us. If you don't tell me, someone else is bound to."

MONTANA, Rory said to himself for maybe the hundredth time. *Claimed to have a ranch over that way. Called it home. Easly alleged to have a wife, or at least a woman, waiting. Planned on wintering over that way.*

Montana is a big place but maybe not really. It's one thing to be big on a map, it's another altogether to be big in the settled areas. Rory didn't figure the murderers would be satisfied wintering on the open prairie, spending their days till spring watching the windblown snow build drifts in the yard. No, they would want a town, people, liquor, women, and activity. He would look in the towns, asking questions along the way, not caring if anyone repeated his questions or talked about his search. He wasn't hiding his intent.

The long, lonely ride through eastern Idaho and into Montana, skirting the worst of the mountains, took him to Bozeman while there was still considerable summer left in the open country, although the nights were cooling in that mountainous, northern clime.

Inquiry with the hostler as he was stalling his two horses in Bozeman provided the information, reluctantly shared, that Rory should maybe ride down Pierre way.

"Heard something a while ago." was all the man would say.

The suggestion had led him right.

4

So now, with it all behind him, waiting for his coffee to boil while a roughly cut-out piece of deer meat broiled on a green stick hanging over the small fire, Rory tried to relax. It was over. There were three new graves being dug back up the trail.

Justice. Never revenge. Justice. He had assured himself of that several times.

His father's murder, his own near death, the fight on the trail to Boise, the long ride to Montana, the fight at Pierre. Over. It was all over. His father could rest easy, knowing the son did what the law refused, or couldn't do. He had balanced the scales.

It had been a major disappointment to the young man to have the sheriff at Bozeman tell him to go home and forget it. It wasn't as if the man was simply the town marshal, he was county. He had the authority, and, in Rory's eyes, the responsibility to ride to Pierre. At least check it out. Ask some questions. Perhaps write to the authorities in Boise. Something. Certainly, being sheriff meant more than sitting on a half-barrel chair in front of the small jailhouse.

That Rory, in his frustration, had suggested that the man was more concerned about his own skin than his job, was perhaps not wise or particularly diplomatic. But young men, full of zeal and self-righteousness, and with a solid belief in how things should be, could sometimes misjudge. That didn't necessarily make them wrong. But it did make them out to be unwise.

The world is not a perfect place. To lay perfection as the goal, even on a brave man, might be aiming a bit too high. Rory would bank that experience against days to come when wisdom would again be required.

It went against everything Jacob had taught his son, to take matters into his own hands when there was a choice. To protect himself on the trail down to Boise, when any questionable law was days away, appeared to be a natural and right thing to Rory. To have the law available but of no use was another matter. As he rode from Bozeman, heading south, he knew he had to do it. If he quit or ran away, he would forever live with that truth. That didn't appeal to him at all.

With all of that behind him, he knew he had changed. Had he changed in a good way? He was not so sure.

Did he really want to go back to the ranch his parents had started years ago? His uncle would be firmly in charge by this time and doing things his way. Would there be a place for Rory?

He had plumb no evidence one way or another. He was, nevertheless, slowly headed south. He now had three JJ horses, too many to take on leads. The two stolen by the murderers and recovered in Pierre had been the pack animals on the initial trip to the gold fields. They were all well-broke geldings and would herd easily. So, staying to a steady, mile-eating walk, or the occasional trot, he herded his horses south.

~

JACOB AND SUSANNAH JAMISON came west bare months before the big war worked its way toward their home, took up a piece of land, and bought a small herd of nondescript cattle. Their two children, the eldest was Rory, a son, and then Peggy, a daughter, were to be their only family. Peggy's birth had been difficult in the extreme. The country doctor back in Tennessee had been army trained and knew little about birthing. He was a bit clumsy, but when faced with the challenging position of the baby, he at least managed to keep both mother and child alive. He was correct when he predicted there would be no more children.

Jacob was a good rancher and cattleman. Even with a herd that would never pass muster in the east, with its heavy breed animals and the ever-growing green grass, he managed to take advantage of the fluctuating market, buying and selling, and growing his herd. He had every intention of importing the eastern breeds he was familiar with, but that would have to wait on the railway. In the meantime, he was slowly, in spite of threats from free-range ranchers, planning the fencing of his claimed land. With fences, he would be able to care for the animals himself. He would rather spend his money on barbedwire than wages for riders. The price of fencing was a one-time cost. The wages for riders would never end.

He had never seen barbwire. So far as he knew, there was none being used in the area. But he had read of it in the newspapers that, from time to time, found their way into his hands. In the meantime, he was digging post-holes and cutting posts and rails from the light forest land a few miles to the west. Even a single rail would control most grown animals, and the calves that ducked under would soon return to their mothers.

The big reason for fencing, in Jacob's mind, was to keep the neighbor's scrub bulls away from his eastern breeding cows. Cows that, up until that time, only existed in his mind and dreams. For that matter, there were few enough bulls, scrub or otherwise, in this lightly settled area. But Jacob liked to be prepared.

Life had gone well for a few years, at least by pioneer standards. The children were growing and healthy. The herd was growing too, and gradually improving, although he had yet to import the bulls he knew he needed to upgrade his stock. Rory was becoming a young man to be proud of. An excellent rider and good with anything he could lay his hands on, whether it was in the blacksmith shop or swinging a catch rope. Or shooting with either the carbine or his handgun.

Both children took readily to the teaching Susannah laid out for them on the kitchen table. The town of Stevensville, Colorado, had no school.

That Rory showed some readiness to saddle up and wander the land was a concern to his father. But no family is perfect. Jacob believed that to have recognized a potential problem was to have already half-solved it. Perhaps he was correct. Time would show soon enough, as Rory reached further into his teen years.

LIFE CHANGED FOREVER when a neighboring family took ill. With the rancher needing help, Susannah had ridden to their assistance on the third day of the illness. The closest doctor was miles away. No one knew the early indications of smallpox.

At first, the child and then her mother were uncomfortable, with aching bodies that failed to respond to any treatment the rancher knew to offer. When Susannah arrived, the patients were showing signs of a combination of fever and chills. Serious suspicions grew when the little girl broke out in a rash that quickly turned to blisters. Shortly after lunch that same day, the girl died. Her mother, already seriously ill, followed within the hour.

Susannah, wanting to help the family over the crises, and not understanding the infectious nature of the disease, stayed to cook dinner for the grieving father and husband. She then removed the bedding the victims had lain on and soaked it in a pot of boiling water, believing that would cleanse it and make it usable again. By the time she arrived back at the JJ Ranch late that evening, she was tired, unusually tired. She blamed it on a busy day and went to bed. A couple of days later, Jacob knew the truth. His wife had smallpox.

Not everyone who comes into contact will pick up the disease, and not everyone who suffers from it will die. But many do. In the case of the neighbor, within two weeks, the entire family were all dead and buried. Only one brave neighbor volunteered to see to the burying. When that unpleasant task was behind him, he lit fire to the house, the barn, and the three outbuildings, in the belief that the disease would linger and the buildings would be unusable.

When Jacob acknowledged that Susannah was ill, he sent both kids to sleep in the loft, keeping a distance from each other. Peggy complained about the cold in the loft on the first night. Rory knew the temperature was fine. When Peggy began shivering, her father brought her back into the house and her own bed.

At Susannah's insistence, Jacob stayed a goodly distance from both her and Peggy, carrying meals no closer than their bedroom doorways and vacating the house himself when one of them had to rise to visit the outdoor facility.

Even with all the cautions practiced, before long, the mother and daughter were lovingly buried in a garden plot Susannah had spent hours cultivating behind the house.

Jacob, for the first time in his life, failed to do the work required of the little ranch. While his father sat or knelt beside the graves, Rory filled in, caring for the animals, knowing what had to be done, having done all of it before.

After three days of mourning, and reasonably certain that he and Rory had escaped the deadly blight, Jacob sat down at the kitchen table and wrote a letter. He told his older brother about the happenings on the Double J Ranch, closing with, "You've talked for years about coming west. Now would be a good time for you to sell out and join Rory and me on the JJ."

Within a month, the brother and his family were standing on the station platform in Cheyenne, looking for information on stagecoaches heading south. At Stevensville, they rented a wagon from the livery and asked for directions. The tobacco-chewing hostler spit on the dirt floor, looked the family over, and said, "You com'n in from the rails like you done, if'n you'd a been look'n of'n to yer east you'd a seen the gate and the sign. Lantern hanging from the cross piece. *JJ Ranch* she says, as if that was something fer a man ta be proud of. And maybe it is, who can tell? Mayhap the most of two to three miles back to the north from town.

"Or you could simply walk across the road there and climb inta that wagon in front of the general mercantile store. Expect Jacob will come along sometime soon. That's his rig. He never spends more time than necessary in town. Not since the bury'n anyway. Course it's costing me a rental fee for tell'n ya that. But then I ain't always been the smartest businessman in town."

He ended that bit of information with a cackle of a chuckle.

A few minutes later, Jacob came from the store with his arms loaded down. When a male voice offered, "Here, let me help you with that." Jacob lowered one arm to be able to see over the package. His startled look caused the owner of the voice to laugh. He was soon joined by the others gathered close around. Jacob leaned over the side of the wagon and dropped the parcels in. Turning around, he said, "George, you rascal, you didn't even tell me you were coming for sure, and here you are."

After shaking hands, he took his older brother by the shoulders. "Let me get a look at you. And here's Eliza. And more welcome faces I've never seen. Now look at these kids. But they're not kids anymore.

"Henry, Thomas, Nancy. Welcome. Welcome to all of you. My, y'all are a sight for weary eyes. Climb aboard. Let's get to the ranch. Rory will be as excited as I am to see you."

With Rory introduced to his aunt, uncle, and the three cousins, and the coffee pot hot on the stove, the visiting began, bringing each other up to date. When the conversation got around to Susannah and Peggy, the voices quieted while Eliza tried gently to express their dismay at the news that came in Jacob's letter.

There was a pause while everyone took an uncomfortable sip of coffee. After a moment, Jacob, looking as if he had forgotten something he should have remembered, said, "Say, I've plumb forgotten Miss Hannah. Right up until this moment. Where's your sister, Nancy? You didn't marry her off already, did you?"

George answered, "No, she's not married off. She's gone away to school. Way up to northern New York State. School for young ladies. Teaches them to be school-teachers and such. Don't understand it myself, but she was bound and determined. So that's where she's at."

"Imagine that." is all Jacob could think to say to the news.

GEORGE and the family settled in on the JJ with the boys, one having recently celebrated his nineteenth birthday and the other at twenty-two years, seeking work on local ranches. A cabin was being planned for Jacob and Rory while the family took over the house. The season was warm, with an early spring. Jacob had buried his wife and daughter amid a snowstorm, but that had long since melted away, leaving greening grass as its gift to the land.

Rory was restless, and Jacob hadn't slept a full night since the deaths of his loved ones. Conversation had almost stopped between father and son as each wept through their loss.

Saddling his favorite horse, Jacob rode the land, thinking, dreaming, plotting. Remembering and planning forward. George was a competent cattleman. He had also brought enough wealth with him from their savings as well as the sale of the Tennessee holdings, that he would be able to build up the JJ in return for a half-ownership. Jacob could ride away, if he wished, knowing the ranch was in good hands.

≈

WITH AS MUCH research as the small town allowed, mostly from talking with the publisher of the weekly paper and studying back issues, Jacob made a decision. To most, his decision would make no sense, but he wasn't asking for advice. He was seeking release from pain and memory. He went first to Rory with his thoughts. They talked long and earnestly as they rode the property. With that done, he called a family council, kids and all. Eliza had outdone herself with the dinner she prepared, finishing it off with a dried apple pie.

The dishes were picked up and stacked on the counter, the fresh coffee pot was laid on the table, ready for whoever wanted a refill. Chairs were pushed back, and all eyes turned to Jacob.

When he finished outlining his plan there was silence, until George asked, "Exactly what do you know about panning for gold, little brother?"

"All I can tell you for sure is that it doesn't involve staying on the JJ. I know that sounds weak. Many men lose their wives in this hard land. But I'm not many men. I'm me. That's all I can tell you. I can't explain my feelings. Talking to Rory, I find that he feels much the same. We're both kind of lost. Aimless, you might even say.

"You will manage the ranch just fine and have a good life here. This is a good country, if hard at times. Rory and I will be back in a year or two. If we find gold, that will be a bonus. Mostly what we want to find is ourselves. Half of me is buried out behind the house.

And beside that half, another big piece of my life, my beautiful Peggy. Rory has lost his mother and sister.

"Call me weak. Call me melancholy. Call me anything you want. But I need a new view on life for a while.

"In many ways, Rory is the stronger of the two of us, but he needs to see the sun come up over a new horizon for a while too."

There was more talk, but within a week, Jacob and Rory were sitting high in their saddles, with two well-loaded packhorses waiting to be driven, heading to Idaho, a land they knew little about.

Now, nearing three years later, Rory was within a few days' ride of the Double J, and he didn't know what the future held for him. What he did know is that the gold fields had been kind to them, at least up until the murder. There was money in the Boise bank. Quite a lot of money when it all was added together. At least he wouldn't have to beg for his food and shelter.

5

Reaching the welcoming gate of the JJ Ranch, Rory's two loose horses, trotting about one hundred yards ahead of him, turned into the driveway with no directions from him.

'Well, looky there, if ever proof was needed that these were JJ horses, that might just about do it. They know their home.'

Although Rory kept to his easy trot on the long driveway, the loose horses picked their pace up until they were in a slow lope. Rory heard a shout of alarm as two men ran out to slow them as the geldings approached. With no hesitation, the animals allowed themselves to be caught. There was much arm waving and talk that Rory couldn't hear, but could surmise, as more people came from the house and yard.

'That's a lot of folks down there. More than just family. Wonder what's going on.'

It was a woman, judging by size and clothing, that first noticed Rory. When she drew the crowd's attention to his approach, all conversation seemed to stop. One of the men who were holding the other horses let an animal loose with a light slap on the rump. The other followed suit, turning to place all their attention on Rory. As the distance reduced with each step of his horse, Rory could identify his uncle, George, and could now see that the woman was his aunt, Eliza. There was no sign of cousins Henry or Thomas. He had no idea who the other men were, but he saw no welcoming smile from any of them. George and Eliza, on the other hand, had gathered closely together and were slowly stepping toward Rory, even as his horse drew him nearer.

George gently took hold of the bridle on Rory's tired gelding, offering a smiling welcome and a firm hand-shake. Rory remained mounted as he returned the welcome and nodded to his aunt Eliza, but he couldn't take his eyes off the three men who were clustered together, seemingly led by the man in a business suit. Two of them wore stars on their vests. One star was imprinted with 'town marshal', the other with 'county sheriff'. The third man wore a too-tight woolen suit and a stiff countenance. He was the perfect image of official-dom, an image that would bring nothing but gloom into any gathering of well-meaning men. That would be his buggy and horse tied off to a nearby fence.

Rory, holding his eyes firmly on the three visitors, said, "Uncle George? What's going on?"

"What's going on, Rory, is that this so-called judge has taken it upon himself to try and impound the JJ, land, and animals all."

"And exactly what gives him any authority to do such as that?"

"It might be interesting if you were to ask him that question."

Rory, still studying the judge, said, "You heard the question." There was a surprising firmness to his voice. Young he might be in age, but not in experience.

The judge puffed himself up, seeking to lend authority to his voice.

"I'll answer to no one. On the contrary, those on this ranch will answer to me."

"And exactly who are you, and where do you come by such authority?"

The judge tried his best to ignore Rory, but the young man was having none of it. He was tired from riding. He was weary from fighting, always seeming to be doing what the law should have been doing. And he wasn't about to accept any challenges to the ranch his parents had worked so hard to build. He nudged his horse two steps closer to the judge, stepped to the ground, and with an open hand and no warning, slapped the man across the cheek. The judge staggered but didn't go down. The marshal tried to step between them, with a shout of objection and protection for his boss, laying his hand on his holstered gun. With a quick glance at the man, and then back at the judge, Rory simply backhanded the marshal across the side of his head. Unlike the judge, who had managed to stay on his feet, the marshal fell to the dust of the driveway, stunned from the impact of the work-hardened knuckles. He lay still, with blood running from his lips and nose, as Rory bent and relieved him of his weapon.

Everyone in the yard fell to silence, until the judge managed to sputter, "I'll have you arrested. I'll have you jailed for assault. Sheriff, arrest this man."

The county sheriff, elected in the adjoining county, who had no jurisdiction on the JJ in any case, said,

"Judge. I believe the young man asked you a perfectly reasonable question. Might be easier to simply answer the question than to go around and around again."

His dignity hammered as badly as the marshal's nose, but seeing the hopelessness of the situation, the judge gathered what remained of his dignity and said, "The county is impounding this ranch and its stock until a full probate can be formed and heard. The original owners are all dead, and it is the business of the government to assure that any heirs are located and compensated. The herds will be sold off and the money deposited under my care until the probate is completed. These people living on the ranch must leave."

Rory was slow responding, casting his eyes from one badge wearer to another before he spoke.

"And exactly who are you two?"

The judge, sensing he had to take control, answered the question.

"This is Mr. Wasson, town marshal, and Mr. Clare, county sheriff from the next county over. But perhaps it is time you told us who you are and exactly how any of this is your business."

The talk was interrupted by a frantic, feminine scream that drew everyone's attention to the big gate adjacent to the barn that led into the pastures. A quick glance showed a group of a half-dozen riders, with two of them now dismounted. One was gripping a young girl by the wrist while the girl's other hand was holding an overly heavy shotgun in the air. As the man pushed the struggling girl against the wooden gate, another scream rent the air, just as a blast from the shotgun overshadowed all other sounds.

Rory leaped back into the saddle and, with a simple

nudge of his heels, had the gelding racing across the half a hundred yards to where the struggle was taking place. All eyes turned toward the sounds of the thundering hoofbeats. Rory, with a single goal in mind, pulled one of his big .44s, reversed his grip, taking the weapon by the barrel, and plunged into the crowd of horses and men. One man on foot tried to dodge out of the way but was unsuccessful. Rory laid him on the ground with a single blow from the heavy pistol. Although it was a firm strike to the side of the head, the heavy felt of the man's hat saved him a broken skull. Turning the gelding, he was on the grappling man in a single step. The man let go of the struggling girl and attempted to protect himself with a raised arm. Rory's first blow hit the man's elbow, breaking bones. With the second blow, the man folded like a broken reed and fell to the ground with blood flowing from his scalp.

He reversed the .44 again, pointing it at the startled riders.

"Whether you ride off this ranch or get hauled out in a wagon is of no never mind to me. Now pick up these two and get out of here. Don't ever come back. Men who would fight with a girl are no men at all. Now get out. You touch a gun, I'll shoot you dead and forget it ever happened."

Slowly, two of the men dismounted and lifted their comrades onto their saddles. Holding the two from falling off, the little band rode toward the ranch road.

Rory turned to the girl

"Might I be guessing that you're Cousin Nancy, mostly grown and fighting for what's yours?"

"If you're Cousin Rory, returned from the gold fields and ready to make war on a moment's notice, then you could call me Cousin Nancy."

"Well, Cousin, put your foot into this stirrup and hang on. We'll go see what more this so-called judge has to say."

Nancy, a pert, saucy, seventeen years old, lifted herself up with Rory's help, hanging onto the cantle with one hand and her shotgun with the other.

Rejoining the group assembled at the gate, Nancy stepped down. While Rory moved his horse a bit out of the way and dropped to the ground, Nancy broke the double-barrel shotgun open and inserted a new shell withdrawn from a pocket of her loose, flaring dress.

Rory took the few steps back to where the stunned judge was still standing. Before he could say anything, George said, "Thanks Rory. I had no idea Nancy had gone to protect the herd from these thieves. I'm not armed and have no horse nearby. Glad you were here. Did you hurt those fellas to where they need medical help?"

"I certainly hope so. I don't know any other way for them to learn how a man treats a lady."

As if there had been no break in the previous conversation, Rory looked back at the two men wearing badges.

"Mr. Clare. Mr. Wasson. Neither of you have one speck of authority in his county or on this ranch. And as for you, Mr. Judge, I'm reading you for a liar and a fraud. Probably a thief. A thief that hires other thieves to come and do his dirty work. Now know this. I'm Rory Jamison, son of Jacob Jamison, he who was murdered by thieves such as yourself. I own fully half of the JJ Ranch. My uncle George, standing right there, owns the other half.

"The three of you have just a half minute to step into your saddles and get off my ranch. And take those brave woman fighters with you."

Into the stunned silence that followed, the town marshal, recovering some bravado, if not true bravery, said, "I've been here this past full year as marshal and I ain't never laid eyes on you before. What makes you think this is your ranch?"

George put his arm around his nephew's shoulder.

"Men, Rory's my nephew and sure enough the owner of the JJ, although I've been half owner these past three years. Now, you've used up the most of your thirty seconds. But if you hurry, you can still get aboard your animals and on your way before the time is up."

With a laugh, the county sheriff said, "Sorry folks, I should have known better than to get mixed up in such as this. The deal stunk from the start, but being it came from a judge and all, it was hard to question the official order to impound. I'll be on my way. Marshal, don't you and the judge bother catching up to me. You carry a smell with you that upsets my stomach."

Silently, with pursed lips, the judge walked to his buggy. The marshal had nothing to say as they rode out of the yard.

The three strangers who had caught and then released the horses now caught up their own animals. Stepping aboard, one said, "You'll be alright now, George. Welcome home, Rory. Don't expect you'll remember me. Hanson, from down the road a piece. Noticed this bunch turning into your lane. Saw no good in it, what with that self-appointed judge included. Thought I'd just ride over and give 'er a look-see. These others came along for the ride.

"I'm truly sorry to hear about your father. I'm guessing we'll hear the full of that story by and by. We'll be getting back to our own work for right now. Nancy, I apologize for not seeing what was going on down by the barn."

As they rode away, George said, "Always have appreciated good neighbors. Now Rory, step down here so's I can give you a welcome, me and your aunt both."

6

WITH THE HUGS AND THE HANDSHAKES BEHIND THEM AND the horses cared for, the family sat around the big kitchen table with Eliza's good cooking laid before them. Rory told the shortened story of the past three years, pausing and choking up a bit with the repeat of the shooting that took his father's life. He made no mention of the justice rendered on the trail to Boise or in Montana.

After listening to Rory's story and considering the happenings of the morning, George chuckled a bit and spoke to the young man.

"I don't know where you got your drive from, Rory. The Jamison side of the family can be a bit easygoing, almost casual sometimes, your father and me, both. I don't see much of that in the short time you've been home. Comes from your mother, I guess. Susannah was a lovely woman. A lady in all respects. And beautiful. I'm supposing you remember that about her, Rory. But when the chips were down, she could be a mama grizzly protecting her cubs. When Susannah voiced her opinion, there was not one soul on the face of the earth that could doubt what she believed. I never saw her really challenged by a stranger, like you were this morning, but I can imagine her acting just about the same. Not altogether wrong, either. You sure set things to rights with that bunch from town."

Rory didn't care to pursue that conversational direction, so he made no response other than to say, "What I remember is her smelling like freshly baked bread and tucking me in at nights and praying with me when I was small."

Nancy, a sassy, very pretty and self-assured seventeen-year-old, grinned and said, "You ain't told us nothing at all about the gold. Did you make yourselves rich, Cousin?"

Eliza chimed in before Rory could answer.

"Nancy, that's not your concern. And such language you use. Why the poorest peasant back east uses the language better than you. I fear all my teaching around this table has gone for naught. Your cousin is going to think we're a bunch of hillbillies."

"Ain't noth'n wrong with bein' a hillbilly, Ma."

When George burst out laughing, the moment was broken. Rory joined in the laughter with just a smile, while Eliza buried her face in her hands and shook her head.

When the room quieted down, Eliza said, "You speak very well, Rory. I'm pleased to hear that."

"My father was a stickler for doing things properly, Aunt Eliza. Whether it was pitching a tent or digging a hole by the creek in search of gold-bearing sand, or reading from one of the books he was forever dragging out. It doesn't seem to have hurt me any."

When the table settled down, Rory asked, "Where are the boys?"

"They've taken up work with a big ranch down southwest a way. I've never been up there. It's mostly mining country further to the south. High country, at least higher than here, but I'm told there's grass valleys and plateaus the ranchers are making use of. Most of a day's ride away, so we don't see them often. Not often enough anyway.

"Your father was a planner, Rory. The way he has this place fenced, the care of the cattle is little trouble. I care for most of it myself. Can't keep Nancy off a horse, though. She insists she could give the animals all the attention they need if I wanted to find something else to do with my time. I've thought about it too. Might be better to keep her busy here on the ranch. No telling what might happen if we were to burden the town with her presence."

Nancy showed her lack of patience with this conversation but said nothing.

Changing the subject, Rory asked, "How has the time been since we left? I haven't heard about cattle prices for three years."

"We've done well. Slowly replacing the original breeding stock with heavier animals. Not what we eventually want, but surely an improvement. Sold all the others off as pregnant cows. Got a better price that way than the beef market allows for older stock. We drove the mature feeders to the rails the past two falls. What we need now is an upgrade in bulls. Like to bring in some of those white-faced animals. Herefords, they're called. But that will have to wait until we have another couple of shipments sent off and paid for."

Nancy could see the gears going around in Rory's

head when her father mentioned the bull upgrade. She figured he wanted to say something but was holding back for some reason. *Probably wants to talk man-to-man with Dad. Such foolishness.*

Eliza said, "What are your plans, Rory? I know you will want to take a few days to sort out your thinking and maybe catch up on your rest. But you need to know we've kept you in our minds and hearts all the while you've been gone. Your place is here when you're ready for it. The cabin was finished and never used. It's all set up for you when you're ready to settle here on the Double J."

There was more discussion, but before long, Rory tired of the talk. His had been a very quiet world on the gold stream. He and his father did little small talk, both being of a more serious personality. But his father was also a teacher by natural giftedness. He never seemed to tire of explaining life and happenings to his son. They had a few good books, first brought with them and, after that, traded in Boise as they wintered there. For the times and circumstances, Rory could be considered as well-read.

7

THE NEXT MORNING, RORY ALLOWED HIS UNCLE TO SHOW him through the various fenced-in pastures, explaining his planning as they rode. Rory was interested, but he couldn't get his mind off the judge and the town marshal. Saying only that he was going to town, he left George at the barn and headed to the town road. He was a quarter mile away when he heard hoofbeats behind him. Looking over his shoulder, he saw Nancy. Her hat hung down her back, suspended by a tie-down string, with her long blond hair floating at will. She bent over the neck of her horse while urging him onward, as if Rory were miles away and she had to rush to catch up. In fact, she caught up in a matter of seconds.

Pulling up beside Rory, she grinned, dragged her hat back onto her head, and teased, "Thought you could get away without me, did you?"

"Never gave it a single thought. Can't see why I would want a girl-child tagging along anyway." He was grinning openly as he said it.

"Girl-child, is it? Well, Mr. Gold Hunter, you're

not hiding out in the Idaho forests now. This is the big settlement. Got a mayor and all. Figured as how you should have a guard riding along with you. Someone to kind of watch out over you. Someone to see that the town girls don't take you prisoner so's they can run their fingers through that long hair of yours."

"That long hair is one reason I'm going to town. I don't suppose the mayor cuts hair, so I'm hoping there's a barber. And perhaps somewhere I might be able to buy some new clothes. Everything I own is pretty much worn out, even my boots."

"Your guns and belt appear to be in pretty good condition. Not sure I ever before saw a gun rig quite like yours. Were conditions that doubtful up in the mountains?"

"Just pays to be cautions, is all."

They rode along quietly for a while and then Rory asked about the situation in the town. Who was the mayor? Who had real control, if not the mayor? Was there a lawyer besides the would-be judge? Who seemed to control the marshal?

Nancy answered the questions and added several opinions of her own. Rory figured his aunt and uncle were wasting their time trying to hold her back. She sounded as if she was familiar enough to make a person believe she lived in town.

"How do you know all of that? You break away from the ranch once in a while just to prowl around finding things out?"

"From time to time, I get to town on my own. Ma worries, but there's nothing to worry about. Mostly though, I visit after church service is out. The town girls are always full of news. And then there are some simply awful gossips. If a body hangs close by and just keeps quiet, it's a caution what can be learned."

She emphasized that bit of information with a big grin.

Seeing the humor in it, the two young people found themselves grinning at each other, as if they were in a secret club of some kind.

Reaching town, Rory stalled his horse in the livery. The hostler, only ever known as Tippet, remembered Rory as a young man. He greeted him warmly and asked about his father.

"Buried up in the gold fields." was all Rory said.

"Sad thing, that. Jacob was one of the best. How you holding out, boy?"

"Fair to middl'n Mr. Tippet. It's good to be home."

"No 'mister' to 'er son. Jest Tippet. Good ta have ya back. Come in some time. You an' me, we'll have us a visit."

"Thanks. I will. Now I'm for a haircut. Do you have time to check the shoes on this animal while I do that? He's walked many a mile these past weeks."

As if the answer to the question was too obvious to bother with, Tippet said, "I see ya brought that girl cousin of yours in with ya. That girl has every young sprout within a day's ride look'n fer prairie flowers to pick 'n bring in, hope'n she'll reward 'em with a smile."

Rory looked across the street where Nancy had tied her horse to a railing in front of the mercantile. Next door was a ladies' wear shop. He watched to see which one she would choose. When she entered the mercantile, he glanced back at Tippet, smiling.

"She has a practical nature, though, that's plain enough to see."

"Thet may be so, but don't ya ever suppose she don't spend time look'n in the other windows."

With the subject of Nancy's shopping habits about worked out, Rory doffed his hat to Tippet and crossed the road. A half block from the mercantile, he found the barbershop, exactly where he remembered it. The shop was the same, but the barber was new. There was no one waiting, so Rory went directly to the chair. As he settled in, adjusting his holsters between the high side arms of the chair, the barber flicked a pinstripe apron once and then pulled it around Rory's neck, leaving Rory to drape it over his own shirt and pants.

The barber spoke as if he was already halfway into a conversation, making Rory wonder if he talked to himself during the quiet hours.

"Been a while."

The man was running his fingers through the course, black growth.

"You want 'er all off?"

Rory wasn't sure what the man meant by 'all', but the idea bothered him enough that he gave a detailed description of what he wanted. He had no intentions of looking at a bald man in his mirror every morning.

Rory hadn't had more than a short dozen haircuts in all his years. For the past three years, one cutting in Boise at the end of the season did for his father and himself alike. He wasn't sure of the approved etiquette, but he was actually hoping the man preferred silence. Unfortunately, that wasn't to be.

"New round 'round here?"

"Some. Been away for a while. As far as that goes, I don't remember you from before."

"Been here two years now. Not even sure why I came. Small town. Men getting their hair cut every few months. Hardly worth getting up some days. Maybe should have gone to the big city."

"There's nothing stopping you from taking your scissors and getting on a stage. There are cities enough around."

"Paid a handsome sum for this shop. One hundred and fifty dollars. Of course, that included the building. That's a lot of money. Can't find a buyer and can't afford to move on leaving that investment at the mercy of wind and rain."

Rory remembered the building as being about the size of a chicken coop, and the one chair was easily moved. He figured the man just enjoyed complaining. He could be a source of information, though. He probably talked with every man in the district over a year's time.

"I don't remember there being a marshal here when I left three years ago. Town always cared for its own. And I hear there's a judge. Don't know what he would have to judge in a place like this. Man could throw a rock from one end of the main street to the other. Can't imagine there's much crime."

The barber commented on Rory's hair before he got back to the matter of the marshal and judge.

"It's a caution how dirty most men's hair is when they sit in that chair. Can hardly pull a comb through it most times."

"I had a long, dusty ride the past couple of weeks. Heated bath water last night back on the ranch. It sure felt good to get the sweat off my body and the dust out of my hair."

"I wish everyone that took a seat in that chair would do the same. What ranch are you from? Somewhere close by, I'm guessing."

"The JJ. Double J, some call it."

The barber fell to silence, which troubled Rory. But finally, the man cautiously said, "Heard there was some trouble on the Double J. Marshal rode into town last evening, not looking so good, his nose all swole up, and one eye turning to black. Sure had his tail between his legs. Him and the judge both came into town looking almighty grim and unhappy. Ain't seen the marshal yet today. I expect he might be hiding out until he's feeling and looking a bit better."

The barber laughed a delighted laugh.

"Those two, the judge and the marshal, they seem to spend an awful lot of time together. Ain't seen no improvements in the town come from any of it so far. I expect they're up to no good too. It will be a happy day when we see the last of the two of them."

Rory listened without comment, but the words had him thinking, adding to the thoughts he had formed the afternoon before on the ranch.

The haircut came to a sudden halt when the barber's fingers found the groove in Rory's skull under all that hair. The man almost sounded excited, as if there might be a story here to brighten his day and provide gossip for a week.

"That was a close one. Don't know as the hair is ever going to regrow here. Reckon it might have caught your attention. Near enough to too close."

All Rory said in response was, "Near enough, for sure."

The barber couldn't disguise his desire for more information, running his finger along the groove again and waiting. When Rory outwaited him, he finally finished the cutting.

After scrubbing his fingers over his scalp to free any loose hair and digging his fingers under his shirt collar for the same reason, Rory settled his now loose-fitting hat onto his head and placed a two-bit piece in the barber's hand. His next stop was the mercantile, where he hoped to find some clothing to his liking. He might manage to squeeze some information from owner Browning too, although the man was notorious for having a closed mouth. Without exactly going from person to person, Rory was determined to get as much information as possible on the judge and the marshal.

"Good morning, Mr. Browning, Rory Jamison, perhaps you'll remember me from years before."

"Well, young man, I might not have known you at first glance, but besides the fact that Nancy is skulking around the back aisle, fingering everything she has no intention of buying, after telling me most of what I'd already heard from others about your welcome home yesterday, you do have a distinct look of your father that might have identified you. Awful sorry to hear about Jacob. One of the best if anyone was to ask me. The country will be the poorer for his loss."

"Thank you, Mr. Browning. Now, as I'm sure you can see, my clothing is about worn out. I'm hoping you can outfit me, including a good pair of boots."

"I can outfit you, but I'd never hear the end of it, and neither would you, if you didn't let Nancy show you the stock on hand. She never spends a penny of her own money, but I'm guessing she'll have no trouble spending yours."

From a voice behind a stack of ready-made dresses came a voice. "I do too spend what little money I get my fingers on. Why, it ain't more than just a bit ago I bought me one of these here fancy dresses. House dresses you called them."

"Nancy, that has to be a full half a year ago. Of course,

you've been known to splurge on a penny candy, time to time."

Rory figured the two were just having a bit of verbal fun, so he ignored the rest and walked to the display counters. An hour later, he arrived back on the sidewalk after changing in Browning's back room, wearing a full new outfit, with more wrapped in brown paper and tied with a string. The new boots he carried slung over his shoulder by their tied-together laces.

Refusing to add to the ranch credit, he had counted out over a month's wages for the average cowhand. Nancy stood in awe as he laid down the gold coins.

At his simple attempt to gain information on the town's happenings, Mr. Browning had answered, "Rory. My advice, for whatever worth you lay on it, is to let it go for now. There're things going on with the town leaders. We've had some questions we couldn't find answers to. But we're still working on it. Give us a bit of time."

Rory had listened and agreed, silently saying to himself that the promise didn't mean he couldn't still do his own thinking. He then asked Nancy, "How's the food at the hotel dining room? It's getting to be about lunchtime?"

Dining out was a rare treat for the girl. That her cousin would suggest such a thing was startling.

"I've not eaten there but once or twice. But I'd be willing to risk it if you have another of those coins you're prepared to part with. You'll have to be careful of Sonia though."

"Who, or what, is Sonia?"

"Who or what. Now that's a good question. I probably wouldn't put it quite that way to her, though. She'd be liable to burn your toast or serve you half-cooked eggs. No, Sonia is really very nice. I visit at church with her most Sundays. Some folks shy away because she has a bit of trouble with English. Speaks with a bit of an accent. I don't know where she's from. I've never asked, and she doesn't volunteer the information. She's very pretty, but the boys mostly still leave her alone because of the way she talks. Let's go see what they're cooking today."

"Is Sonia the owner of the business?"

"No, that's still Ma Gamble. Sonia just works there."

Nancy introduced Rory to Sonia and then turned to the chalkboard that displayed the lunch menu. Sonia offered Rory a firm handshake with a hand that was strong, showing calluses from much work. Ranch women's hands were strong hands. Milking cows, feeding and caring for chickens, gardening, and the multitude of other chores faced daily. Sonia, it turned out, lived in the boardinghouse in town while she worked at the diner. She rode home from time to time when she could find someone with the time to ride with her. She wasn't prepared to ride the long, isolated trail alone. Her parents were settled onto a small holding just a few miles west of town, higher up, on a bit of a foothills plateau.

Riding slowly back to the ranch on his newly shod horse, the big bundle of clothing balanced on the saddle horn in front of him, and Nancy riding by his side, Rory said, "Guess I've done about what I can do in town. Don't see where I might fit on the JJ, though. Even your brothers went off to find paying work."

"They mostly wanted to see some new faces from time to time. Still, the way your father laid out and fenced the ranch, and with the few things Dad did to improve on that, the cattle need little care."

"What's been done since I was last here?"

"Mostly making the watering easier. Dad had two wells drilled and windmills put up. There's water on every piece of fenced-in land now. Then, of course, Dad has dealt for some upgraded cows. What's really needed now are some new bulls, but I believe Dad mentioned that to you."

8

RORY AND HIS UNCLE GEORGE WERE DEEP IN conversation, sitting on upturned buckets. The chill, early morning wind, and the promise of rain had driven them indoors. They had chosen the barn for their private talk.

"It's not like I don't include your aunt in my decisions, Rory. It's just that I like to have my thoughts clear before I lay them before her. She's a good sounding board and often sees things I missed. But sometimes, our conversations go sideways, into trails leading nowhere, if we don't establish a direction before we start. And now that you're back and wanting to take a part in the JJ, we need to think that through together."

Rory listened to this and more before saying, "Nancy figures there's little to do, what with the layout you've established. That the ranch almost runs itself."

"Nancy figures a lot of things. Often enough, she's right. She's a caution, that girl is. Don't know where she gets her hard-driving nature from. Her mother and I know hard work, but Nancy goes a bit beyond that with her energy and enthusiasm. She'll bear watching, lest she goes off in some direction she can't find her way back from.

"But, now for you, Rory, are you filled with the wandering bug after your time away? Or the gold hunting drive that has called so many men away from home and hearth? Or are you ready to ranch in a serious way?"

"I'm home Uncle George, as far as I'm thinking now. You'll have to tell me where I fit and what work I might take up."

"Well, first, let's drop the aunt and uncle titles. You're an adult and deserving of equal treatment. Besides that, the titles are cumbersome and unnecessary.

"As for the JJ, your father laid out his goals before you left three years ago. He knew it would take some time, years, in fact. But his goal was to work toward a top-notch herd. As close to purebred as possible when the funds were available for upgraded animals."

The two men sat in mutual silence for some time, as George whittled on a broken piece of wood and Rory chewed on a wheat stalk. Both men were lost in their own thoughts, not sure where to take the conversation from that point. But wanting to find out a bit about the business of the ranch since George and his family had taken it over, Rory finally formed a question.

"How has it been for the past three years? I'm completely out of touch with stock prices. Has the ranch made money?"

"We've made money. Not a lot, but not too bad either. Your father left a small bank loan that we paid off with his half of the proceeds. Eliza has a complete set of accounts up at the house. You could go over them any time you wish. There's a balance available for whatever must be done, but most of the profits have gone to buying better cows. We have the first calves from those cows just about ready for weaning."

"I'm seeing yearlings that are about ready for market too. How is the price right now?"

"We're not exactly in the center of the informed world here, Rory, but the last I heard, a couple of weeks ago, we'll make money this fall if those prices hold."

"So, what does the ranch need to move it into a better position? Nancy suggested you've done about all you can do with these cows, that what you needed now was better bulls. Is that your thinking too?"

George whittled a bit more before he answered with, "Nancy is often right. She's sharp. Sharper than me sometimes, and that's a bit hard on my ego. She was forever a challenge to her brothers, although they don't seem to have suffered any permanent damage from the experience. And she's right on the herd too. Not that it's entirely her thoughts. We've talked about it as a family, wishing. Well, wishing won't make it happen, so we'll bide our time and save our money. There'll be bulls enough when we can write a check that big."

"I take it you're avoiding bank loans."

"Like the plague. I don't altogether trust bankers, on top of I don't need the stress of a bank loan."

Rory let that statement soak a bit before saying, "How many bulls do you need for a herd this size?"

"Now that's a question that will bring you different answers from different ranchers. With the three hundred fifty cows we have, some would tell you we need eight bulls, others as many as fifteen. Myself, I'd like to take the comfortable, but surer path. I'm aiming for a dozen good two-year-old bulls, ready for the herd."

"How much money are we talking about, George?"

George studied his nephew for a moment before he answered. Rory had not said anything specific about the profitability of the gold diggings except that there was money in an upcountry bank. If Rory was offering to buy the bulls, that fact would soon become apparent.

He finally put a number in front of Rory, expecting the young man to slap his knee with his hat and let out a big sigh of hopelessness. No such thing happened. Instead, Rory asked, "Where would a person have to go to find these bulls?"

"What are you asking, Rory? Are you seriously interested in getting involved financially, or is that just a curious question?"

"It's a serious question, George. I'm assuming you're talking about high-grade animals brought in from somewhere down east. Back in the older, more established ranches. Is that correct?"

"It is. And there are many places to find such animals. A big-city newspaper somehow found its way to town a few weeks ago. Browning, over at the mercantile, passed it along. There was a half-dozen ads for bulls. Mostly white-faced Herefords. But some others too. Available from as far away as upper New York state, south to Kentucky and Tennessee. The closest was in Illinois.

"The railway makes provision for moving livestock, shipping either direction. Running straight through, it really wouldn't take long from somewhere as close as Illinois. Just a couple or three days, depending on conditions. Unfortunately, a rancher making a shipment can't necessarily depend on a through train. The mixed trains take a lot longer.

"My understanding though, is that the new cars have feed and water facilities built into them. There's also some unloading and reloading too, to provide better care of the animals."

After a longer than usual pause, Rory said, "I need some time to think on this. I want to ride to town again. But we'll continue this conversation right soon."

OTHER THAN WANTING to talk to the banker, Rory had a growing curiosity about the town itself. How had a clearly dishonest marshal and judge gotten so well established among a group of good people? Who really held the power? And why would anyone want to be top-dog in such a small, unpromising place? None of it made sense to Rory's eighteen-year-old, inexperienced mind.

George was a be-and-let-be kind of man, and that suited his life as a small rancher just fine. But, even inexperienced in the broader aspects of life, Rory had an inquisitive mind. There were things he wanted to know. He needed to talk to an older, sensibly intelligent man. Or woman, he quickly thought. But in the existing culture, it would more than likely be a man. Mr. Browning was the obvious first choice, if he could get the man to talk.

Perhaps Ma Gamble. Eventually, everyone takes a meal in the hotel dining room. She had probably heard more than just about anyone else in town, except, probably, the bartenders in the small saloon that was actually nothing more than one side of the Mexican chili café located to the south side of town.

When he set out for town, the morning's chill was off the land. The sun was brilliant in the sky. There were still a few summer wildflowers remaining, giving color to the land, slowly being replaced by the reds and golds of the alder, poplar, and the few aspens that grew at that elevation. Within weeks, even those would be gone, leaving behind bare stalks and branches. But fall had a way of hanging on for a time before a reasonably mild winter took over this semi-arid country.

He rode slowly and casually, thankful for time alone. He had enjoyed his bit of time with Nancy, but now he wanted solitude. After three years on the gold fields with only his father for company, he had learned to treasure solitude and quiet.

The north-bound stage passed with a wave and a shouted greeting from the whip, leaving dust, the echo of hoofbeats, and the crunch and rattle of steel wheels behind it. Rory turned the horse until the rolling dust was on his back and out of the face of his horse.

Arriving in town, he avoided the single main street, choosing instead to swing onto one of the back streets. Here there were modest houses, most with a small barn or shed at the back of the property. He didn't remember so many fences and well-kept yards from when he last visited the area. He took it all as a good sign, an indication of prosperity and permanence.

When he swung back toward the main road, he passed the small church. Somehow, with just the single church and its one pastor, the congregation managed to hold itself together in spite of the variety of beliefs and backgrounds. Rory figured that was no small accomplishment. It was a modest structure, in keeping with the homes of the parishioners. The clapboard siding was freshly painted white, and the yard was well-kept, showing a mown lawn, now turning toward the brown of winter. A man was walking from the manse at the rear of the property toward the back door of the church. He acknowledged Rory with a small wave and a bright 'good morning', showing by his actions that he would welcome a visit, if the rider wished to stop. Rory returned the wave and the greeting but made no motion toward stopping.

After slowly riding two more residential streets, where he found one area with slightly larger, grander homes, he made his way to the mercantile. He wandered the store, fingering a saddle and a couple of fine carbines, as well as one bolt-action rifle. He saw Mr. Browning glance his way a couple of times, but nothing was said until the other buyers had made their purchases and left the store. Only then did the greeting come.

"Good morning, Rory. You seem to be spending a lot of time in town. I thought you might be kept busy on the Double J now that you're back."

"Not much that needs doing, Mr. Browning. George has it pretty well in hand. He and Aunt Eliza have certainly made me welcome, but they've been handling the chores without me for a long time. I'll have to figure it out soon, but right now, I'm kind of enjoying doing nothing for a few days.

"I do have a reason for riding in this morning. Two reasons, in fact. I need to visit the bank, and I wanted to ask you who the town mayor is. You said a couple of days ago that it would be best if I stayed away from the judge while you sorted some things out. I promise to do that, but I would still like to know who the mayor is."

"There's no harm in telling you that. Anyone in town could tell you it's Hip Dawson. Hip owns the bakery down the street. Good man. Can be rough around the edges at times. Determined in his beliefs, you might say."

Rory grinned and asked, "Do you suppose he makes donuts? I'd sure smile to have a donut or two. Haven't seen one since we left here three years ago."

"If he doesn't have donuts today, I'm betting you can find something else to tempt you."

"Thanks, Mr. Browning. I'll check that out after I see the banker. And I'll hold to my promise. No questions of the mayor. I'll just be on the hunt for donuts."

A few minutes with the banker, Jesse Ambrewster, assured Rory that moving the deposits in the Boise bank was, indeed, possible, and reliable, although not necessarily fast. With no telegraph in town, it would be necessary to wait until the banker made a trip to a larger center with that availability. Rory thanked the man without making any promises of further business and left the bank.

It was nearing early afternoon, and Rory had been thinking of lunch. Most of the citizens would be back at work. He expected the dining room to be quiet, which suited his purposes. He wandered across the street and entered the dining room. Sonia greeted him from across the room and approached him as he chose a table beside the window.

"Mr. Jamison, welcome. Rory wasn't it?"

"Rory. No 'mister' about it. It's good to see you again, Sonia. What's available for lunch today?"

He placed his order and sat studying the scene out the window while he waited. A bit later, after enjoying the roast beef and brown gravy over his mashed potatoes, he sat, half studying the town and half daydreaming, while he enjoyed his last cup of coffee. Sonia walked over with the coffee pot and a tea setting. Rory waved off the coffee refill. Sonia placed the empty fine china cup and the porcelain teapot across from him. At Rory's unasked question, indicated by the raising of one eyebrow, she said, "Ma Gamble will be right here."

The dining room owner approached, wiping her

freshly washed hands on her kitchen apron. After taking a seat, she said, "Always enjoy my tea when it's made the way it should be. Slow steeped and in a fine cup. The way I remember from my youth in the big house back east. And I wanted to talk with you. Welcome you back proper. I remember your mother, of course. And your sister. Terrible sad what happened back then. But tell me about your father?"

Rory shortened the story to the bare essentials while Ma sipped on her tea. When he was finished, she shook her head in sadness.

"Terrible, awful thing, that. An experience like that could change a young man. Leave scars that no one has the healing for. You come from good stalk, Rory. And I suspect you're a good man yourself. I know you'll do what has to be done. You showed that in dealing with the judge a couple of days ago. But don't let that become your life pattern."

She sounded as if she would like to pursue the story of the murderers, but Rory ignored that subtle invitation by changing the subject to the topic that interested him —the judge, the marshal, and the happenings in town and the surrounding countryside. The young man and the much older lady sat for a full thirty minutes discussing the topic, with Ma doing most of the talking. When the conversation slowed, Rory slid his chair back and said, "Thanks for trusting me with that information. I'll hold it private, I promise. But for now, I had best see if the baker has the donuts I've worked up a fierce hankering for, and get back to the ranch."

~

He rode into the JJ Ranch yard a while later with a white, light, cardboard box, sealed with a wrapping of string, containing fourteen donuts, all that was left from that morning's baking in the little shop. He passed them to Nancy as he rode past the house and said, "There's a treat for our coffee. If you don't know how to make coffee, just wait. I'll be right up as soon as I deal with this horse."

Nancy took the box of donuts and smirked up at her mounted cousin.

"Maybe I'll take this in and drop the bar on the door. You can watch through the window as the rest of us enjoy whatever it is."

9

AFTER SOME FURTHER DISCUSSION BETWEEN GEORGE AND Rory, about bulls and the fall shipping of market-ready yearlings, it was decided that the yearlings could benefit with a few more weeks on grass. Rory would go alone to Cheyenne, take a train east, stopping at locations close to where the bull advertisements originated from, check for other ads in the local papers, and attempt to find the best deal for bulls that would enhance the JJ Ranch.

Although Rory had worked regularly with cattle until he and his father left for the gold fields, he still had much to learn. George used their existing herd bulls to describe their deficiencies while Rory listened carefully. By the time he stepped into the saddle for his ride north, Rory felt he had a pretty good handle on the situation. There was also the matter of trust. Eventually, he would have to place at least some trust on the rancher that bred the bulls.

Rory had missed Cheyenne on his ride south from Montana, choosing instead to hug the mountains, which took him to Laramie. Knowing Cheyenne by reputation from before he went in search of gold, Rory was surprised to see how large it had grown and how active the place was. There seemed to be several trains either loading passengers or sitting on sidings. One cattle train was stopped alongside the loading pens. Shouted orders from the cowboys who worked at loading cattle, mingled with the rising dust and the fresh cattle droppings.

Avoiding the entire loading area, Rory crossed the tracks and found the main street. He was looking for a livery barn. Within a few hundred yards, he found three. Choosing what appeared to be the best managed of the three, he turned that way. He stepped down at the door and tied his two horses at the rail. Before he had a chance to enter the darkened interior, a young man stepped out, greeting him with a cheery 'afternoon'.

Getting right to business, Rory said, "I'm traveling east on the cars. No telling how long I'll be. Maybe one week. Maybe three. Like to have good care for these two animals and my saddle and gear. Am I at the right place?"

"Nowhere better in the entire state of Wyoming."

Rory thought of mentioning that he had ridden through a big part of Wyoming and figured the livery didn't have all that much competition. Most of the state was uninhabited, was his opinion.

"Can you tell me the cost per week?"

"Certainly. Do it all the time."

The numbers and the negotiations about exercise, stabling, feed, etc. took only a few minutes. When that was behind him, Rory untied his traveling satchel from the packhorse, left the animals in the care of the livery, and headed toward the downtown. He would find the depot first. He wanted the earliest train heading east. He would then find a hotel if he had to wait until morning. It turned out he was in time to catch an evening train.

~

THREE WEARYING days and two indescribable nights later, after interminable stops and clattering of couplings and clacking of wheels on rails, Rory stepped off the train at a little town called Battlement, Illinois. Pulling into the town, it didn't look like much from the train car window. Just the normal collection of clapboard homes with small stables at the rear to accompany the many outhouses. The main street, feeding directly from the terminal, held more promise. Standing on the wooden platform with his bulky travel kit resting at his feet, Rory took a quick study of all he could see. Directly behind the depot, the main street welcomed the traveler to a hotel and dining room. Next was the normal collection of small-town offerings, hardware and farm supply, general merchandise, including groceries, a tavern—which would have been called a saloon in the West—the doctor's office, and a small building housing the barber on one side and a lawyer on the other. At the far end of the street, safely separating the dust and odor from the finer properties in the town, was the livery barn. That was important to know because Rory was figuring to rent a riding animal.

Most of the crowd on the platform had only stepped off the train long enough to stretch their legs. At the conductor's shouted warning, there was a rush for the entry steps. Rory found himself standing almost alone.

"Help you, mister?"

At the question, Rory turned to the other end of the platform. There sat a top buggy hitched to a single horse. A smallish, pleasant-looking man, wearing a black top hat, smiled to reinforce his question.

Knowing he could use some advice, Rory picked up

his satchel and walked toward the man. The smiling welcome turned into a business offer.

"Take you anywhere you wish to go, tell you the history of the town and where the name came from. Interesting enough story on its own. Even better when I gussy 'er up some. Introduce you to the mayor, should that be of some strange interest to you." How the man held his smile through all that talk was a mystery Rory allowed to slip right through his mind, judging it to be of no importance.

"I need to find a couple of farms. By that, I mean after I secure a hotel room and find a decent meal."

"Train grub leaves you something to talk about and wish to avoid in the future but doesn't do much for the state of your health."

The man managed all of that through the continuing smile.

"Only hotel in town is right next door. Best dining is in the hotel. There, I've already helped you. Should charge you a dollar, by rights, but we'll let it go this one time."

The smiling somehow continued.

Rory laid his satchel on the platform beside the buggy.

"I need to get to the Galen Farm. After that, I need to find the Washington Hereford Farm. If you can deliver me to either of those, you might have an afternoon's work ahead of you."

"I can get you to Galen's easy enough. About seven, maybe eight miles south. Washington's is a longer drive. North, maybe twelve miles. Best to start in the morning on that one."

Rory studied the man and rig, judging that the buggy

and horse both would hold together for the time required.

"You don't look to have a lot of folks ready to take you up on your offer of transport. How would it be if you tie the rig off at the hotel? I'll sign for a room and get a meal. You can join me for coffee if you wish. Then we'll see if you can really find this Galen place."

Rory grinned to show the man he was teasing.

Rory had worn his hip-length, tanned deer hide jacket on the train. He kept it on during his room registration at the hotel and in the dining room. The many stares on the train and since he had landed in town confirmed that a lot of people saw the leather jacket as a curiosity. But he treasured the item, purchased from an Indian lady in upper Idaho. Finely tanned, almost to a dull white color, and trimmed with fringes and enough beadwork to confirm its Indian heritage, Rory had seen nothing like it in any of his travels. It took some time to air the smoke odor from the tanning out of the leather, but Rory could discern no lingering odor now.

The temperature of the fall air would suggest that the jacket was excess to his needs, but he felt comfortable wearing it, and it hung low enough to hide his belt and guns. He had no knowledge of how the locals would react to the hardware, but he felt naked without them.

As he ate a good dinner of fried pork sausages and boiled potatoes, the buggy driver, who introduced himself as Driver Walsley, drank several cups of coffee. Rory tried to watch the man on the sly, to see if he could somehow drink hot coffee while still holding his smile. He didn't, but it was a near thing, the smile sagging to a mere slit in his lips. He then offered the unsought information that Driver was a handle he had attached to himself.

"My folks hung Aloysius on my shoulders, as if any young sprout wants to carry that around with them. I couldn't shorten it to Al because my older brother already claimed that. I've used three, four names over the years, but now I drive a rig, so why not?"

Rory grinned and answered, "It works for me. Easy to remember anyway."

Driver talked almost nonstop on the eight-mile journey. Slowing for a few muddy patches leftover from the last storm, and not pushing the horse overly hard on the low, sloping hills, the ride took a little less than two hours. The subject that interested Driver the most was the town of Battlement and the surrounding areas. Rory learned more than he felt he needed to know about the northern and central area of Illinois. But he was thankful for the ride, and Driver's fees seemed fair, so he said nothing as the man prattled on.

Pulling into the farm road and passing under the big gateway with *Galen Farms* chiseled into the heavy top railing, Rory saw a prosperous-looking, well-kept farmyard. Judging by the miles of fenced land of the numerous neighbors, who all claimed to be farms, Rory figured farm would be a more accurate title than ranch. Ranch held to itself a vision of size, of mastery of a goodly chunk of land, of cattle and horses in large numbers, of men and women both, riding the range like emperors of their chosen or claimed domain. The idea of a farm awoke thoughts of a man walking across the yard at the break of day with a milking bucket in his hand, or of a woman scattering uncrushed wheat for the chickens to peck.

A middle-aged man stepped from the barn door and shaded his eyes against the afternoon sun, studying on the arrivals.

"Howdy, Mr. Galen. Brought you a visitor. He hasn't told me just exactly why he wanted to come out, but I'm guessing he has a purpose. Long trip if it's for nothing."

"Well, pull up here and let's talk."

When the buggy wheels quit turning, Rory dropped quickly to the ground on the offside. He met Mr. Galen just as the farmer stepped around the horses.

"Mr. Galen. Rory Jamison. I'm from the JJ Ranch out in Colorado. Double J, some call it. We don't get a lot of outside news, but a big-city paper somehow floated our way a month or more ago. It held several advertisements offering quality Hereford bulls for sale. One was from the Galen Farm. I'm wondering if that offer still holds, or have the animals all been spoken for?"

"We're in the bull and pregnant heifer business, Rory. We try to have a goodly choice on hand, although the season is about over, and we hope to not have to hold any over the winter. What exactly are you looking for?"

"We run a herd of three hundred fifty fair-quality cows. Mostly white-faced but not quite all. We're looking to upgrade the next run of calves. Changing the entire herd of cows is impractical and may be well-nigh impossible. Our next thought was to get a better grade of bulls. That would be a smaller buy-in and probably more easily done. I don't know if we need purebred animals or if we will have to be content with something approaching, but not quite in that category."

"I'm assuming you ride, Rory."

"That's my preferred method of travel, Mr. Galen. That buggy is alright if a man was to be courting or taking his grandmother to church. But my posterior fits a saddle better than a wooded board."

Mr. Galen laughed, while Driver's smile disappeared for a moment.

"Come with me. Driver, if you walk up to the porch with your hat in your hand, Mrs. Galen may take pity on you and find some coffee. You can enjoy the shade of the porch until we return."

Within a few minutes, the rancher and the farmer were riding side by side among a scattering of cattle that set Rory's eyes to watering and his mind reeling. He had never seen bulls that carried so much flesh or any that had among them the picture of pure health and strength. He noticed the heifers and even some of the older cows, but he put them out of his mind as he studied on the bulls.

They reached the far end of the close-up pasture and swung off to return through a different section of grass, studying bulls all the while. There weren't as many as he thought there would be, but he liked what he saw.

Rory swung his leg over the saddle horn when they reached the gate again, turning the horse so he could study the entire pasture.

"I'm not seeing many breeding cows, Mr. Galen. Or any recent weanlings. This is nice grass, but there isn't much of it. That's a lot of animals for so few acres of graze. Do you, in fact, breed all the bulls, or are you a broker for a collection of farms?"

"Excellent question, Rory. No, we don't represent anyone else. These are all our animals. We have some other land a couple of miles further south. This is mostly our calving and weaning grounds, although these have all been weaned long ago, as you can see. Right now, I have them up because of that advertisement.

"Do you see anything you like?"

"I like them all. But let's be frank with each other, Mr. Galen. You can easily see that I'm young. Too young for making this decision, really. I was raised on the ranch, working stock, but I've been away for the past three years. My uncle runs the spread now with me as half-owner. My uncle couldn't be away from the ranch because of other things he has to care for, so here I am. I'm not completely inexperienced, but still, I know I'm in over my head if we insist on pure honesty. There's some trust involved here.

"I think I'm seeing quality animals. And I'm sure you would confirm that. But here's the question. I'm looking to purchase a dozen good bulls, mature enough to turn in with older cows. If you and I came to a deal on finances, would you guarantee me that the animals you recommended would prove themselves over the years?"

"I can't guarantee they will actually make calves. We don't have the veterinary science to test the sperm yet. But I will guarantee that these boys will put in their best efforts. And I'll guarantee that they are healthy and all purebreds. You would receive the papers on each one with the purchase."

"So, what are we talking about for cost?"

Mr. Galen said a number. Rory silently multiplied it by twelve. He had one further question.

"Do you value all the bulls the same, or are there some who don't show as well?"

"Rory, the ones that don't show well are cut young and sold to beef growers at weaning. We cut them because we can't have others using our off grades and claiming purebred stock. All Galen Farm stock is guaranteed by three generations of quality breeding and a reputation of trustworthiness."

"Uncle George and I picked out two farms close to Battlement. Driver says he can take me to the other in the morning. And there were more advertisements in the same paper, some as far away as New York. But if I can deal here and not punish myself with any more miles or hours on the railroad seats, I'd be just as happy. Can we hold our conversation for one day? It's only right that I look at the other local choice too."

"If you're talking of Washington Hereford Farm, and I suspect you are, I can save you and Driver a day in the buggy. I'm good friends with the folks up there. They have a fine operation, quality animals, and good people to deal with, but it's much smaller. We ran into each other in town a few days ago. They sold off their last bull a week ago."

Rory slowly moved his eyes away from Mr. Galen to the herd. Was that the truth? What should he think? And could he expect to find any better stock anywhere? What about the price? He'd had no idea on cost when he boarded the train, except what George had said, and he wasn't too sure how much George knew. Now, he had to say something to Mr. Galen, but what?

With a deep breath, he turned back to the farmer.

"Mr. Galen, I have no reason to doubt you. So, I'm going to save myself that ride and trust you. I'll have to go to town to see about a car for transport to Cheyenne. They'll have to be driven to town and the rails. We'll have to make sure the Battlement bank can handle a draw on my Boise bank account. But those are all details. All important, but still details. The central issue now is your price. I'm assuming the price you quoted was for a single animal. I'll be wanting to hear you sweeten the pot some for a dozen head."

There was a stillness in the air as the two men studied each other. Rory wasn't sure what he would do if the price didn't come down for the larger purchase. Would he walk away? Did he really want to start all over again looking for another Hereford farm? And if he did, he might end up paying as much or more.

His thoughts were interrupted when Galen said, "I'll tell you what we'll do, Rory. For a cash sale on twelve bulls this late in the season, we'll sweeten the pot, as you said, by ten percent. Can you live and be happy with that number?"

Rory stuck out his hand. With a handshake, both men acknowledged a completed deal. They would sort out the details in the morning.

"I'm assuming you can find the help to drive the animals to the rails."

"I can. They're not hard to drive. A bull has things other than running away on his mind most of the time. If you wanted to pick up a livery horse in the morning, you could come out and help me sort out the twelve you want. We can go to the bank together. It shouldn't be a problem. I've sold animals all over the country. The banker gets approval on confirmation of funds over the wire. I don't really understand that, but then, I don't have to understand it. As long as it works, I'll leave it with the banker."

Rory dropped his foot back into the stirrup, turned to Galen, and said, "We'll call it done. I'll wait for the bank to open in the morning. Get him going on the transfer and then see about a rail car. Then I'll come out here. We'll see you in the morning.

"And when the banker receives his confirmation from Boise, we can sit together and wind it up."

10

EARLY THE NEXT MORNING, RORY ARRANGED TO RENT A horse. Swinging into the poorly fitted and uncomfortable saddle, he rode to the depot. There he placed an order for a single cattle car. The agent confirmed that the car would be available the next afternoon and sold Rory a ticket for himself, including a sleeping room, which he hadn't realized were available on the trip east. The sleeping rooms were next to a car with upholstered and padded seats. He gladly paid the difference in cost.

His next stop was the bank, but he had to wait until the banker showed up for work. He sat in the dining room drinking coffee by the window until he saw a man wearing a business suit walk down the opposite sidewalk and unlock the bank door. Leaving his cup half full, Rory made his way across the street.

At the banker's invite, he took a seat in an office chair, being careful to hold his jacket over his belt and guns. The last thing he needed was a misunderstanding.

He explained his business, calculated the amount of

money to be transferred, and laid his Boise bank book on the desk.

"I'm hoping you can wire that bank with my information and have the price of the cattle purchase transferred to the Galen Farm account. And I'm hoping that can be done today."

"That's a lot of money, young man. Do you have that much on hand, in Boise, or anywhere else?"

Rory had to hold himself in check or risk losing the deal because of an arrogant banker. Carefully he said, "I have the funds and more. Considerably more if that will put your mind at ease. You can look at the balance in that book, which I'm trusting you to hold in confidence, and judge for yourself. But in any case, you will know when the wire transfer is complete, will you not?"

The banker didn't answer the question, simply leafing through the bank book as he glanced at Rory over the top rim of his glasses.

With no further comment, he wrote out a wire request on a blank piece of paper and called his clerk, who had just arrived.

"Take this to the telegraph office immediately. The charges will go to the bank's account. Have a rush put on the wire. Tell Tony to get the answer over here the very minute it comes in."

Rory couldn't help wondering if the evident suspicion and aggressive nature were a daily habit for the man, or had he reacted to something he didn't care for about himself. But, like the other frustration, he let it go. He simply picked up his bank book, thanked the man, and stood to leave.

"I hope you're not wasting my time, young man."

"The name is Rory Jamison, as I have already told you, and that you could well see in my bank book. And I also hope you are not wasting my time or costing Mr. Galen a sale."

The banker watched him until he stepped out the door and stood to his saddle.

AFTER THE HALF-HOUR ride to the Galen Farm, Rory was settled down again and not quite so prepared to get back on the train and go further east for his bulls. The bright greeting from Mr. Galen helped to move his feeling toward quality animals and away from the sometimes-necessary acceptance of fools. He pushed the banker out of his mind and returned the greeting.

"How is it in town, Rory? Did you get a car?"

"I did. For tomorrow afternoon. I checked the railway holding pen. There's feed and water available, so the animals will be alright until the car is ready. I saw the banker. He put in the request for funds to be transferred. He sent the wire, but he is not a happy or particularly pleasant man. He was very suspicious of me. I hope it all goes well."

A female voice came from behind him.

"The banker is a sourpuss. I've told him so several times. His daughter is a good friend of mine. He's as miserable at home as he is at the bank. Someone needs to take a stick to him and explain some things."

Rory and Galen both turned towards the voice. A very pretty girl, or woman, Rory corrected himself, was leading a horse from the barn. She was dressed for riding. She was just a wee bit husky, but on her, and in the clothes she was wearing, which were filled out delightfully, she looked just fine. She appeared to Rory's inexperienced eyes to be a year or two older than he was himself, but how does a man judge a woman's age? Or was it just best to let it go, like he so often did with other matters that came his way? His father's training had become a fixture in his mind and makeup. *Stick to the important. Don't waste yourself on the unimportant.*

"This is my daughter, Willow. Willow, this is Rory. Mr. Jamison. He has purchased a few bulls for their Colorado ranch."

"Yes, father. I understand that. I wish to go to town anyway, so I've decided to help you drive them to the rails, just in case you've forgotten how."

Rory, taken back by her forwardness, glanced over at Galen. That man grinned and said, "I'll try to remember which end of the bulls should be pointed toward town."

"Good. That will leave time for Mr. Jamison and me to get acquainted. Perhaps he will tell me all about Colorado. I've never seen a snowcapped mountain or a big ranch. Oh, there's so much to talk about. And at the rate these bulls walk, we'll have the time for it.

"A girl can never tell, there might even be a marriage proposal before we reach town."

She seemed to be particularly delighted by the flush on Rory's face and the question in his eyes. She didn't quite laugh out loud, but it was a near thing.

Rory nearly choked as those words entered the conversation. Grimly, he pulled his hat down tighter and turned his horse toward the bull pasture. He wondered how many customers the outspoken girl had driven off.

With a warning look at his daughter, Galen opened the pasture gate and rode in. Willow stopped beside the opening to hold back any animal besides the bulls that decided to escape and explore the world outside. To give Rory a good look at the animals on offer, Galen picked them all out and drove them into the yard. Rory helped, once he understood what the farmer was doing.

"There they are, Rory. All we have left for this year. Fifteen animals. Pick which twelve you want, and we'll push the others back."

Rory could see little difference in the bulls. They were magnificent. The differences between these and the resident bulls on the Double J were remarkable. He knew George would be pleased. He found his mind asking questions and a moment later offering competing answers. But he finally settled on the question he wanted to ask.

"Mr. Galen, it hardly seems to make sense to leave you with just three bulls. What kind of a deal could we make if I took all fifteen?"

Galen whipped off his hat, looked at his daughter, and started to laugh.

"Now you see here, Willow? There's a lesson for you to heed. Back east, this young man would never be allowed to take on the responsibilities for his ranch that Rory carries on his shoulders. But in the west, they grow them up fast and young. Men younger than Rory have driven herds hundreds of miles, bossing the crew and dealing with the buyers. Handling great sums of money. And he has me in a corner. I could easily get out of the corner, but that's not the question. The real question is, do I want to get out of the corner? Do I want to stick with my price, in which circumstance, I risk the possibility that my customer will pick out twelve animals and leave me with three to possibly hold over the winter? You can feel fall in the air of a morning. Will I find a buyer for three bulls this late in the year? What say you, daughter?"

"Well. Let's look at both sides. You could keep the

bulls and sell them as three-year-olds in the spring, but then you'd have to drop hay in front of them every morning and evening all winter. Or you could sharpen your pencil and move all fifteen out today. Now another factor to consider is that the buyer is kind of cute, perhaps just a bit shy of outright handsome, in a rough-around-the-edges sort of way. And he has come a long way to find you. So which side of the balance scale do you think holds the most weight?"

Rory was glancing from one to another, feeling as if he was watching a well-rehearsed stage play.

A FULL FOUR HOURS LATER, the agonizingly slow drive reached the town and the corral at trackside. The herd carried all fifteen head, with the final three having an additional ten percent removed from the asking price. Rory offered none of his private plans, but he was thinking he could find a buyer for the extra three, and probably make a profit by it, once he was back home.

HAVING REACHED the end of the short trail and housing the young bulls in the railway corral, Rory said farewell to Willow. As she returned the thought with a small wave, he watched her ride away toward the shopping district in the small town. After the many words spoken by Willow that morning, and the few returned by Rory, he now knew more about Battlement, Illinois, than he would ever have use for. In return, he told her what he could about Colorado ranching and just enough about panning for gold to keep the conversation going.

AT THE BANK, the news of the completion of the transfer relieved Rory and put a smile on Galen's face. The sour banker's manner didn't appear to have improved. That his bank would receive a handsome fee for the trouble of making the transfer of funds wasn't enough to allow a smile to rise from wherever it was that smiles come from in most men. Strangely, he looked a bit put off when Rory explained that a second purchase had been made, requiring a second transfer.

The banker filled out the forms for both buyer and seller to sign. Rory signed the paper and then stood and walked out with no comment. As far as he was concerned, his dealing in Battlement, Illinois, had been completed. Galen stayed behind for reasons of his own.

11

THE COMBINATION PASSENGER AND FREIGHT TRAIN WAS rattling its slow way west with many stops along the way. The newly boarded passengers were settling in and eager for the experience, thankful that the days of covered wagon and horse and buggy were easing toward an end. The weary faces and aching bodies of the travelers, who had suffered the indignities of the many miles from further east, were evident. Some sat with eyes closed, their heads bobbing with the train's movements. Some stared vacantly into the aisles or out the windows, no longer interested in anything but the end of their tedious journey.

Watching from his aisle seat, Rory's eye fastened on a young woman who fit the latter description. The seat beside her was held by an equally young man with a distinctly eastern, city look about him. From the fact that the two spoke infrequently to one another, Rory assumed they were together. The girl was just short of beautiful, like Nancy, back on the JJ Ranch. In fact, the resemblance between the two was startling. The young man was thin, narrow-shouldered, and pale, as if he had never been reduced to doing manual labor and had spent his life indoors. Rory couldn't see from where he sat, but he imagined the man having small hands.

Why was he even thinking that way? He didn't care. And it was surely none of his business. His business was those cattle housed a few cars behind the one he was seated in.

Although he found the many stops frustrating, they were also an advantage, in that they gave him the opportunity to look in on his precious bulls from time to time.

The hours dragged past until even the newest travelers were showing their fatigue. The girl and the thin man were no longer showing much life or any sign of conversation between them. Rory could not have adequately explained his interest, but no matter what he said to himself, his eyes kept wandering down the aisle. The sun had gone down, the few lamps that were meant to light the car had been lit. Some folks had picked up their belongings and disappeared through the door leading to the sleeping car. Rory assumed they were the ones who had the foresight and the funds to reserve a sleeping room.

Absently, he touched the shirt pocket that held his ticket. When the agent offered the sleeping room at an additional cost, he remembered the long, body-punishing two nights in the hard, uncomfortable chairs on his eastward journey. The car he was in, with the padded seats, was a significant step up from the bench seats. He held no regrets about the additional cost, but now he wondered at his own wisdom. How was he to enjoy a night's sleep and care for his animals at the same time? His concern had to remain with the large investment in the bulls. He thought of the sleeping room fondly but doubted he would even muss the blankets. It would be better to continue to check on the animals. He was sure the conductor would find a spare lantern for his use.

While these thoughts were working their way through his mind, he was drawn back to the seat up the aisle. With a loud, arrogant, "Well, now, there's a sweetheart I hadn't noticed before. Good evening, little darling." a young man dressed in cowboy garb and wearing a single .45 hung on a leather belt with a large silver buckle, leered at the woman Rory had been studying since boarding the train. He saw her physically cringe at the intrusion.

With a single, violent action, the crude but arrogant man grabbed a fist full of the thin man's jacket, twisting it until the lady's traveling partner could hardly breathe. He lifted the slight fellow out of his seat, dropping him onto the facing seat. He then sat himself, taking up the space just vacated. The slight-built man immediately stood to his feet, as if to make a defense of the girl, and was just as quickly pushed back down.

Several surrounding passengers gasped at the totally inappropriate action. It was a general rule that a decent woman could walk any street, ride any conveyance, or take a meal in any restaurant, without fear.

A cowboy sitting two rows in front of Rory stood to his feet, lifted his carbine to his side, with his eyes firmly fixed on the action fifteen feet away, and was about to step into the aisle. Rory was there before him.

With a half-dozen quick strides, Rory stood beside the young lady. The intruder glanced up at him and then turned back to the girl, as if to dismiss any threat from Rory. Wasting no time, Rory flipped the man's hat into the air. Dropping his hand only a couple of inches, he grabbed an ear and twisted cruelly. With his other hand, he grasped a hand full of filthy hair. With these two handholds, he lifted. Unable to resist the pain, the man stood to his feet, wobbling and seeking balance. Rory dragged him into the aisle and kicked his feet out from under him. As the man fell, he released his hand holds and stood straight, looking down at the prone man. Before the man could move, Rory placed one boot on the side of his head, pressing firmly and grinding his ear into his skull.

"Mister. You're done here. I'm going to lift my foot so you can stand. Then you git. You git now. Don't come back. Be thankful that nothing more has come your way. You won't get a second chance. In fact, it would be best if you got off this train. If I even see you again, I'll shoot you as dead as you'll ever be. Now, you stand up and apologize to the young lady and her friend. And you make it sound like you're serious."

Watching every move the man took, Rory stepped back. The downed man struggled to his knees and was about to reach for his belt gun. The heavy-set woman sitting across the aisle and one row back spoke loudly. She held a Colt .45, a weapon too large for most women's hands. She held it with firmness and familiarity.

"Mister, you touch that weapon, I'll shoot you dead like any other varmint and never give it a second thought. You've plumb wore out your welcome here. Best if you were to do what you've been told to. Git. Apologize and git."

The voice and the wooden handled .45 held steadily in her hand suggested that she meant what she said.

Rising carefully to his feet, with his hands kept well away from his holster, the passengers close by heard the mumbled apology. Figuring there was nothing to gain by pushing for more sincerity, Rory and the large woman let it go. The intruder stumbled hatless to the door and was gone. The cowboy with the carbine sat back down, and the woman tucked her revolver back under her belt, grinning and nodding at Rory as she did so.

Rory went back to his seat, saying nothing more to either the lady or her friend. He hadn't been seated for more than a minute when the thin man made his way up the aisle. Coming close, he held his hand out to Rory.

"Wiley Hamstead, sir. It came to me that neither I nor my friend offered our thanks. I wish to correct that now. It is clear that I am neither fit for nor knowledgeable about life on the frontier, if that is where we now are. I know something of books. That has been my life. I am trained to be a teacher and, possibly, a lawyer. But I can plainly see that I am going to have to expand my horizons, broaden my outlook, if I stay in the West. In the meantime, please accept my deepest thanks for myself as well as for Hannah. That man was clearly more than I could have handled."

Rory shook Wiley's hand, adjusting his opinion as he did so. He had shown himself to be more of a man than Rory had first judged him to be. A simple thank you and an acknowledgment that he, himself, was inadequate for the task confronting him impressed Rory. He could hear his father advising him to be careful in his judgments.

"No problem, Mr. Hamstead. There were others ready to step up if I hadn't."

On the way back down the aisle Wiley shook hands with the cowboy who had stood to the ready, and then moved on to the lady with the big .45. He retook his seat next to Hannah, but Rory thought he sensed a bit of reluctance in the girl, demonstrated by her leaning far to the side in her seat.

A quiet half hour clacked past, as full dark enclosed the car windows, when Rory had another thought. Fingering the sleeping room ticket in his shirt pocket, he studied Hannah again. She looked to be totally exhausted. Wiley did, too, but that didn't concern Rory. He wasn't quite sure why he was bothered about the girl either. But thinking no more about the reasons, he rose to his feet and moved to where the two were sitting, now both with their eyes closed and their heads pressed against the seat backs. Rory could see by the occasional flicker in her eyes that Hannah was not sleeping. Lifting the sleeping room ticket from his pocket, he held it out in front of her.

"Ma'am, I know how exhausting the nights are on these seats. I found that out on my trip east. Now, I purchased a sleeping room that I'm not going to be using. I'll be busy with my cattle. I'd like if you would take this ticket and have the porter show you to the room. You can lock yourself in and have a good night's sleep."

Hannah barely glanced up at Rory, but her lips pursed, and she seemed to stiffen in her whole body. Without looking up, she whispered, "No, thank you. I'll be fine."

Rory was taken aback to where he didn't know what else to say. He was standing there with the ticket held out, feeling foolish, when the lady from across the aisle spoke up.

"Take the ticket, girly. I'd sure take it if it was offered to me."

Rory suddenly understood. Somehow both the girl and Wiley had taken the offer completely wrong. With that thought flashing through his mind and his face flaming in embarrassment, he half stumbled back to his seat.

Fortunately, the train pulled to a scheduled stop within a couple of minutes. Rory rose and made his way to the door, keeping his eyes firmly fixed on the floor in front of him. The cowboy with the carbine stood and followed.

On the platform, the cowboy caught up to Rory. "Skip Tandy. I'm a bit bored with all this travel. Mind if I tag along?"

"Welcome, Skip. Rory Jamison. There's not much to do unless one of my bulls somehow got himself tangled up. But perhaps you know more about life than I do and can explain some things to me."

"Not to worry, my friend, you're doing alright. It's the girl that needs to open her eyes."

Rory glanced at the man but said no more. He lifted the latch, and together, the two cowboys slid the heavy door partially open. Rory passed the lantern to Skip and boosted himself into the car. Taking the lantern back, he made a quick tour through the quiet bulls. They all appeared to be either sleeping or at least at rest. Within a half-minute, he was back on the ground and the door was being slid closed.

~

THERE WAS a dim light shining through a smoke-encrusted window in a small building beside the track. Over the door, Rory could make out a night-darkened sign that read *Eats*. Indicating the sign with an upraised hand, he said, "I wonder if they have coffee on?"

Nothing was said, but his walking partner veered that

way. There was, indeed, coffee and a choice of sandwiches served by a tired-looking, middle-aged woman.
Two track workers and three other passengers were
already eating. Rory ate two roast beef sandwiches and
put down three cups of coffee. Skip chose one ham and
one fried egg. He ate the ham while the woman dropped
two eggs into a greased pan. She stood yawning as the
grease bubbled and the eggs cooked until their edges
were just a bit crisp. They were served up, hot enough to
melt the generous layer of butter on the bread. Skip
licked up every bit as he rolled the sandwich this way
and then that way.

THEY WERE BACK on the train at the first sound of
"boooo'rd" and rolling their monotonous way toward
Cheyenne. With no words, the two young men parted.
Skip retook his seat beside his valise and his carbine.

When Rory saw the porter coming his way, he had an
idea. Lifting the sleeping room ticket from his shirt
again, he motioned for the man's attention. The porter
stopped and with a quiet "Yes sir, is there something I
can help you with?" He stood waiting.

Rory held the ticket out, keeping his voice very low
so no one nearby could overhear, he indicated Hannah,
still seated where she always had been, and explained the
situation.

"I'm afraid I was misunderstood when I first offered
this room to the lady. I'm sure I embarrassed her, and I
know for sure I embarrassed myself. Please take this
ticket and try to encourage her to use it. I have no intention of intruding."

With a glance at the ticket, then a small nod and a

wink, the porter tucked the ticket into his closed hand and made his way back down the aisle. In his quiet, diplomatic way, he bent close to Hannah's ear and whispered for a few seconds. Hannah's eyes flashed down the car toward Rory, but he had his head tilted back, as if asleep or at least resting. He was holding his eyes open just a slit. He caught her look and then, with some satisfaction, saw her rise, pick up her satchel, and with no words to her traveling partner, she followed the porter out of the car.

12

MIDMORNING TWO DAYS LATER, WILEY HAMSTEAD MADE his way to Rory's seat.

"Good morning, Rory. When you get a moment, Hannah would appreciate a word with you."

The face-to-face seating arrangement allowed Rory to sit directly across from the girl. He eased into the chair and waited.

"I'm told your name is Rory. I believe Wiley has already told you mine. In any case, Hannah will do just fine. I confess, I wearied of calling everyone mister, missus, or miss, back in school. It's a relief to escape from that formality. I also owe you an apology and my thanks. First, I thank you for coming to our rescue. Neither Wiley nor I quite knew how to react to that dreadful man who confronted us so brutally."

Rory smiled and said, "You need not worry about him any further. He left the train two nights ago."

Wiley looked astonished.

"I confess, I'm surprised at that. The way he was

carrying on, I believed he would be a nuisance during the entire trip."

"He changed his mind. Got off at a stop back down the line."

Hannah asked, "How did that come about, and how do you know this?"

"It was during one of our many stops. I was there. I had a bit of a talk with the fellow. He seemed to have repented of his actions and agreed it would be best if he rethought his travel plans."

Wiley and Hannah stared at him, not knowing what to think or say on that. The safe position was to leave it alone.

As the car had become overly warm, Rory had removed his coat, believing that the weapons he wore would not be an issue with the travelers. The truth was that most of the passengers were carrying weapons, some hidden away and some in plain sight. Both Hannah and Wiley had taken a serious study of the two-gun rig. With Rory saying that the unruly passenger had decided to disembark after having a talk with him, they had scrambled visions of matters they knew nothing about filling their imaginations.

Wiley said, "I'm not even going to ask what you said or did that made him change his mind. I might be better off not knowing."

Hannah glanced from Wiley to Rory and then offered, "In any case, sir, I owe my grateful thanks for two nights in that wonderful sleeping room, and my deepest apology for misunderstanding your intention when you first offered it.

"But it has occurred to me that you have not had much rest yourself. I understand from Wiley that you are caring for some livestock in a car somewhere behind this one. But that still leaves you with trying to sleep on these chairs. Regardless of the good intentions of the people who manufacture these seats, three days and two nights on one is still an endurance trial.

"May I ask where the livestock are bound for?"

"I share a ranch with an uncle. South of Cheyenne just a bit. I'll be driving them there."

"I am hoping to go south as well, if I can connect with some kind of conveyance, a stagecoach perhaps. My family are also ranchers, although I have never been to the ranch. My family moved out west at the same time I started school. They call their ranch the Double J. It is apparently near some town called Stevensville, Colorado. Perhaps you have heard of it."

Rory didn't answer right away. He sat staring at the girl who he had already identified as the visual match for Nancy. Getting over his shock, he asked, "Would your name perhaps be Hannah Jamison?"

"Why yes. JJ Ranch. The Jamison family ranch. I see you have indeed heard of the place."

"Oh, I've more than just heard of it. I own half of it. My father started it. Jacob Jamison, JJ Ranch. My mother and sister are buried there. My name is Rory Jamison, and we must be cousins, if that doesn't stretch the possibilities too far. It's good to meet you, Cousin. You look enough like Nancy that I should have wondered, but somehow the thought never occurred to me. You are sort of the mystery cousin among our small family. But tell me, please, do your folks know you're coming west? They said nothing to me."

"No, it was a last-minute decision. I knew that they often were several days between trips to town. If I sent a wire, I could easily be there already before they got the news. I'll have to chance that there will be some kind of a welcome when I arrive unexpectedly."

"You have no fear on that matter. They miss you and talk of you often."

Hannah thought for a minute and then said, "Perhaps, Rory, since we are cousins and you have proven yourself to be trustworthy, and knowledgeable of the area and customs, I could ask you for assistance in finding a stagecoach and whatever else I might need to get to the ranch."

Rory had an answer ready, but he glanced at Wiley, wondering how he fit into the story. Hannah caught the look and came back quickly with the answer to the unasked question.

"Oh, Wiley won't be going to the ranch with me. We're friends from school, but that's all. When he heard I was coming west, he offered to escort me, hoping to fend off the types of intrusions we experienced a couple of evenings ago. Now he's thinking of staying in Cheyenne or somewhere close by.

"I would still appreciate your assistance since we are going to the same place, and I don't understand how things work out here in the West."

Wiley shook his head at his obvious inadequacy and said, "I'm afraid I wasn't much help when the chips were down."

"Perhaps more help than you know, Wiley. But what are your plans when we arrive at Cheyenne?"

"I'll be seeking some kind of work. Outside work if I can find it. It seems I've spent my life indoors. I would enjoy the change."

Rory accepted that without comment and turned back to Hannah.

"When we get to Cheyenne, the passengers will be

off-loaded first, then the cattle cars will be shunted over to the loading ramp and corrals. If you could wait in the depot until I have the bulls dealt with, we can go together into town. Then we can do what has to be done."

SLOWLY AND PAINFULLY, the time passed. Although not particularly warm outside, with the windows in the passenger car closed, the air became rank and stifling. With the windows open, the car filled with coal smoke that the engine exhausted in amazing volume. The first night. The long, wearying second day. The unbelievably tiring second night. The half of the third day that finally came to a gratifying end at the depot in Cheyenne.

When the doors opened and the step was in place, every man, woman, or child was up, with their luggage at their sides, hoping to be among the first to be released from the imprisonment of the railroad car. By the standards set by covered wagons, it was an amazingly fast trip across the frontier. Everything else about it was written on the other side of the coin in most passengers' minds.

HANNAH STOOD outside the depot enjoying the cool, fresh air while Rory unloaded the bulls and arranged for their care. The two of them then made their way to the closest hotel. Entering, and setting their simple luggage out of the way, Rory approached the registration desk.

"Two rooms, please. One for me and one for the lady."

He indicated Hannah as he said it.

The young man behind the counter stumbled a bit, looking embarrassed, but finally said, "I'm sorry, sir. We do not allow unescorted ladies to stay in the hotel."

Rory had never heard of such a thing. It took a few breaths for him to sort out his thoughts and come back with a comment.

"Now, see here. The lady is not unescorted. She is with me. And before you say anything you will regret for the remainder of your days, understand that she is a lady in every sense of that word and, in addition, is my cousin. We are traveling home to our family ranch. I've politely asked for two rooms. We are both weary from travel and I'll have no nonsense from the likes of you. Now get the register out here and lay two keys on the desk. And they had better be the best rooms you have."

When the half-frightened clerk still hesitated, not knowing what to do, an older man stepped up beside him.

"It's alright, Peter. You might have misunderstood the hotel policy. Give the man and his cousin rooms 212 and 214."

With that bit of unpleasantness behind them, Rory carried both pieces of luggage to the rooms and told Hannah to lock her door.

"I'll go find the stage office and make the arrangement for you. Stay here or in the dining room until I get back. Do not go outside."

The firmness in his voice left no doubt in Hannah's mind that he was serious for a reason. She had seen many rough-looking men on their walk from the depot. But then, Rory looked pretty rough himself, so how could she judge the men around the town?

Rory soon returned with the stage fare paid and the

times sorted out. The stage would pick up her small trunk from the depot on the way out of town.

A quiet rap on her door brought Hannah, with her face washed and her dress changed, cleaned up as best as the situation allowed.

Rory noticed but made no comment, simply passing the stage ticket through the partially opened door. He then said, "Put your coat back on and let's get you some warm clothing. You're not going to do well with that eastern coat on a two-day stage trip."

Hannah was clearly troubled by the suggestion, not knowing what to say or do. But finally, she said, "I'm going to have to make do. I left upper New York state with just enough money to cover the train costs and a bit for food. I can pay you for the stage costs, but I can't afford another coat."

Rory smiled and said, "How would it be if we talk about that some other time? Now come on. I don't know how late the stores stay open, but the afternoon is nearly gone."

Hannah put on her coat and locked the room door. As they were walking down the hallway, she said, "You didn't hear a word I said, did you?"

Teasing, Rory shook his head as if in wonder. "Now you've got me. Did you say something?"

Frustrated and not really understanding, Hannah followed along, seemingly having no choice. She had to take a couple of quick double steps to catch up.

At the general store, Hannah stood in wonder at the clothing piled high on the counters separated by narrow aisles. The racks of coats and ready-made pants and dresses took up several feet of the next aisle. From the roof hung all manner of items, from expensive farm tools near the checkout stand to bridles, halters, camp gear, and every imaginable implement for working with horses or cattle. Along the wall, where they could be easily seen through the window, lay four beautiful saddles slung over saddle stalls.

Rory went directly to the rack of coats. He lifted down a finely tanned leather coat with a sheep hide lining.

"Here, try this on."

Hannah started to say, "I can't-"

"Try it on, Hannah. We'll talk about the costs another time."

The third coat she tried fit beautifully. Hannah hugged it to herself, wrapping her arms to hold it tight.

"It's wonderful."

"Good, now let's find you a lap robe."

With that done, they picked out a woolen scarf and a pair of warm gloves.

"What else do you think you need?"

"An explanation."

"We're repeating ourselves, Cousin. Let's get this paid for and try out the dining room. I believe it's been at least a month since I've had a good meal. I'll take you back to the hotel, and then I have to see to my horses. They're in the livery down the street."

"I'll come with you."

Carrying the cumbersome, paper-wrapped package from the general store, Rory entered the barn and called out, "Ash. You here or have you run off with my horses, knowing you'll never see the better of them?"

A grinning, middle-aged man, strong and wide in the shoulders but with a limp and a bent spine, came from the small office.

"You are quite correct, my good man, about the horses. Fine animals. Fine animals. Double J is known far and wide for their horses, including up in Montana." The hostler paused there, giving Rory the opportunity to comment. When that didn't happen, he continued, "But alas, my riding days are all in the past. My body won't put up with the abuse anymore.

"But she was a glorious couple of minutes on that outlaw stallion that did this to my poor old self.

"Your pair are fit and ready, but you're not riding out this late in the day, are you?"

"No, but I'll be back in the morning. Just checking it all out."

"Come when you're ready. The horses are in fine shape."

~

AFTER A DINNER TO REMEMBER, Rory escorted Hannah to her room, leaving her with firm instructions to lock the door and jamb a chair under the doorknob.

"The stage leaves at eight sharp. I'll meet you in the dining room for breakfast at seven. One night on the trail and you'll be home soon enough."

With expressions of thanks and wonder at all that had happened so quickly, not the least being the warm coat and accessories she had put on and worn from the minute Rory had paid for them, Hannah moved into the room. Rory stood there until he heard the chair being jammed into place.

He went immediately to a saloon close by. The bartender shuffled his way toward Rory with a curt, "What'll ya have?"

"Just a moment of your time if you don't mind. I have some animals to move south, I'm looking for a couple of experienced men that have some time on their hands. Any suggestions?"

Without answering the question, the barman hollered out, "Caesar, Blade, get yourselves over here."

Two, thirty-something men lifted themselves from their chairs and sauntered over, as if they had all the time in the world. Without a word, they stared at the barman.

"Fella here looking for a couple of men for a few days. I'd like to not see you here for a while, what with you sitting around, eating free peanuts and pickled eggs, and not spending a red cent."

Rory looked the two men over, liking what he saw. He liked the casualness of them and the worn nature of their clothes and boots, showing all the signs of work, not just sitting around a saloon. Grinning at the men but talking to the barman, he said, "This the best you got? I don't want fellas that can't stick it out. We'll be on the trail for, oh, I don't know, three, maybe even four days. Could be one or two longer than that, depending on happenings. Fifteen head to move, and I can't afford to lose any. And it looks to be coming to rain. Can't have any quitters."

The barman, catching on to the humor of the words, came back with, "Might be a few women in town that would like to see a little less of their men and a bit more money coming in the door. You could ask around. Even try the ladies' aid over at that church down the street. Of course, that wouldn't get these fellas out of my hair, which is the reason I called them over in the first place."

The man who answered to the name of Blade finally spoke up.

"When you two are finished flapping your gums, perhaps one of you could outline the job while the other goes and washes some beer glasses, which are never any too clean at the best of times."

The bartender laughed and walked away. Rory said, "Rory Jamison. Double J Ranch, Stevensville, Colorado. I've got a small job I need some help with. I have fifteen unbranded purebred bulls in the railway corral. I just hauled them in from the east. I plan to leave them where they are for one more day to kind of let them get their feet back on the ground after being in that rolling contraption. It's only about sixty miles to the ranch, but these bulls are in no hurry to get anywhere. We'll do well to hold it to three days. Could be four. That's assuming no trouble.

"I am not experienced with driving animals, having been away from ranching for a few years. I need men I can trust and who know what they're doing. If one of you knew your way around a frying pan and a campfire, that would be good too. My cooking might try the patience of Job. I'll pay one month's salary each for those few days. But you have to know what you're doing and be willing to stick it out through the rain I'm sure is coming. Not much shelter on the grasslands we'll be covering. Any of that sound right to you?"

The two men looked at each other and Rory thought he saw a slight nod.

Blade said, "We'll take the job. We always finish what we start. We'll stick to the end, but you'd best not be fooling about having the wages available. Wouldn't want to have to go round and round over wages. Caesar here is a fair to middl'n cook."

"Welcome, fellas. Don't worry about the wages. You'll get your pay. If you can do some cooking, Caesar, how would it be if I give you some money and you go tomorrow and gather up some easy-fix grub? And don't forget the coffee. You'll have all day tomorrow. Then we'll meet at dawn the next morning at the railway yards."

Rory held out a twenty-dollar gold piece. Caesar folded it into his hand and the two men returned to their table.

13

Rory walked Hannah to the stage depot, carrying her small overnight satchel. Tell your father I'll be along with the bulls in something less than a week, although this rain may complicate things.

"Now, hear me well. You trust the stage driver and no one else, man, woman, or child. You're not likely to enjoy the ride any more than you did on the train, but it will get you there. And I know you can look forward to a grand welcome when you arrive at the JJ. Now, step up, choose a seat, and relax as best you can. Good travels. I'll see you in a few days."

He stood there watching while the driver climbed to his elevated seat, picked up the reins, and flipped the whip in the air, ending with a resounding crack, all without touching the horses. With a loud shout from the driver, the team lurched into their collars and had the stage approaching top speed within a few yards. For some reason, stage drivers loved entering and leaving town with a dramatic flourish, one known to have scattered men, horses, dogs, and chickens in all directions.

Some towns were forcing the practice to a halt before someone was seriously hurt.

Rory then made his way to the rail yards, where he checked on the bulls. The rail crew had seen to their feed and water, and the animals looked fine. He probably could have hit the trail that morning, but he wasn't going to change his plans. The thunder and lightning during the night, and the dark clouds over the western mountains, promised a plodding, wet drive. The western hills had disappeared behind a gray haze of falling water. There was no doubt which direction the storm was heading. He would wait one day. There was no point in rushing off half-prepared.

As he was leaning on the top rail studying the animals, the only thing that bothered him was that they were not branded. If one somehow managed to slip off in the dark of night, he could have a misery of a time proving it was his. Still, he didn't want to delay his arrival at the Double J either. To have the smithy make up a JJ brand and then spend the necessary time branding would be more of a delay than he wanted.

He was still standing in the same spot when a stranger rode past on a solid black gelding. Glancing into the pen, he suddenly pulled rein, staring long and hard at the bulls. He spoke to no one. After a full minute, he jigged his animal back into movement, turned his eyes, not his head, sideways to study on Rory, and rode on into town. A couple of minutes later, a rail worker walked up behind Rory and spoke quietly.

"I'd watch that fella if these animals were mine. Saw him here last evening just at dark. Seen him before. Got a reputation, he has. Never works and hangs with a few of the same. Seems to have money. Now, in case you think that chain and lock on the corral gate is a normal thing, it's not. After that fella rode off last evening, I went to the workshop and rigged that up. Wanted to be sure your animals would see the sunrise from this very spot, not ten miles out on the grass."

Rory turned to listen and then glanced over to the gate.

"I noticed the chain and lock, of course. And you're correct. I took it as a normal practice. Thanks for doing that and for the warning."

"Between the two of us. Right, Mr. Jamison? Wouldn't do to have my name bandied about in the saloons, calling me a snitch and such."

"I've already forgotten you were even here. And I don't know your name."

With a grin and a nod, the railman moved on to the other cars that needed unloading.

The last few things necessary for the small drive were assembled during the day, including a warm lining to place under Rory's rain slicker. He had asked Hannah to take his beautiful leather coat along with her so that, at least, would not add to his burdens.

Caesar and Blade showed up at the livery in midafternoon, hauling a canvas sack of provisions. Together, they sorted it into the panniers, trying to keep a balanced load for the JJ packhorse. Rory had found a two-sided canvas satchel that he could sling across the packsaddle under the panniers. Scouting around town, he managed to locate enough unclaimed firewood to fill the satchels. The thought of the dearth of trees and other fuel on the broad grasslands had been bothering him. It was the hostler who suggested taking his firewood with him.

When everything was set up and ready for an early

morning start, Caesar reached into his pocket and held out a small gathering of coins.

"That's all that's left of your gold piece, Boss. Cheyenne is an expensive town. Don't know how the saloon can afford all those pickled eggs."

With that, the two hired riders broke out into a guffaw. Rory, knowing the two were eating on the good nature of the saloon man, laughed with them but finally said, "You fellas keep that. Take a meal or a glass of beer. But be ready in the morning."

BY MIDMORNING, riding in the pouring rain, the bulls were five miles away from Cheyenne. Their only knowledge of being held in a group and driven was on the short trail from the farm of their birth and raising, and Battlement, Illinois. The first couple of miles required a good bit of Caesar and Blade's previous experience. Rory watched and learned. The trio finally settled for having one of the experienced men on either side of the small group, while Rory rode drag. Unlike most drag jobs, with the flourishing grass and the rain, there was no concern about dust.

Rory looked behind him frequently, repeating the railway man's warning in his mind. It wasn't until early afternoon that he saw just the image, the slight glimpse of something or someone, through the rain.

There were few reasons for anyone to be riding on such a miserable day. That there were at least three riders following along, bothered him considerably. Even with the desperately slow travel of the bulls, the followers didn't seem to get any closer, as any normal riders would. When the herd was passing a considerable thicket of trees, mostly stunted poplar with an under-growth of a few shrubs filling in between them, Rory hollered over at the others.

"Going to drop off here for a bit, fellas. See who that is dogging our trail."

"You want help?"

"No. You keep the animals heading south. I'll handle this."

A little less than a half hour later, the three followers pulled up even with the poplars. The stop gave two of them the opportunity to roll cigarettes in the shelter of their held-open coats. The smoke rose into the rainy sky and drifted towards the third man, the same one who had been attracted to the bulls a couple of evenings before.

As he had in the incident up in Montana, Rory unbuttoned his knee-length slicker and flipped one side over each leg, giving him access to both his weapons. As he often did when there was something needing doing, he heard his father's voice in his mind. *When you've got something to do, there's no gain in waiting.*

Rory stepped his horse out of the brush, to the surprise of the other riders. Wanting to give them no time to think or react, he quickly said, "There's no logical reason for you men to be out here following our trail. That means you're almost certainly up to no good. You need to know that rightly, I'm a man of peace. But when put upon, I'll hold my position. If you care to test that, I can assure you that not everyone will be standing when the sun goes down. Now I'd appreciate if you would just go back to Cheyenne and save us all a bit of misery."

The obvious leader, the one from the railway corral, came near to sneering.

"Kid, I already sized you up back in town. You worry

me not at all. You would live longer if you just turned those bulls over to me and my friends and go on your way."

Rory smiled in spite of the rain and the warning.

"I don't like to be reminded of this, men. It was a troublesome day for all involved. Best forgotten. But there were some gents that thought the same up at Pierre, Montana, a few months ago. Perhaps you've heard the rumors or the story. Of course, they couldn't tell the story themselves, they being dead and all. You might want to think that over and then turn around. Life is just fine, even on a rainy day in Wyoming. It would be a shame for you not to live through it."

One of the smoking men was fidgeting, looking nervous. He barely glanced at Rory, as if doing more might be misunderstood. Talking out of the side of his mouth, he said, "Poge, I've heard that story. Boys up Laramie way were talking about it."

Poge had never taken his eyes off Rory. Slowly he studied his adversary, clearly glancing at the JJ brand, as if he, too, had heard the story and that it was in connection with that very hide mark. Then, with no words, he turned his horse back north and spurred the animal into a trot. The other two were quick to follow along. With a sigh of relief, Rory buttoned his coat and turned to catch up to his bulls.

FOUR DAYS LATER, three of them having been suffered through driving, cold, late-season rains, Rory kicked his mount into a trot and pulled to the front of the small drive. When he was abreast of the lane leading to the JJ Ranch, he turned the lead bulls. Blade dropped back to allow the gather to make the left turn. Caesar turned a couple of animals that were intent on continuing their southern march. When all the bulls were slowly walking toward the ranch yard, Rory waved the two men over to himself.

"I can take it from here, men. You did a great job and it's time you got inside where there's a bit of warming comfort and better food. We have no bunkhouse on the Double J, but about two miles up ahead there's a nice little town. Pretty fair hotel and a good dining room."

He reached into an inside pocket and retrieved two small envelopes. He then dug into his pants pocket and pulled out a ten-dollar gold piece.

"Got your pay here, fellas. And an extra ten. Take the ten and get a room. Get some rest and good food in you, and come back out here in the morning. We'll get the branding done, and you'll be finished with this little chore. A couple of long days will put you back in that Cheyenne saloon, eating free peanuts and pickled eggs. You did well here, and I thank you for being patient and for teaching me along the way. In the morning, you can continue your teaching with the branding, although George has done considerable hide burning too."

With a simple touch of their spurs, the men turned their horses back onto the trail, waved a farewell at Rory, and rode for town.

Rory had been watching the ranch yard as he talked with the men. He could see George standing in front of the house and two riders hurrying his way. They could only be Nancy and Hannah. With shouted greetings, the girls eased past the bulls and pulled in behind them. Rory sat still, watching the action unfold. Driving the languid bulls was about as easy a drive as could be imagined, but still, he admired how the girls handled the chore. In no time at all, George had opened the corral gate and stood aside while the girls completed the drive.

With the bulls confined and the handshakes and greetings behind them, Rory and George stood looking at the purchase that they hoped would begin the future of the upgraded Double J. The girls sat their horses, also studying the bulls.

Rory turned to the girls and said, "On that packhorse, you'll find all kinds of camp fixings. Most of it has never been touched. We geared up for doing our own cooking along the way but found out there were enough stage stops that we were able to purchase our grub. We even managed to corral the bulls at night and sleep inside. Good thing too. Except for today, it rained nonstop. There's no reason that grub can't still be used if you wanted to unpack the horse and sort it out."

14

THE BULLS WERE BRANDED, EXCEPT FOR THREE THAT RORY planned to resell. Caesar and Blade, shaved and looking none the worse for the days of work in the rain, had waved their hats in the air as they rode away from the Double J. They weren't heading back to Cheyenne. They had decided that the warm south held more promise for a contented winter than cold and snow-choked Wyoming.

Rory, also rested, shaved, and bathed, was restless. George had mentioned sorting the two-year-olds for a drive to the rails. But that wouldn't be for a couple of days yet.

He pushed his chair back from the breakfast table. To no one in particular, he said, "I'm thinking of taking a ride to town. Might find a sale for those three bulls."

Nancy glanced over at her sister. A silent message passed between them. With a nod at Hannah and a grin at Rory, Nancy said, "Might just as well saddle three horses, Cousin. We'll come along. You know, to kind of keep you from getting lost and to fight off the girls, lest you get yourself in some kind of trouble you can't get out of."

"Your mother must have some work for you here. Wouldn't be right to leave her with everything to do alone."

"She'll be happy to have us out of the house for a few hours."

"Now you've said something I can understand."

Nancy ignored his last remark. Instead saying, "Come on, Hannah. We'll clean up these dishes and be ready to go while Rory saddles the horses."

Seeing no way out and finding no good reason not to ride with the girls, Rory obediently walked to the barn. Within a half hour, the three were on their way.

FEELING the need to keep his own finances separate from those of the Double J, Rory visited the bank with the intention of opening a personal account. Again, he sat with Jesse Ambrewster, giving directions for the transfer of a small amount of funds to be transferred from Boise. Although he had no evidence, and he knew it wasn't fair, he harbored serious doubts about the banker. Or perhaps it was the smallness of the bank. Trusting him with more than a few months of walking around money didn't seem prudent. He had his eye on the bigger bank down in the city for a larger transfer and deposit.

With that completed, Rory walked over to the livery. Tippet knew everyone in the territory that had anything at all to do with horses or cattle. He might be able to drop a name on Rory, a possible link to the sale of three purebred bulls. As it turned out, the only suggestion he had was for a rancher, miles away, far too long a ride for what remained of the day.

"Too many folks are content with what they've got. Anyway, most run their cows on the loose range, mixing cows and bulls, never knowing, or caring what the progeny is. I suspect it won't change until there's more miles of posts and wire sorting out the holdings."

He was wondering where the girls had gotten off to when he heard a whistle from the walkway across the dusty road. Wondering what that was all about, he looked around. The only ones he saw in the direction the whistle had come from, were his cousins. But surely it wasn't one of them who had whistled. Just as he passed that thought through his mind, dismissing the idea as preposterous, he saw Hannah curl her lips. The same shrieking, piercing noise emanated from them. Both girls waved and giggled at his startled look.

Feeling he had no choice, Rory sauntered across the road and stepped up onto the boardwalk.

"You didn't learn that at a school for young ladies, Hannah."

"You bet I did. That and a lot more the headmistress didn't know about. We didn't spend all our time reading fine literature and ironing petticoats."

Rory had no sensible response. When he stood there soundlessly wondering what was to come next, Nancy said, "Hannah has been telling me about the midmorning tea break back at that fancy school. We're not much for tea on the ranch, but we thought it might be fun if we were to see if Ma Gamble would share her private stock with us. And since neither of us has any money, we knew you would be gentleman enough to come and cover that small expense."

"You came to town with no money? Not even enough for a cup of tea?"

"Town isn't always about buying or spending. It's, well, it's just town. Every girl likes to get to town now and then. You know, see the bright lights and all."

"The only bright light here is the same one that's shining on the ranch, where you should be, helping your mother, gathering eggs and whatnot."

Hannah looped her arm through one of Rory's arms. Nancy grabbed the other. Together the girls half dragged their wealthy cousin, or at least he was wealthy enough, into the dining room. Once inside, they headed to a four-place table beside the window. Being midmorning in an early-to-work town, there was no one else there. Nancy plopped into a chair as if she was settling onto an upturned bucket in the barn. Hannah hesitated, giving Rory an opportunity to pull her chair out for her and seat her as they had been taught. When Rory sat across the table, Hannah pulled out her own chair and settled in.

Sonia came from the kitchen, wiping her hands on a white cloth.

"Sorry. I didn't see you come in. I was washing dishes."

Feeling like pushing the girls just a bit, Rory said, "I'm guessing either of my cousins here would be glad to help."

A glare from Nancy that could have frozen boiling water put an end to that half-born conversation.

The girls inquired about the tea. Assured that Ma didn't just hold the tea in stock for herself, the order was placed. Sonia turned to Rory, waiting. When he said nothing, she asked, "I'm assuming you'll stay with coffee, Rory?"

When Sonia returned with the tea, after boiling water on the big wood stove in the kitchen, she was in time to hear Rory say, "I was hoping to find a buyer for those purebred bulls. Tippet had just the one suggestion, but to ride to that ranch, way out east into the flat country, would take longer than what's left of this day."

Sonia's ears perked up at the talk of bulls. She carefully lifted the tea setting off the silver tray she held and set it down on the table. Knowing the three customers well enough to enter their conversation, she asked, "What's this about purebred bulls?"

Rory gave a brief explanation while Sonia listened carefully. Quickly mulling over what she had heard, she said, "My father has been talking about upgrading the stock. I'm guessing he would like to know about that opportunity."

Nancy asked, "Where exactly is the family ranch, Sonia? I know you've said it was up in a high valley. But where exactly?"

"It's only, I'd guess, a couple of hundred feet higher than where we are now. It's west, up in the hills. It's pretty level once you climb the hill, but the road is steep in places. It's about a two, maybe three-hour ride from here, depending on what a person is riding."

Rory wasn't intimidated by either a three-hour ride or the steepness of the hills. After nearly three years in upper Idaho, he felt he had done it all when it came to difficult rides.

"If you could sketch me a map, Sonia, I'd make that ride. These are good bulls. I'd like to find a good home for them."

Sonia hesitated before making the offer but finally decided there would be no harm in it.

"I start my few days off tomorrow. I live here in

town, of course, but every few weeks, Ma gives me a few days away to visit the folks. If you wanted to ride up with me, it would solve two problems, one for you and one for me."

Nancy asked, "What is your problem that needs solving?"

"The road home is long and mostly unpopulated. Both my folks and Ma have insisted that I not ride it alone. I wasn't at all sure who I could ask to ride along this time, but you could be that solution, Rory."

RORY TOOK some good-natured teasing on the way home from town. When the girls pulled up outside the house yard to dismount, their mother was standing there. Nancy couldn't wait to say, "Rory's going courting tomorrow, Ma. Be gone all day. Could be gone several days. Maybe even forever. There's simply no telling."

"Courting, is it? Well, it's about time. Might settle him down to home."

Rory didn't bother correcting his aunt or arguing with the girls. He simply took their bridle reins, as they held them out to him, and rode to the barn. In the quietness of that animal shelter, he told George about the potential sale.

Rory could see his uncle's mind sorting something out before he spoke.

"I've been thinking we should get the boys to come home. We'll need to put a crew together to get these yearlings to Cheyenne. The ranch they're on is up in those hills somewhere. I wonder if there's any way to ride through the hills between where you're going and the Triple T, where the boys are?"

"Do you have any directions?"

"Only that it's up in the hills to the west."

"I hadn't figured on it, but I'll take a bedroll and some trail supplies. I'll ask around when I'm up there. Do you want them home for the long haul or just for this one drive?"

"I can't insist on anything. They're of an age to make their own decisions. But if they want to be involved in the Double J when I'm ready to take my ease, they had better get at it now."

~

RORY AND SONIA were well underway by the time the sun was fully up. Sonia fixed herself an early breakfast in the boardinghouse she lived in. Aunt Eliza was at the big iron range when Rory tied his horse to the rail outside the house yard fence.

The two young people visited as they rode, learning about each other's families. Rory had said, "Not too much to say about my family. They came out from Tennessee and took up the ranch we still live on. You've heard the story about smallpox and my mother and sister. No need to repeat that. And you know my father and I went to the hills to hunt gold and get our minds off our losses. Uncle George came west and took up the ranch. He's done a good job with it too."

Sonia waited to see if Rory had more to say. When nothing came forth, she said, "My family has much history, but the memory of it is dying out. My parents were happy to put it all behind them. They don't talk much about it anymore. Except my youngest brother. He somehow thinks he would like to have lived in the past, with the old ways.

"My parents, they have said that if it wasn't one faction or one king or pseudo king or one ruler or one country bringing war to the people, it was another. Everything seemed to be up in the air. They could never be quite sure who were their friends and who were their enemies. The countries around our old home are small. While there are many very large nations in Europe, there are also small ones. As far as that goes, I am not sure if we are from Europe or if the territory is called something else.

"Men rule everything, allowing the women no choices at all. Many marriages are arranged between fathers, mostly for the father's benefit. My parents had an arranged marriage. Fortunately, they learned to love each other. Sometimes I think they even like each other. Our lands are bordering the Black Sea, where there is much shipping. Somehow my father arranged to work his way across the sea to America, taking his family with him. My brothers and my sister were very young. My sister died on the ship. I was not yet born.

"We love it here. We have freedom to work and keep what we make. My father is a good cattleman. He has done well. One brother will follow in his footsteps. The other brother, I don't think he will."

The horses had trudged along, making good speed, but Rory could see the trail becoming steeper not far ahead. He had one other question for Sonia.

"You speak very good English. How did that happen with no schools up in those hills, and your parents speaking another language?"

"My English, I think, is good, but there is still the accent behind it. I fear I will never lose that. I learned my parents' language first, of course. Many of the pronunciations in my native language are different from English.

"Growing up on a remote ranch, we all swung from one language to another with hardly a thought. It is too late now to correct the pronunciations I learned then. My speaking bothered some of the kids in school. I fear it still keeps some away, not wanting to be associated with the bohunk.

"But for my parents, there was an Englishman who came to our land to preach and begin a church. He had much opposition from the established churches, but he stayed. To feed his family, he taught school. He learned our language very quickly. My parents made the change to his church. He was often in our home, I am told. From him, my father learned the English. My mother, not so much. She is improving all the time, though. I refuse to talk to her except in English. At first, she objected, but now she simply laughs at her mistakes, and we enjoy our times together.

"Anyway, I have lived in town for many years. Since my twelfth year, I have been at the boardinghouse, first attending school and then working with Ma at the dining room. My parents know there is nothing on the cattle ranch for me. My one brother, who is still longing for the old ways that he really knows nothing about, believes I should be on the ranch, taking orders from him, if my father won't follow the old paths. He can be very difficult. I mostly ignore him. He will leave the ranch one of these times."

IT WAS NEAR ENOUGH three hours later that the weary horses stepped into the yard of the I-5, which Sonia had said stood for the five members of the Ivanov family. Rory was startled by the beauty of the place.

He knew that some called these lands hanging valleys. Of course, they are no such thing. They are merely plateaus between mountain upthrusts. The plateau the Ivanov family had settled was like a flat dish, with the sides sloping upwards, ending in rockslide moraines that separated the grassed flat lands from the rocky peaks. Except near the buildings and the yard, there was little need for fencing. The cattle were captive within the rocky edges.

That Sonia's father was a good rancher was obvious from the log buildings, painted and well cared for, to the house garden enclosed in a white-painted picket fence and the flowers carefully tended in window boxes and along the face of the log house. That the man who had put all this together might be interested in his purebred bulls, was easy for Rory to accept. Here was a family who valued what they had and cared for it well.

Sonia's mother was hanging washing on the line beside the house. At Sonia's call, she whirled around, dropped the bedsheet she was just lifting out of the rinse tub, and screamed. Running more quickly than Rory had believed a woman well into middle age could run, she was there almost before Sonia managed to step from the saddle. Grasping her daughter in her arms, she squeezed tightly, before leaning back and kissing her on each cheek. She then hollered out, "Grigor. Grigor, Sonia is here!"

With that, she unwrapped her arms from around her daughter and, looking up at Rory, asked, "And who is this that has brought you to your home?"

"Mother, this is Rory Jamison. He wanted to talk with father about the cattle, so I asked if I could ride with him. He is from a ranch near the town. I know his family well."

By this time, Sonia's father was nearing, hurrying, but not so spryly as her mother had. Behind him were two big men, handsome and strong looking, as if work was no stranger to their lives.

Sonia made the introductions.

Grigor Ivanov, Sonia's father, shook hands with Rory and said, "Welcome to our home."

Without a word, Pavel, the older son, also shook hands, sizing up Rory as he did so. Ivan, the younger son, stood well back, staring daggers through Rory. He offered no welcome of any sort.

Sonia's father turned to his son, "Ivan, have you forgotten your manners? Your sister is here, and this young man has escorted her safely home."

"My sister should have never left this home, and who is this that she rides with? How can she trust such a man, and why would I greet him?"

Rory was still seated on his horse and had not spoken. Now he said, "Mr. Ivanov. I would talk cattle with you if you were interested. I am in possession of three purebred Hereford bulls, two years old. They are available to you if you have use for them. Otherwise, I will simply turn and ride away. Sonia is home and safe. I promised I would return in four days to escort her back down the hill."

Grigor answered, "Of this, I am interested. Please step down. Ivan, who does not wish to greet his sister, he will care for the animals. We will talk bulls and the cattle business. We will do it over coffee and food."

"I will care for my own animal, sir."

Grigor hesitated, looking between Rory and his obstinate son.

"Ah, yes. Of course. Come. Pavel will take Sonia's

packages to the house. You and I, Mr. Jamison, we will care for these two horses."

Side by side, the two men led the hard-ridden horses to the shade of the lean-to on the side of the barn. There they found water and hay and a selection of brushes and heavy cloths for working over the horses. Pavel joined them after a few minutes to discuss cattle. Ivan was not seen again until there was a call for food.

AFTER THE LENGTHY stop for lunch, Rory said, "I must be going now. I have another ranch to find, somewhere in these hills. Is there any chance that any of you know the Triple T Ranch?"

All the men were familiar with the ranch. Pavel was able to outline a clear trail that would not require dropping down the hill again. He estimated a two-hour ride would get Rory to his destination, if he didn't miss any of the turnoffs.

"It is a trail for one horse only. Very narrow. In some places steep. But it will take you to the Triple T, and the other ranches out that way."

Rory thanked Mrs. Ivanov and shook hands with Pavel and his father. Again, Ivan sat silently and sullenly, stewing in his own unhappiness.

Pavel asked, "What is at the Triple T? If it is the bulls you are going to talk about, we would like to have first chance, after we see them."

"No, it is not the bulls, although I will sell to the first ranch that shows me the color of their money. I am hoping that will be the I-5. No, it is my cousins I look for. I have two cousins riding for the Triple T. They are needed at home. We are putting a drive together. We have about 250 two-year-olds that must be driven to Cheyenne. We need their help."

Pavel glanced at his father before saying, "We would help you with the feeders if we could join our small bunch with the others. We will have about one hundred fifty head."

"You round them up and drive them down when you come to see the bulls in four days. I have given you directions to the Double J. You can escort Sonia at the same time. You, Pavel, and your father would be welcome on the drive."

The wordless rebuke stung in Ivan's mind. It hung in the kitchen like a thundercloud. No one could be quite sure what was coming next from Ivan. But Rory was firm. He had done enough work with cattle to know that a malcontent had no place in a bunkhouse or on a drive with other men.

Roughly, Ivan pushed back his chair and stormed from the house. His mother folded her hands in front of herself and bowed her head. Very quietly, she said, "My poor son. His heart is so angry."

Rory was a bit surprised when Sonia's father and brother didn't hesitate to shake hands. That he left tension behind him was beyond doubt. It was quite likely not the first time there had been tension in this family. He made his goodbyes, mounted his rested horse, and rode from the yard, looking for the first turn in the trail Pavel had outlined to him.

15

THE TWO-HOUR RIDE MENTIONED BY PAVEL TURNED INTO three, but Rory finally saw the name, *Triple T*, carved into a gate transom. After slowly riding the quarter-mile-long lane, he was met by a man standing in the center of the two-track trail, holding a carbine tucked under his folded arm. Not unfriendly, but not exactly friendly either.

"Help you?"

"If that sign is accurate and this is the Triple T, I'm thinking you probably can. Do you have a couple of Jamison boys on the payroll?"

"Well now. I might like to know who you are and just why you're asking."

Rory lifted his hat and wiped the sweat off his forehead with the sleeve of his jacket. He grinned at the questioner and said, "I should tell you that I'm the sheriff, come to arrest them for being lazy and of no account. But since you might not believe that, I'll own up to being their cousin. Rory Jamison, by name. I bring them news from the Double J Ranch. The Jamison ranch."

"Step down."

Pointing with the carbine, he said, "Walk over there where I can see you."

Rory kept pace as the man strolled nonchalantly across the yard toward the cookshack, as if there was all the time in the world. And perhaps there was in this high-up country. He suspected winters up that high, where the land was totally enclosed by snow-topped mountain peaks, were long and hard. But still, it was a beautiful country. Different from the Ivanov lands, but still beautiful. It wasn't as closed in as the Ivanov's ranch. He had seen the buildings of a couple of other ranches as he searched for the Triple T.

His guide held the cookhouse door open and motioned for Rory to enter ahead of him. Even before the door had been opened, Rory's stomach was rumbling at the odor of fried steaks and onions. He truly had a love for fried steak and onions.

He stepped inside to see, by quick count, fourteen riders arranged around tables with seating for four each. Years had passed since he had last seen his cousins, but he thought he could identify them at a table near the back. There was one other man sitting with them. He stepped that way, studying the men to assure himself of their identity. On close inspection, there could be no doubt.

Speaking loudly so everyone in the cookshack could hear, Rory said, "I haven't seen you in some years, but you're just as ugly as I remember, so you must be the Jamison boys, run off the Double J for being lazy, and for continually falling off your horses."

Silence filled the smoky room as men from every corner stared to see if this was a challenge to be taken seriously. When loud laughter came from the challenged couple, everyone relaxed.

"You must be Cousin Rory. You're the only one unaccounted for all these years."

With that, they both stood to their feet and shook hands with the newcomer.

The cousin who turned out to be Henry hollered across the room. "Hey, Slim. You suppose the T can afford to feed a wayward and half-starved wanderer? I'd take it as a kindness."

When no answer came, Henry took it as approval.

"Washbasin outside the door, as you probably saw already. The grub is help yourself style. Set up by the kitchen door. Watch out for the cook. He ain't no picnic to be around, but he can burn a steak as well as anyone. Get yourself fixed up and then come tell us why you're here and how things are on the outside."

An hour later, after the three Jamisons caught up on what news there was, a decision had been made. None of the news startled Henry or Thomas except the death of their uncle Jacob and the return of Hannah. When Rory talked about the murder and raid on the gold camp, they were both silent until Henry quietly said, "I take that hard, Rory. I can't imagine."

Henry and Thomas asked for their time after being assured by Slim that the T could complete their gather and drive the herd down to the flatlands with the remainder of the crew. On a different, and better trail than the one Rory had come up on, it was a six-hour ride to the Double J. That would be two, perhaps three, long days with the cattle. They would leave the next morning.

Rory inquired about the size of the Triple T market herd. Slim, who had joined the cousins after the third man had left, and was again sipping on a coffee cup and listening to the others discuss their plans, answered, "We're going to hold back some heifers for breeding. Not sure how many just yet. Should be near enough seven hundred head going to the rails."

"The Double J will have about two fifty, and the I-5 will have another one fifty. All branded so there could be no mix-up. If we joined together, we'd have more hands, and it still wouldn't be too large a drive. You have any interest in that?"

"I'd have interest in that. You would have to put in enough riders to carry your part of the load. We ain't going to do it for you."

"The best we can do is for myself, and I don't have a whole lot of experience, and these two lazy cousins of mine. I've got a couple of girl cousins that might work out better. We could leave these two back at the ranch and out from under our feet."

Slim accepted that as it was meant in jest before saying, "We'll be camping somewhere close to the Double J four days from now. We'll size up the situation then."

The foreman walked away grinning while Henry and Thomas studied on their long-lost cousin.

LATE THE NEXT AFTERNOON, there was a great welcoming celebration when the three men rode into the yard of the Double J. Henry and Thomas looked at Hannah for the first time in over four years. No one seemed to know exactly how to respond. Do you hug a sister? Shake hands? The boys had no idea. The consequence was that they stood where they were without moving while Henry said, "Don't know that I'd have known you if'n I'd seen you anywhere else. It's good to have you back. We'll have to hear your plans, but first, we have to care for these animals and see what Ma has on the stove."

ONE DAY before the Triple T herd was expected, the I-5 bunch arrived. Both Pavel and Ivan had ridden with the herd, leaving their mother alone on the ranch. They bunched the animals on grass alongside the northward trail. Grigor rode in while the two sons held the cattle. After greeting the man and introducing him to George, Rory threw a saddle on a horse and rode out to the herd.

"I'll hold your bunch. You go ahead and ride in. You'll want to take a close look at those bulls. George is going to clear out a small pasture to hold your bunch for a couple of nights. That will just take a short while and I'll move them in."

Pavel thanked him. Ivan ignored him.

Rory watched them ride in, shaking his head at how a man could hold such anger, or suspicion, over nothing at all.

FIVE MINUTES after seeing the young bulls and being guaranteed of their pedigree and the papers to prove it, Grigor nodded at George.

"Is there some room on the price, Mr. Jamison?"

"Rightly, they're not my bulls, nor do they belong to the Double J. They belong to Rory. The word he left when he went out to relieve you with your herd was that the price was firm. You can see that we bought those other twelve for the Double J. That shows that we believe in the stock and what they can do for our brand. But you are under no obligation to buy. There will be other ranchers interested once the news is out."

Grigor looked at his two sons as if trying to read their minds. For the first time, Ivan spoke.

"Buy the bulls, Father. You've talked enough about this for years. Now it's right in front of you."

A nod from Pavel confirmed the decision of the next generation of I-5 ranchers.

Grigor looked back at George. "Can they stay here until we get back from Cheyenne?"

With that settled, George led the men to a gated pasture alongside the ranch road.

"The boys have cleared out this grass. It is all fenced and gated off from the other land. Run your bunch in here. You can hold them until the Triple T gets here."

Not waiting for an answer, George walked back to the barn. He still had work to do before dinner. His womenfolk, too, had worked a long afternoon preparing for the visitors, along with their own family.

Grigor and Pavel, with Rory's help, soon had the herd moved. Ivan silently rode for home. It would be well into darkness when he arrived, but he would keep going. That was preferable to having his mother alone on the ranch all night.

IN ORDER TO find space with a bit of grazing for the Triple T, they had to move north another mile after reaching the Double J gate. One night of rest with decent graze and good water, and the three herds pulled together and pointed toward Cheyenne.

Rory stayed behind to help the girls care for the ranch. George and his two sons were more than able to hold up their end of the drive.

16

LEFT ALONE ON THE RANCH WITH JUST THE THREE WOMEN, Rory started to feel trapped. He had no desire to ride back up to Cheyenne, so he had volunteered to stay behind. But what he really wanted to do was ride down to the city. He had a few things in mind that could only be done from there.

To complicate matters, the girls were bored. Rory knew that it would take only a simple suggestion, and they would be pushing him to ride to town. But he liked to tell himself he had more sense of responsibility than to leave when there was no one on the ranch but his aunt.

He was fussing over his horse when Nancy walked into the barn and sat on the tipped-over bucket that so often served that purpose.

"Not much to do, Cousin. Dad keeps this place so picky organized that he really doesn't need any help. Mother took her broom to me. Can you imagine that? Brushed me out of the kitchen. She told me to quit moping. I don't think I ever mope. Do you think I mope?"

Rory looked at her and grinned.

"You don't really think I'm going to get into that conversation, do you?"

Then he had a thought. That led him to ask, "How would you like to saddle up? We'll push the old herd bulls out of the big pasture, separate them from the cows, and bring them up here to a corral. That has to be done sooner or later. Why not sooner?"

Without a word, Nancy walked into the tack room. A few minutes later, she led her saddled horse from the barn just in time to see Hannah walking across the yard.

"You might just as well get your horse and give us a hand, Hannah. They didn't teach this in your fancy school either, but we're going to separate the old bulls from the herd. You do know how to tell a bull from a cow, don't you?"

Hannah didn't reward her sister with an answer, but she did saddle a horse.

The bulls didn't particularly want to leave the herd, so the job turned into more work than Rory had assumed it would be. But by dinnertime that evening, there were fourteen bulls housed in the small corral beside the barn. Hannah dumped enough hay onto the ground beside the fence to hold them for at least one day. Rory carried buckets to fill the water trough, while Nancy pumped. With feed and water cared for, they called it a good day's work.

THE NEXT MORNING, the same boredom set in. Rory could feel it even before they were finished with their breakfasts. Aunt Eliza offered a possible solution.

"As soon as he's home, your father plans to wean the calves."

She said no more, leaving it to the young people to decide what that might mean. On any ranch in the West, Rory was well past the age of adult responsibility. He only hung back because he didn't want to get in the way of George's plans. There was also his lack of experience to consider.

Hannah knew nothing at all about working cattle, but Nancy, full of energy and self-confidence, stood to her feet and declared, "Let's us get it done."

The girls rushed from the house, ready to go to work, while Rory hung back for just a moment to drink up the last of his coffee. As he stood to leave, after thanking Eliza for the breakfast, she said, "I'd appreciate it if you would explain to Hannah that the mamma cows won't be happy being separated from their babies. And that cow horns are sharp and dangerous. She needs to take care. You can remind Nancy, too, but it might not do much good."

A WEEK LATER, when George and the boys returned from Cheyenne, Henry and Thomas turned into the ranch yard with the Ivanovs. George carried on into town. They were all carrying a considerable amount of money, all in cash, from the sale of their animals. They would provide security for each other until the money was safely deposited in the Stevensville Bank.

Grigor and Pavel rounded up their three new bulls,

and in a matter of minutes, were trailing the larger bunch of riders on the town road. They would spend one night in the hotel so they could get a good start in the morning with the slow-moving bulls.

～

HENRY AND THOMAS busied themselves with caring for the horses, while George, as soon as he got home, sunk into the big easy-chair that took up a considerable space in the corner of the kitchen.

Eliza looked at him with a grin.

"Long ride?"

"Long ride. But a good ride. The buyer grabbed up all three herds. Paid cash money. Higher price than I had hoped for. That gives the Double J a good year. Now I have to get those calves weaned and the old bulls separated out. Get this place set up for winter. May get a bit more hay off that south field yet too."

Eliza didn't want to spoil the surprise, so she simply said, "When you get your breath, you need to take a look at what your daughters have done. Them and Rory."

At dinner, a couple of hours later, George wanted to talk to the family while they were all together.

"We've had a good year. Makes up for two years ago and a bit more besides. With the bulls sorted out and the calves weaned, the other work can wait, all except that field of hay. But even that can wait one or two days. So tomorrow I'm declaring to be a family holiday day."

He reached into a shirt pocket and pulled out a fold of paper money. He peeled off one ten-dollar bill at a time and passed them around the table, including one to Eliza.

"That's not wages. We'll sort that matter out another

time. That's a bonus with my thanks. You can do with it whatever you wish. Tomorrow is Saturday. If you want to go to town, you can ride along with your mother and me."

Rory immediately offered to stay on the ranch, saying he had no desire to see the small town again. He slid his ten dollars over to his Aunt Eliza.

"You've treated me kindly, Eliza, and I appreciate it. You take that and add it to the other and buy yourself something nice. Something you wouldn't normally think of."

Without a word, Henry slid his ten over to his mother. Thomas immediately followed suit. Eliza glanced from one man to the other with a strange look on her face.

Henry had been studying Rory across the table all through the dinner. With no easing into the matter, he said, "Heard mention of your name once or twice up north."

Rory didn't wish to get into any conversation of that sort. He said nothing in response. But Nancy, who had the habit of blurting out the first thought that came to her mind, said, "A good mention? Did he break some poor girl's heart? Did he get arrested and break out of jail?"

Henry was slow to answer but finally figured out what he wanted to say.

"I would say it was good. Or at least good enough. There are some who would see it otherwise. But no matter how it's seen, it set the matter to rights, there can be no doubt of that."

Hannah added, "I was with him on the return trip with the bulls. Nothing happened during that time that anyone would remember."

Henry said, "Rory, we're all family here. We're all on your side. You need to fear nothing from any of us. It's fair to say that the story will soak down this far someday. It would be better if we heard it from you rather than from someone who gets it garbled and inside out."

Rory could have wished for almost anything but what was happening. He had hoped the story would have stayed in Pierre, Montana. But that was probably hoping for too much. Hesitating to say anything at all that might separate him from this family, his only family, he sorted things out in his mind. There was no reason to believe anyone knew about the attack on the trail to Boise on his way out. Hoping none of the men on the trail to Boise had spoken of the matter, and that they never would for fear of their own incrimination, he left that out. In any case, if no one talked, there was nothing to connect the dead men to the group Rory was traveling with.

"There had been some murders and thefts on the river we were working. We heard about it but not the details. Only that there had been three thieves and murderers. Somehow, we convinced ourselves that we would be safe. We weren't.

"I was digging out the old stream channel, taking it down to either bedrock or to the lowest water level. I could tell by the sand and clay I dug out, where the old bottom was. I threw the diggings as close to Father as I could. He was washing it out in the pan. I never did get good with the pan. Not as good as Father, anyway. It was a productive stream. We were fairly high up on it, close to the motherload, or so we figured. Only a handful of miners above us. There were other streams being worked, so there was no shortage of miners, but only those few more on ours. The gather of gold was good.

"We had gone up there hoping to get away from

heartache here on the Double J. Get some distance from the happenings. You all knew that when you came out here. Father didn't really much care if we found gold or not. But we did find it, and in plenty.

"I was just climbing out of the ditch I had dug, and Father was on his knees beside the stream panning out the sand. The attack came from nowhere, it seemed. We didn't hear them coming. The first thing I heard was the shot that killed Father. Hit him square in the head. Then, not really knowing what had happened to me, I found myself lying over the pile of just dug sand with blood pouring down my face and hurting so as to make me cry, but I couldn't move or speak. You can still easily see the groove in my skull where the bullet tore through. That I was unable to move saved my life.

"Father was shot three more times. They didn't bother with me again. I could hold one eye open just a slit. The way I was lying, I could see them. My vision was blurry, but I could see them alright. Three killers, tearing our camp apart, looking for gold. When they found just the bit we had cleaned up at noon, one of them ran out and shot Father again. Shot that good man after he was long dead. I could do nothing, but I could see their faces and hear their voices.

"With a shout, they were gone. It was hours before I was able to move. Even just a little bit. It took me several days to drag Father into the forest and scoop out a hole for him. My head finally stopped bleeding, but it was a couple weeks before I could stand up and move without sharp headaches. And all the time, those faces crawled through my memory. The murderers ran off our horses, four of them, but two got loose and came back. I managed to catch them and hold them until I was ready to move out. I dug up the gold the killers didn't find and readied myself for the long trip out.

"About that time, a group of upstream miners came by, heading out for supplies. I rode along to Boise. Banked my gold and rode out. I got a hint from a fella about where the killers had gone. Montana. A long ride in the condition I was in. But I did it. It took some time, but I found where they were. I scouted around and located the county sheriff, telling my story and asking for help. He said I had no proof. Wouldn't lift a finger. I figured I had it to do, or the knowing that they were alive and running loose would plague me all my days. They had stolen our horses, smashed our camp, and killed my father. I couldn't just let that go. I hung around that one street, ten-building town where the killers had taken refuge. No one saw me. I waited until two of the men took up sitting on the boardwalk chairs in front of the saloon. They had my JJ horses tied to the hitch rail.

"I rode up to the men and called them out, all the time wishing the third man was there. They tried to bluff me, but the JJ horses held them as guilty of horse theft. The folks standing by, listening to the talk, were convinced of that much at least.

"The fella who appeared to be the leader of the three, hoping to silence me, I suppose, shouted and jumped from his chair, pulling his belt gun. The second man was only a breath later, reaching for his weapon. I pulled my .44 and shot them both. The first man, the leader, was only wounded, but he fell to the boardwalk. The second man died with a single shot. The third man, the one with the scratchy, hoarse throat, who had somehow got himself appointed town sheriff, came shouting from the saloon. We exchanged shots. You can see on my fingers here where his first bullet struck. That caused me to let loose of the gun. The leader shot again, killing my horse. I dropped with the poor beast, lifting my carbine from the scabbard as the horse sunk into the dust of the road. Four shots from the carbine put an end to it all."

There was total silence in the room. No one even lifted a coffee cup. All eyes were on Rory. Aunt Eliza and Hannah were both quietly crying. Rory stayed silent for only a small part of a minute before he said, "You might ask if I'm sorry or if I feel guilty. The answer to both would be no. And you may ask if I don't remember what I was taught in church about not seeking revenge. Again, the answer would be no, I don't forget.

"These men were killers and thieves. They had shot me, killed my father, and stolen gold and four horses. I took the problem to the county law, who would do nothing. These men could not be allowed to live to repeat their crimes.

"Someday soon, I hope we will have law in this wonderful West. Some parts have reasonable law now. But not the wilderness of Idaho or the foothill country of Montana. Or even right here if we were to be honest about it. If we are to be safe, we must look after ourselves."

Again, there was silence as Rory looked around the table. He had just one more thing to say.

"If I make you uncomfortable by my actions and you want me to leave, I'll understand, and I'll go now. If you want to buy out my half of the Double J, I'm alright with that. I would even just ride off, and you can have the ranch. I can't change anything, and I can't find any other path I might have taken. I'm sorry the story got out, but I suppose it was inevitable."

Eliza was still crying quietly. Hannah was wiping her eyes. She was no longer crying. Nancy was staring hard at her cousin. Rory couldn't find a message in any of their actions. George cleared the air with, "I never do this, Rory, but I'm going to just this once. I now speak as the owner of half the Double J and the head of this home and this family. I know the Scriptures too. And I know we would all be better off in a perfect world, or at least in a much better world. That world, however, does not exist. Especially in this half-settled West, it doesn't exist. In my eyes, you did what the sheriff should have done. You cut a couple of corners, shortened the process some, but the end result was as it should have been. I find no fault in your actions. And I now understand why you riveted your father's gun to your belt.

"This is your home. It will always be your home, until you decide to move on to a better opportunity. I hope that time never comes. We want you here. You belong here. And we'll not talk of this anymore. I don't want to hear anyone asking questions or bringing this up again. It is done. Finished. I'm glad you came home to us, Rory."

17

TRUE TO HIS OFFER, RORY STAYED ON THE RANCH THE next day while the family went to town. George put a horse on the buggy and helped Eliza onto the seat. The young people were all on horseback. Everyone was dressed warmly. Eliza had a lap robe she spread over her and George's legs. Rory wondered how much of their ten dollars either of the girls would bring home with them. Henry and Thomas had been earning wages, so they had money of their own.

Rory puttered around the yard, making use of a rake and shovel where the horses had been turned loose to graze the grass of the yard.

He saddled a horse and rode slowly through the just weaned yearlings, studying the heifers with an eye to holding some for breeding.

The new bulls had been turned out with the cows who were all heavy with calf. They wouldn't be ready for breeding until after the calving season, which would come in February or March.

He seemed to keep himself busy, but still, the day

dragged. He cleaned out his own cabin with an eye to inviting Henry and Thomas to move their bunks out of the house. With everyone home, the space was at a minimum.

As evening was nearing and another drizzling rain was overtaking the land, the group returned. Rory was obliged to look at the wonders the girls had picked out but was spared any details about the others' day in town.

THE NEXT DAY WAS SUNDAY. Again, they all trouped into town to attend church. It was the first time Rory had gone with them. He found he liked the young minister and the thoughts he shared. The music was uplifting, even though a good singing voice was not one of the birth gifts his parents had lain on him.

His day was brightened a bit from a short visit with Sonia. She again thanked him for escorting her up the hill to her home. Nothing was said about her difficult brother.

ON MONDAY MORNING, Rory approached George.

"I'm fixing to ride up to the city, George. Is there anything I can do here on the ranch before I go?"

"You go and do what you have to do. We're all under control here."

Rory rolled his bedroll as tightly as possible with a change of clothes and his fine deer hide coat tucked inside, and a rain slicker wrapped around it. It made a bulky roll behind his saddle, but that was better than being burdened with a lightly loaded pack animal. The fall air was chilly enough that his fleece-lined coat was a comfort. He didn't bother with food or camp fixings, figuring he would have no problem breaking a two-day trip with a stop at one of the several small villages or stage stops along the way.

He nudged his gelding into a trot and, after waving a farewell to the onlookers, headed out the ranch trail on his way to the city.

His early morning start and the steady ride put him into the city by midafternoon of the second day, after a stopover in a pleasant little village that appeared to exist mostly for the comfort of travelers.

In the big city, the hotels on the edge of town looked pretty rough. He wasn't there looking for a challenge or for trouble, so he put the rough-looking ones behind him and kept riding. Further toward the center of the city, the buildings and the folks walking the sidewalks showed a considerable improvement. Studying out his options, he stopped at a hotel he liked the looks of, hoping it was affordable. He felt like a country boy coming to the city for the first time. Of course, that is exactly what he was. The two winters in Boise had helped, but Boise was still small-town compared to where he now was.

With his gelding tied to the rail in front of the hotel, he whipped as much travel dust off his clothes as he could, rubbed the toes of his boots on the back of his pant legs, adjusted his hat, and stepped onto the board-walk. Two young, well-dressed ladies strolling past looked him up and down, giggled, and moved on. He had no idea how to take that, so he pushed it out of his mind.

Entering the hotel, he was startled to see what, to him, was grandeur. The couches and chairs in the big lobby spoke of elegance and expense. The few women in attendance were dressed in gowns, as if they were waiting for a golden carriage to carry them to a fancy-dress ball. But that seemed unlikely in the middle of the afternoon.

Every man, decked out in black broadcloth suits with white shirts and bolo ties, appeared to have a cigar in his mouth or clasped between his fingers. Several, sitting in the big easy chairs, were in deep conversation with other similarly dressed men.

Rory's first glance had him backing the door, thinking to ride back to one of the lesser hotels he had seen. He was stopped in his tracks when a smiling hotel employee, dressed in what must have been the hotel uniform, approached and said, "Good afternoon, sir. May I help you? Were you thinking of a room, sir?"

Rory stumbled and hesitated but finally managed to nod toward the finely dressed hotel guests and mumbled, "I need a room, but I might be in the wrong place."

The hotel worker responded, "Don't take any of that seriously. Those are all either ranchers or mining men. The salt of the earth, them and their wives, if you take my meaning. Some of them arrived here wearing far rougher clothes than I see on you. Come, let's see about that room."

To Rory's relief, the room rental was affordable and the room clerk friendly. He signed in, received his key, and walked out to his horse to untie the bedroll. He was ready to step back onto the boardwalk when the same two girls walked toward him, heading the opposite direction. Feeling mischievous, he openly looked them up and down and then forced a small chuckle.

The girls stopped in their tracks. The one standing on the outside of the boardwalk, closest to Rory, stared at him and demanded, "Did you just laugh at me? That's pretty rude."

"Is it more rude than you laughing at me a few minutes ago?"

That he said it with a smile probably saved the day. Into the brief silence that followed, Rory tipped his hat and said, "Rory Jamison, ladies. And yes, I'm just in from the ranch. New to the big city, you might say. But I'm figuring I'll manage to sort it all out by and by. I'm not figuring to waste my money on clothes as fancy as I see around me, but I'm hoping you, who are obviously my betters, will have some sympathy for a country boy."

"I'll have sympathy if you promise not to laugh at us again."

"That's a deal. No more laughing. But if you won't take me wrong, I must say seriously, you girls look mighty fetching today. Why, if I was looking for a girl, I just might call on one of you. Or perhaps both of you. That is if I knew where your ranch is."

The talkative girl answered, "I'm thinking we'll leave it at that. Good day, sir."

Without further words, Rory smiled and tipped his hat. When the ladies had moved on, he stepped into the hotel and headed toward the stairs. The same employee who had first spoken to him spoke again.

"That was smooth. For a country boy, as you called yourself, I'm thinking you'll adapt to the city before you know it."

Rory grinned and answered, "I have no idea what you're talking about."

∿

His FIRST STOP after washing up in the hotel room and getting a bite of lunch in the dining room, was to seek out a bank. It wasn't unheard of for banks to go broke and close their doors. He would have to be cautious and ask the right questions. Diagonally across the street from the hotel, the sign over the big door said, *Ranchers and Miners Bank*. Stepping off the boardwalk, he angled his way through traffic and entered the establishment. As a precaution against misunderstanding, he had left his gun belt in the hotel room. There was no need for the fleece coat on a warm afternoon, so he left that in the room also.

Easing up to a teller's wicket, he said, "I'm hoping to talk with someone privately. Is there a space where that can be done?"

The teller stepped into the back room and was soon back with a more senior employee beside him.

From behind the safety of the teller's brass wicket, the suspicious manager asked what it was about.

"If we can meet in private, sir, I'll be happy to tell you."

After a serious study by the manager, he was led into a small room off to one side. When both men were seated, without preamble, Rory opened the account book from the Boise bank. He flattened it out and laid it before the suspicious man.

"As soon as you say something that will assure me of the stability of this bank, I would like to transfer these funds."

The manager studied the bank book. As if copying the banker back in Battlement, Illinois, he asked, "Is this your money?"

Rory reached over and closed the little book.

"That's my name on the front, so it seems to be a reasonable assumption."

"I'll need some proof that this is really yours and that there were no crimes involved in you having it."

Rory stood to his feet and reached for the book. Sternly he said, "No, you don't. But what is clear to me is that I am in the wrong place."

With no goodbye, Rory left the building. A block down the street, past the hotel, there was another bank. He walked over that way expecting the worst. But it turned out completely differently. He was given a friendly handshake and an escort into a pleasantly deco-rated, private room. Within minutes, the transaction was completed. He had moved half his gold money.

With that behind him, he still had to deal with the remainder of the funds. He had no intentions of depending on just one institution. A full block further away, he found a second bank that wanted his business. In both places, he had inquired about the security of his deposit, receiving the same answer. There was no real guarantee. It was up to the management of the bank, and sometimes, events that happened far away. It wasn't quite the luck of the draw, but it leaned that way. With no real choice, he completed the remaining transfer.

By the time banking affairs were in place, and he had walked several blocks along the busy street, studying out the wide range of retailers and services on offer, the business day was at an end. His call to government offices would have to wait.

18

Looking toward a long evening with little to do, Rory decided to make the most of it, beginning with a slow, fancy dinner. That was all the time assuming the hotel dining room would qualify within those parameters. He had no intention of leaving the hotel in search of something better.

He returned to his room with a cold wash and a shave in mind but was delighted to discover that hot baths were offered to hotel guests. He hadn't had a hot bath since sitting in Eliza's big, round laundry tub back when he first arrived at the ranch. Many times, he had gotten reasonably clean sitting in a cold-water creek or standing before a basin of water with a wet rag. Neither compared well against a real hot bath.

With the bath and a shave behind him, he unrolled his bedroll and dug out the clean pants and shirt he had carefully folded there. He dressed, combed his hair, and studied himself in the mirror in his room. He knew his clothing wouldn't compare to the men he saw in the lobby earlier in the day, but it would have to do.

He wiped a wet cloth across his boots, donned his freshly brushed hat, and stepped out. Walking through the crowded lobby toward the dining room entry, he was amazed to see the room filled. Every table held guests laughing, smoking, drinking, and eating. There was no maître d'. Seating was catch-as-catch-can, every man for himself. He stood in the doorway, glancing over the room, trying to decide what to do. He knew no one, and no one looked his way. And then someone did. A man, well-dressed, sitting with two women at a table for four. The look was direct. He could not mistake it.

The table was set sideways to the room so that all three diners were able to glance at the entryway. As far as he had noticed, neither of the women had looked at him. But one woman leaned across the table and whispered something to the man, giggling a bit as she spoke. Rory could see the questioning look and the slight movement of lips that returned the whisper. The woman appeared to speak more emphatically. That brought about obvious resignation from the man.

Again, the man looked directly at Rory, this time with a raised finger that seemed to be signaling him.

Rory had never seen the fellow before, but he couldn't mistake the steady look and the upraised, beckoning finger. Rory fixed his look at the man with a question in his eyes, as if to say, "Me? Are you flagging me?"

This time, in obvious frustration, the finger beckoning turned into a whole-handed wave, calling Rory to the table. By this time, other people were looking at the scene being enacted out before them. Rory figured he might just as well see what it was all about. He slowly made his way through the maze of tables and chairs and the scurrying waiters, arriving at the table to see the women were the two girls from the sidewalk earlier in the day.

"Sit down, young man."

It was more an order than an invitation, but Rory sat, holding his hat in his hand and then laying it on his lap. He looked at the two girls and then back to the man. Judging by similarity of looks and their ages, this had to be two sisters and their father.

Into the silence that greeted his seating, Rory looked at the man and asked, "You called me? What can I do for you, sir?"

The returning voice was deep and strong but not gruff. It appeared to be the fellow's natural speaking voice.

"You can tell me your name, where you're from, and what was the meaning of speaking to my daughters on the public street this afternoon."

"Rory Jamison, sir. Double J Ranch. Stevensville, fifty or so miles north of here. In town on business, same as most here, I'm guessing. As to your daughters, who I respected and properly introduced myself to, they were, by looks, so obviously what they are, good decent ranch girls in town and dressed for strolling the walkways of the big city. They took me a bit by surprise when they sized up me and my work-worn clothing and giggled. I know I could often pass for an uncared-for scarecrow, so I didn't take it personally. Not much anyway. But a bit later, when they came past going the other way and I was there again, I made a point of letting them see me returning the favor, followed by a bit of a chuckle. I meant it all in good fun, and I'm sure the ladies did as well. But if I gave offense, I am truly sorry, and I apologize."

No one spoke for a few seconds. The man finally said,

"Gale Strombeck, GS Ranch, up on the plateau. My daughters, Allie and Polly."

With that, he turned to the girls with an amused look.

"You didn't quite tell me the whole of it, girls."

Through a glorious grin, Allie, or perhaps it was Polly, Rory wasn't quite sure as the father hadn't singled them out when he named them, said, "Well, Father, a girl who gets to the city once in a year, and perhaps not even that, can surely amuse themselves, and not confess every little detail. And you must admit, he's the kind of fellow you just have to notice. So, there's no harm done, and we have a dinner guest to abuse at our own will."

Gale Strombeck leaned back in his chair and studied his two daughters. He then turned to look at Rory before saying, "Young man, do you feel like being abused over dinner? Or perhaps the real question would be, is it worth some abuse to have a seat in a busy dining room? I'm assuming the abuse will only be verbal. I took their guns away from them as soon as we came to town."

"So, there you have it, Mr. Jamison." said Polly, or perhaps it was Allie. "We are helpless. Unarmed. At the mercy of the cruel world."

As she said this, a waiter approached with a menu. Offering it to Rory, he said, "Will you be dining here, sir, or are you just visiting?"

Rory finally heard a question he could answer. "I'll stay, and thank you. I'm staying mostly to see what happens next. Do you have anything special that I should try tonight?"

"We have a special, but it's nearly gone. I would recommend the schnitzel. It is excellent with a side of dumplings, some mashed potatoes, and cream gravy."

Rory passed the menu back before saying, "That

sounds great. And I'd like a glass of cold water, if you please."

The meal and the visiting progressed with nothing of note being discussed, after Rory and Strombeck gave a brief description of their ranches. But before they left the subject, Strombeck said, "Somehow, I feel I've heard of the Double J before. Perhaps one of your riders found his way to the plateau and mentioned something."

Rory didn't pursue the topic, choosing instead to ask the girls how long they were in town for.

The speaker was Allie. Rory had finally figured them out from little things said along the way. "One more day only. I have no idea what we're going to do tomorrow. We intend to ask the hotel desk for suggestions. Father will be doing business, and we've done all the shopping we wanted to do. But as soon as we finish dinner, we intend to go for another stroll. We both enjoy looking at the wares in the windows and watching the folks going by."

Strombeck quickly said, "You're going nowhere in the evening unless you have someone with you. The city isn't exactly the same place at night as it is during the day. Perhaps Mr. Jamison would have time to accompany you for an hour or so."

Polly, who had spoken very little, asked, "Do you have other plans, Rory, or would you escort us for a few blocks up and down the town?"

"You let me go upstairs and get my warm coat, and I'll walk along for a while. I'm thinking it's going to rain. Rain or snow. It's cold enough for snow. We wouldn't want to get too far from the hotel."

Suddenly, as if the other conversation wasn't happening at all, Strombeck almost hollered, "Got it."

With that, he turned in his seat to take in a better

look at Rory. He only hesitated a moment before saying, "It wasn't a Double J rider that spread the story. It was a rider heading to a warmer climate after being up in Montana. It was quite a story, young man. I'm assuming it's true. I don't see you mounting any objection to it."

"What story, Father?"

"Never you mind. Rory can tell you if he wishes to, but I won't. A man deserves some privacy."

Allie looked at Rory with unasked questions, as if they would be asked soon enough, and said, "Go get your warm coat, Rory. We'll get ours too. We'll meet you in the lobby in ten minutes."

19

WHILE RORY HAD VERY LITTLE EXPERIENCE WITH YOUNG ladies, he managed to hold up his end of the conversation as the three visitors to the city strolled the boardwalks. That the girls were ranch raised became evident after the parading and the giggling of their first encounter was set aside. Awkward, at first, not knowing where to walk—beside the girls, ahead of them, inside or outside of the walkway—Allie finally solved the issue.

Grasping Rory's right arm with her left, she pulled up beside him. Polly quickly grasped the other arm. Arm in arm, they proceeded. Doubtful at first, Rory finally settled in and found himself enjoying the closeness. But evening dusk was giving way to night-time darkness, and the storm clouds continued to build over the western horizon.

"I believe the time has come to return to the safety of the hotel, girls."

"Aw, just one more block and then we'll go back."

"If you girls will take a serious look up ahead, I

believe you will see the reason for my wanting to go back."

Stopping to look, Allie said, "You're right again. I can barely see in the dark, but that looks like a pretty rough crowd up there."

With no further words, they made a three-person turn without unlinking their arms. But it was too late to avoid controversy.

"Well, well, what have we here? Two lovelies come to enjoy the evening with us. And just one kid holding onto the two of them. Doesn't seem hardly right, does it, boys?"

The speaker turned to look at his three friends, seeking approval and support.

One of the others slurred out, "Beat it, kid."

Understanding that these were cowboys out on the town, filled up with whiskey bravery, Rory didn't try to talk or negotiate. He simply shook himself free from the girls, unbuttoned his heavy coat, and spread the sides far apart, exposing his belt and double holsters. He said nothing at all, simply waiting, with his hands hanging loosely at his sides, while the men took in the dual .44s and considered their odds. Even through the whiskey cloud they were operating under, the thinking didn't take long.

One of the previously silent men, perhaps a bit more sober than his pals, said, "Sorry there, girls. It appears we made a mistake. If y'all don't mind, we'll just keep walk'n along. No harm meant."

With that, the four men squeezed against the adjacent building to allow Rory and the girls to pass. Rory was green, but he wasn't that green. And as far as no harm meant, he didn't swallow that for a moment. Instead of walking along, he eased the girls to the side of the boardwalk and said, "You fellas move out now while I can keep an eye on you. If you turn around, I'll assume you mean a threat.

"The next time the whiskey leads you to insult a lady could be your last. And if it happens to be these ladies, I can guarantee it will be your last. Move out now."

As the image of the four men faded into the darkness of the next business block, Rory led the girls toward the hotel. The excitement and romance of the evening had disappeared just as surely as the last of the day's light. It was a silent return walk.

At the hotel, Rory was set to bid the girls goodnight, but they weren't ready to be alone.

"The dining room is nearly empty now. Let's sit for coffee."

Without a word, Rory headed that way. They chose a table where they could see the doorway and a glimpse of the lamp-lit boardwalk yet be somewhat hidden themselves. At Rory's suggestion, they had a piece of apple pie each to go along with the coffee. There was little conversation, with each one considering the events of the past half hour. Rory was again ready to bid goodnight when Gale Strombeck walked into the lobby, shaking a mixture of rain and snow from the shoulders of his coat. He removed his hat and was beating the moisture off on his pant leg when he noticed his daughters in the dining room. He walked in and was about to speak, but Allie spoke first.

"Father, I want my gun back. And I want it back tonight. It was a mistake not to have them with us all the time."

The firm words caught her father by surprise.

"Tell me."

"I'll tell you, alright. Four drunks accosted us, taking

us for something their evil minds thought up. If we hadn't been with Rory, there's no telling what would have happened. As it is, I don't know what he did for sure other than open his coat and tell the men to get lost."

Gale didn't know for sure either, but he suspected that Rory had been wise enough to arm himself before venturing out.

"I'm not going to ask you to show me what's under that heavy coat, young man, because I probably already know. But I'm going to thank you for going with the girls and for being prepared."

Turning his eyes to Allie, he said, "I'll get your guns when we go upstairs. But don't be showing them around."

In exasperation, Polly said, "Father, we've been handling weapons almost from before we could walk. We won't be showing them around."

Suddenly the girls weren't giddy, starstruck town visitors. They were ranch girls. Strong, competent, self-assured, and ready to face whatever came upon them. Rory liked the change.

BY MIDAFTERNOON THE FOLLOWING DAY, Rory expected to be on the trail back to Stevensville. He had only three calls to make. He didn't think any of them would take long. He checked out of his room, carried his carefully rolled bedroll down to the livery, and saddled his horse. With everything checked out and snugged down, he rode back to the hotel for breakfast. He was in time to join Gale Strombeck and his daughters.

"Good morning, Rory, come join us. The girls and I

have just ordered. By the looks of that bedroll behind your saddle, I'm guessing you're about done with the city."

"It's a nice enough city, and I guess I'm not really done with it since it's going to be here a while, and I expect to be also. But I'm about done with my business. Just a couple of stops that I hope to clear up this morning. I'd like to be home tomorrow evening."

Allie smiled and said, "I know it was rude, but I'm glad we giggled at you. Otherwise, we wouldn't have met. And we are both very thankful you were with us last evening. We completely misjudged the city. Or at least the night-time city. We pretty much know our way around the ranch but have a lot to learn in town. So, thank you again."

The conversation went along easily but faded when the food came. When they finished their meals, Rory insisted on paying, reminding Gale that he had bought dinner the evening before.

They all followed Rory out to his horse and bid farewell one more time. Polly spoke for all of them when she said, "Come visit us on the GS sometime. And if we're ever up north, we'll look in on the Double J."

Rory nodded his head in agreement and kicked the gelding into motion. His first stop was the state offices. He had asked for directions the day before. He was surprised at the smallness of the office. He had somehow thought there would be more to it. He suspected that, as time went along, there would be growth in the government control and administration, but for now, it was two rooms with four desks spread among them, but with only two people in sight.

A middle-aged woman, with her graying hair tied into a knot at the back of her head, looked up from her work. There was no friendliness in her expression. She said nothing, simply waiting for Rory to speak.

"I'd like to talk with someone who can tell me about counties and how they're put together."

"Now, why would someone too young to even vote care about that? We're busy here. We have no time for foolishness."

Before Rory could form a response, a man hollered from the second office, "Come in, young man. And Bertha, please try to remember that we are public servants."

Bertha harrumphed as Rory walked past her desk, heading toward the other office.

As he entered, the man behind the desk rose and held out his hand.

"Oscar Cator, administrator, how can I help you?"

"Rory Jamison, Double J Ranch, Stevensville. I'm wanting information on how a county works or is supposed to work."

"That's a good question. Have a seat, and we'll talk about it. But first, to narrow the answer, tell me your specific concern."

"I'm wondering how a county with no organization of any sort gets itself organized. And I'm wondering how law and order get established on a solid footing."

After a lengthy, silent study of Rory, the administrator said, "Well, one thing Bertha is right about is that you don't appear to be old enough to vote. Are you asking on behalf of someone else? The village council, perhaps?"

"No, sir. I'm just me. But it may help if I told you that having the county organized is less important to me than the establishment of law."

Oscar smiled, and again, he was slow to answer. But

finally, he asked, "Would this have anything to do with a matter that came to my ears a few weeks ago? A matter of a judge who isn't really a judge and a town marshal that isn't really a town marshal?"

The surprise on Rory's face couldn't have been more real. The look caused Oscar to laugh out loud.

"We live in a vast, open country, Rory. Hundreds of miles, if not thousands, where we could travel and see hardly a soul. But in reality, we are very small. Even as our population is small. There isn't much news, but what there is travels fast."

He got up and closed the office door.

"You answer my question, young man, and then I will answer yours."

With a relieved grin, Rory asked, "Would I be close to the truth if I assumed you have been talking to sheriff Anthony Clare?"

Now the two men were grinning at each other. Oscar changed his grin to just a few confirming words with, "You see, Rory, it really is just a small world."

With a nod, Rory asked, "So where does it go from there?"

Oscar got down to business, explaining the situation as it dealt with declaring a county seat, establishing a county commission, working out a tax structure. Creating a voters' list, and on and on. Rory's head was beginning to swim with new information. Oscar wound it up with, "Normally, Rory, a county sheriff would be voted in by all the ratepayers of that county. But baby steps can be slow and cumbersome. And it always requires a leader, and there are few of those in a small town or village.

"So, when there is a clear and pressing need, I have taken it upon myself to shorten the process a bit. I have only done that twice before, and thankfully, it worked out alright. And thankfully, too, no one from any higher office than mine has chosen to challenge my decisions."

"So where does that leave it, Mr. Cator?"

"No need for the 'mister', Rory. Oscar is fine. As to where it leaves matters, here's what I'm prepared to do. But first, tell me, are you interested in a position in law enforcement, or do you hope to recruit someone else?"

"I hadn't thought seriously about myself, but I would discuss it with you if you thought I would be a fit."

"Strangely, you have to be a certain age to vote but not to protect the voters. But then, no one ever said that every law makes sense. If you were interested, I would appoint you as deputy sheriff under Anthony Clare. He spoke highly of you even though your meeting was brief. You would be assigned to your home county for a one-year appointment. By that time, hopefully, someone up there can pull the people together and apply for county seat at least. Perhaps work up a voters list. That would be a good start.

"For now, and until there is a tax base to support the needed staff, you would be best to rely on a circuit judge. We have three of them in the state, all good men."

THERE WAS MORE TALK, some of which Rory failed to truly understand, but the result was that he left the office with a sheriff's badge in his pocket after swearing the oath administered by Oscar and witnessed by the ever-sour Bertha.

He had come to town with the full intention of inquiring about having a telegraph line strung into Stevensville. As soon as he mounted his gelding, he gave the idea up. His head couldn't hold any more that day. *There will be another time.*

～

THE NEXT AFTERNOON he rode through Stevensville without stopping. Nor did he pin the badge onto his shirt. He wanted no one to know about the assignment until he was ready. He rode directly to the Double J.

A fine supper, a long talk with the family, while his sheriff badge was displayed in the center of the big kitchen table, a good night in his own bed, and a refreshed bedroll, this time carrying warmer clothing, and he was off to his first attempt at lawing.

20

WISHING TO APPEAR AS HE ALWAYS HAD AND GIVING NO hint that there was a sheriff's badge in his pocket, Rory dressed in clean, but slightly worn ranchhand clothing. He didn't really expect to be gone overnight, but he packed a bedroll anyway. Inside the tightly rolled blankets, he had tucked a change of warm clothing in acknowledgment of the season. In mountain country, the weather can change while a man is having lunch or saddling a horse. It was best to expect the worst and be prepared.

It was just past first light when he rode from the Double J, heading for town. He would be early for the bank, but that suited the habits ingrained after years of his father's instructions and influence. While he waited for the bank to open, he might drop in to see Sonia and have a coffee. Ma might have a minute for a quick discussion too.

Right from his return from the gold fields, he had been troubled by a lingering mistrust of the banker. He had no good reason for it. He could not really explain it.

Now, with nowhere to start except for the few people he knew in town, he had to decide, trust the banker or not. He used his short visit with Ma as a starting point.

Sitting opposite Rory when the busyness of the restaurant allowed, she quietly asked, "So, what's happening?"

Rory had not yet said a word, but the woman had already sensed something. Rory was again impressed by her knowledge and her wisdom.

Rory pulled his chair a couple of inches closer to the table and leaned in. He reached into his vest pocket and wrapped a couple of fingers around the badge but didn't pull it out until he again glanced around the room and out the window. When he was sure no one else was watching, he carefully removed the badge and, wrapped into the palm of his hand so no one else could see, turned it to Ma. No words were spoken until their eyes caught and he slid the badge back into the pocket.

Ma leaned even closer than she had been and quietly said, "You had better tell me. I have the sense that you could be on a dangerous path."

"It's temporary. Or at least I'm thinking of it that way. The state people are aware of the happenings down here. We had a long discussion on it a couple of days ago, up in the city. The administrator jumped past the need for an election by posting me as a deputy to the sheriff from another county, but to only work this county. I want to keep it all secret until I have some solid evidence. I've shown you, hoping you might have heard something about other folks who were treated to the same crime that the judge tried on the JJ. I've heard rumors but no names.

"Before you answer that, perhaps I should tell you that I'm thinking of leveling with the banker. I haven't had any real reason to distrust him, nothing I can put my finger on anyway. Still, there is a lingering doubt. And if I trust the wrong person, the whole deal will be lost."

"Rory, I like you. And Sonia believes you're the answer to every girl's prayers. Browning, down at the mercantile, thinks highly of you. You're on solid footing in the community, and I know most will support you in what you're doing. But the only ones you should trust are the ones who might have helpful information. Jesse Ambrewster would be one of those.

"Jesse is sometimes cranky and even a bit rude. He's never gotten over some things that happened in that dreadful war. Many others are the same, but Jesse has been unable to hide his feelings. But I believe I am correct when I tell you he would not be a party to the doings that you're hoping to stop. I also don't think he would do anything to stop it himself. He would just sit by, running his bank, all the while telling himself it had nothing to do with him. I've told him a few times that a man can get real sore sitting on the fence."

Rory leaned back in his chair, having listened closely but also noting that the banker was walking down the opposite boardwalk toward the bank. Plus, Sonia was looking toward Ma. Several customers had come in. Ma was needed in the kitchen. Without words, they rose from their chairs together. Ma leaned in and quietly said, "Ambrose King, east of here. Be very careful son."

Rory asked if they could shut the office door when Jesse Ambrewster invited him into the inner office. With a questioning look, the banker stepped back and gently closed the door after telling the clerk not to disturb them.

With shivers of worry and doubt, Rory went ahead with his plan. He laid the badge on the banker's desk and waited. Ambrewster looked at the badge, up at Rory, and then back at the badge. He leaned back in his chair, folded his hands over his startlingly thin waist, and said, "I won't ask how or why. But I will ask how it is that you are showing me this and what it has to do with me or the bank."

"Mr. Ambrewster, I'm showing you this in absolute confidence. It's important that no one else knows about it for the time being. And I'm showing it because I don't have time to waste, and I believe you may have information that could help."

"You were so abrupt and doubting when you were last in here, I came to believe there was something between us. Now here you are asking for my help."

"You knew my father, Mr. Ambrewster."

"Indeed, I did. And a finer man I never met."

"I'm pleased to hear that about him, but he also had other attributes. You might remember that he was well known for saying a man had to finish what he started. And less known was his inner cautiousness. He was a careful man. Both of those traits were deeply imbedded in me.

"I have taken on a task that I fully intend to complete. And I, too, am cautious. If my fixing something should hurt others in the doing of it, I would have failed. You are correct in thinking I approached you and the bank with some trepidation. Perhaps I took too much from a couple of rumors I had heard. Gossip, really, and I know better. So here I sit after deciding to trust you and level with you.

"You, of course, know that Ronald Thrasher, who passes himself off as a judge, together with the phony marshal, attempted to grab off the assets of the JJ. He's done the same to others. It's those others I need to contact. I've heard of at least three ranches, two in the highlands and one east of town on the flatlands. And one name, Ambrose King. All I know about him is that his home is east of town. I have no more accurate information.

"It's a long, cold ride to where I've heard his home is. I wouldn't want to make that ride unnecessarily. And I would not want to disturb him or start more rumors if he is not involved. So, I'm asking you in total confidence, can you confirm any of this?"

Ambrewster was a long time answering, as he studied Rory and fidgeted with the pencil in his hand. He finally said, "I'm sure you understand that confidentiality is uppermost in a bank, confidentiality and security, which are sometimes almost the same thing. But I'm going to lie to myself, hoping that someday I will believe I didn't really break a confidence. I do it only because this thing has to stop, and perhaps you are the one who can accomplish that.

"I will confirm the King situation, without discussing the details."

Rory nodded and rose to leave. Then he thought of one more thing.

"Is Thrasher holding the funds from the sale of stock in this bank?"

"Yes. Whatever he hasn't drawn to spend on himself."

"I think it would be helpful if those funds were locked down until the real law gets to sort it all out."

"I'll have to think on that, Rory."

"You do that. Just for a few days, perhaps."

Rory rode his gelding east, never having been through that country before. The further he rode, it seemed, the dryer the land looked. The recent rains and even a skiff of snow could not hide the natural tufts and sparseness of the grass. The rapid change from the green plateau ranches like the I-5, to the Double J, and eastward to what he was riding across, was startling.

About five miles east of town, he spotted a ranch off to the south. He turned that way to seek directions. His badge was again secreted in the small vest pocket.

As he rode near, a middle-aged man stepped from the hay shed with a pitchfork in his hand.

"Morn'n, young fella, fine day for rid'n. Although I might want some shelter in a few hours. Com'n to rain. Maybe even snow. What can I do for you?"

"Morning, sir. Rory Jamison. I'm new to this east country. Live and ranch up north of town a bit. Double J. Hoping to find the King place. Can you set me right on that?"

"You just angle back to the northeast, mostly east, and in about ten miles or so, you'll see 'er. Greet Ambrose for me. Tell him Earnest Fisher asked about him. Sent his greetings."

As Rory turned his gelding, he said, "I'll be sure to do that, sir. And thanks."

Holding his animal to a ground-eating trot, Rory came in sight of the King buildings two hours later. He had pushed the animal a bit, but he wanted to get his work done and return to town before nightfall. The horse would recover some strength while he visited with the King family.

He saw no more than a handful of cattle along the way.

Riding in, there was no sign of Ambrose King. But a

woman stepped out of the chicken house and turned after closing the coop door. She was older than Rory had been led to believe Mrs. King would be. With her eyes firmly on her visitor, she let herself out of the chicken yard and carefully closed that door, as she had with the other. Shading her eyes with her one hand, while the other held a bucket of eggs, she waited.

Within seconds Rory figured out that the woman was waiting for him to break the silence.

"Good morning, Mrs. King. Rory Jamison. Out from town to talk with Ambrose King, if he's available."

"I'm not Mrs. King, but come to the house. It's too cold to stand yapping out here."

"May I stall my gelding? He could use some rest and shelter. A bit of water, too, if you don't mind."

"I don't mind. There's room in the barn. A bit of feed and some corn too. Help yourself and then come to the house."

When Rory was let in at the kitchen door, there were two women standing there, but still no Ambrose King.

He stamped his feet on the porch mat and removed his hat before stepping inside.

"Morning, ladies. As I said outside, ma'am, I'm Rory Jamison. I'm hoping to talk with Ambrose King."

Working through obvious suspicion, the younger of the two women said, "I'm Katie King. This is my mother, Mrs. Lavinia Flint. What do you want my husband for, Mr. Jamison? I don't believe he or I know you."

"You are correct, Mrs. King, Mrs. Flint. We have not met before. You might know my family ranch though, the Double J, north of Stevensville by a couple of miles."

"Heard of it but don't know anyone from there."

"Is Mr. King available, please? It's important that I talk with him."

Katie King pursed her lips and tightened her hands into fists, as if she was ready to do battle. Instead of that, she said, with some resignation, "Whatever it is you want can't be any worse than what's already gone before. Come with me."

She led him into a short hallway that connected the big kitchen to a sitting room and three closed doors. She opened one door and walked in. Rory followed. What he saw startled him. There, lying crookedly on a mussed bed, was a man who was half asleep but in obvious pain. Rory glanced sideways to Mrs. King and asked, "What on earth happened? Is there something I can do to help?"

"What happened, Mr. Jamison, is that my husband, trying everything and anything he thought might save what's left of our ranch, managed to corral three wild horses. He was hoping there would be a sale for them if he could get them broke to the saddle. The first two he rode gentled a bit. They're in the barn. The third one was the very devil himself. Ambrose stayed with him for perhaps half a minute before he lost his seat. He flew into the corral railing and then to the ground, landing on his shoulder and arm, and giving his head an awful whack on the fence post. He did that just in time for that outlaw horse to come down with his front hoof on Ambrose's leg."

"I'm so sorry, Mrs. King. Are there broken bones? How bad is it?"

"He has a badly broken arm, with a bit of bone sticking out of the flesh. He fades in and out from the injury to his head, and his leg is certainly damaged. Whether it's broken or not, I don't know."

Rory was startled into saying, "Mrs. King, we have to get your husband to the doctor. We have to do that right now."

"Do you somehow think Mother and I don't know that?"

Her angry response was not what Rory was expecting. It took him a moment to recover his thoughts. Mrs. Flint, walking into the room, said, "We have been at our wit's end, Mr. Jamison. Ambrose is too much for either of us to lift. Even together, we couldn't do it. He can't walk. He somehow managed to half crawl, half slide on his belly from the corral to the house. But every move now brings on terrible pain. Can't sit up. Sleeps most of the time. Or is unconscious. We don't know which. He's still in terrible pain. And we're open to suggestions."

Before Rory could wrap his head around all that, Mrs. King said, "I shot that cursed animal. He'll do this to no one else ever again."

That was interesting information, but Rory couldn't see how it would help get this man to town. Sorting it out in his head, studying possibilities, he thought he would start with the basics.

"I saw a buckboard under the shed. Is it in workable order?"

Mrs. King had left the room crying. Her mother answered for her.

"The wagon is fine. So is the team that's stalled in the barn. As soon as this happened yesterday, I caught up the team and put them inside."

"Alright, let me do what I can, and then we'll see. In the meantime, you ladies have to see to what needs doing when you're not here. We'll get to town somehow. You could be a while returning."

Without a word, Mrs. Flint left the room and started putting on her warm clothes. Before going out the door, she spoke to her daughter, "Katie, get the kids fed and dressed in their warmest clothing. Bundle up lots of blankets and get dressed warmly yourself. Pack a couple jars of drinking water and something for the kids to snack on. I'll deal with the chickens and the milk cow, and then we'll see to some lunch."

With that, she was out the door. Rory was right behind her, heading to the barn to harness the team. Before he even reached the barn door, he heard the squawking of chickens as Mrs. Flint caught them, hauling them out six at a time, holding them by one leg each. She carried them to the farthest back corner of the barn and let them go. Before long she was back with others. When she was done with the chickens, she turned the milk cow and her calf loose in the barn. There was hay stacked in one stall. The animals could look after themselves.

Rory turned the two wild horses loose and then harnessed the team, while Mrs. Flint pumped water into a trough fixed inside, adjacent to the big doors.

Within fifteen minutes, the wagon was sitting, ready, outside the kitchen door. Rory had loaded it down with a good layer of hay. Now he spread out the blankets Mrs. King gave him.

The rain had stopped, changing to a pebbled snowfall as the temperature dropped. Mrs. Flint brought an oiled canvas from somewhere and spread it over the top of the bedding.

With a quick lunch, they were ready to go.

With both the bedroom and kitchen doors propped open so they wouldn't get in the way, and with the bedding in the wagon as prepared as it was ever going to be, Rory set his hat on the kitchen table to get it out of the way and walked into the bedroom. The glazed-over eyes that looked out from the covers told him Ambrose King was at least half awake, or conscious, or whatever it should be called.

Not really sure how it was all going to work out, Rory said, "Mr. King. I'm Rory Jamison. I came for another reason, but now it's more important to get you to a doctor. I'm going to carry you to the wagon. It's probably going to hurt you like nothing has ever hurt before. There's just nothing I can do about that. Please don't fight me when I pick you up, or we're liable to both fall, and that won't help anything at all."

Not waiting for an answer, Rory folded the odorous covers back and sized up the heft of the man. This was going to be a difficult lift. He could see that. He could also see no other option. Sliding the bedside scatter rug out of the way and planting his feet as firmly as possible, he reached for King's uninjured arm and lifted. The scream that arose from the man was startling and shocking, but he ignored it and continued to lift.

With King spasming in pain, Rory raised him to a sitting position. He then bent until he could place his shoulder into the man's midsection. When King naturally folded forward, over Rory's shoulder, he stood, straining in every muscle, his knees shouting doubt, his arms wrapped around the man. Once upright, with no hesitation, he shuffled to the door, afraid to lift his feet for a normal walk. The screaming finally diminished, to be replaced by silent sobs, and then to silence as King lost consciousness again.

Mrs. King was crying, in sympathy with her husband, with her two fists jammed against her mouth. The two children were staring in wide-eyed fear, not understanding what was going on. Mrs. Flint was stalwart, knowing by instinct what Rory was doing and what would help. As Rory worked his way through the outside door, he faced the three steps down to the garden path. Mrs. Flint took a firm grip on his one arm.

"Keep coming, young man. You're doing great. Just these three steps. One at a time. I'll hold your balance. Easy now, but steady down."

With that, she said over her shoulder, "Katie, stop blubbering and get up in that wagon. Get ready to help. You're doing no good back there."

With the last of his strength, Rory walked until his legs butted up against the wagon. Almost in the same motion, he bent forward, as gently as possible, which was still a bit rough, and eased Ambrose King onto the blankets. Katie King grasped his head to keep it from flopping around.

When the weight of the injured man was released from Rory's arms, he staggered back two steps and sank to his knees. He didn't know what King weighed, but he knew he had never before lifted such a weight. On hands and knees, he kneeled on the wet ground, gasping in one heavy breath after another as the snow fell on his head and shoulders. The women were busy getting the kids under cover beside their father after pulling him further onto the wagon and straightening him out as best they could. He was still unconscious.

Rory staggered to his feet and went back for his hat and the fleece-lined coat he had taken off before carrying King out. Walking slowly, he then went to the barn for his gelding. He thought to put the saddle and bedroll into the wagon, but there was no spare room for more than just the bedroll. The saddle would stay in place.

With Mrs. King and her children settled under the

blankets beside Ambrose King, Mrs. Flint stood from helping them and swung her legs over onto the spring seat.

"Tie that gelding on back and come up here with me, Mr. Jamison. I'll drive while you tell me why you really came out today."

That Rory's visit was intentional didn't seem to him to need any confirmation, just an explanation.

21

Mrs. Flint drove a quiet half mile with no sound but the huffing of the horses and the rolling of the steel-rimmed wheels through the snowy grass. While both she and Rory were thinking it through, they remained silent. Finally, Rory, needing to know the details of the crime that had brought him to the King ranch in the first place, dug under his heavy coat and pulled out the badge.

First, holding his finger across his lips in a plea for privacy, he opened his hand. Mrs. Flint took a quick look and gasped. She then spoke quietly, confidentially.

"I had a dozen thoughts go through my mind in the past hour but never that."

Indicating the badge, Rory almost whispered, "It's new and I'm new at it."

"If you put the same effort into the job as you put into getting Ambrose out of bed, you'll do. You'll do just fine."

"Mrs. Flint, I think I know the bulk of what happened. The same people tried to pull that very stunt on the Double J, and a couple of others. I don't know anything at all about the other two yet. But I intend to find out. Apparently, they're up in the high country to the west.

"If these thieving rascals had done any asking around, they would have known the Jamison family aren't that soft, nor that gullible. But I'm thinking with you folks being well out from town with no close neighbors and just the one man on the ranch, they thought they had found easy pickings."

"You're correct to a point, Mr. Jamison. My man had just died a few weeks before. Pneumonia. Pneumonia in the summertime. Who ever heard of such a thing? Anyway, we were left with two women, two young children, and Ambrose. Ambrose is a good man. A good father and husband. And, importantly, he is a good cattleman and a hard worker. But he's not hard within himself. Not hard in the way a man has to be to stand and be counted when an injustice is being done. Put another way, he's not really a fighting man. His day will come. Perhaps in twenty or thirty years. But right now, he's a good man living in a sometimes bad time and place. Mind you, I've seen some signs of anger at injustice building up in him the past little while. There's no telling what he'll find inside of himself if he ever gives rein to that side of his thinking."

Mrs. Flint was silent for a short while, first glancing down at the turning wagon wheel beside her and then staring off into the wind and snow-swept miles ahead of them. Rory, figuring they had miles and hours ahead to get down to it, didn't push for more conversation until the woman was ready.

Finally, she said, "If my man had been alive, he would have warned those men off with a load of buckshot. And, believe me, they would have gone.

"I've been to town hoping for some help a couple of

181

times. I got nowhere at all. I have friends in town, but, like many of the town residents, they more than half believe that horrible man is really a judge. Law-abiding folks don't easily go against the law, as it's represented by a judge. I was all set to head down to the big city until this miserable weather came upon us. And then Ambrose got hurt yesterday."

"So, Mrs. Flint, were they saying that because your husband had passed away, there was some doubt about the estate, and they were authorized to impound the assets until a court could look into the matter? That's what they tried on the Double J."

"That's exactly what they said. There would be no chance at all of that working in a settled area, but we're still pretty scarce on the ground around here. No sheriff. No lawyers. No telegraph. No real authority. That's why I thought to go up to the city. Perhaps find a good lawyer. Mind you, we have no money either. We were depending on the sale of our fat yearlings for our winter's needs, and to cover a small loan at the bank. My man's doctor bills took a sizable chunk out of what little we had left. I'm not at all sure how I thought I could pay for a lawyer. There're a few head of our stuff that the rustlers didn't find, wandering the grass somewhere, but Ambrose couldn't find any, although he rode for hours."

"Don't think about lawyers or money. Let me do my job, although I'm just new at it. I may be oversimplifying it, but it all looks like a plain and simple attempt at embezzlement, or at least organized theft. The state people already know about it up in the city. We'll have their backing when the time comes. But I wonder about one other thing, Mrs. Flint. How did they know your man had died, and how did they know my father had died, something that happened hundreds of miles away?"

"You're off to a good start, sheriff. That's the prime question. I've gone over every name and face I know from the town and countryside. No one seems to fit the bill for such as that."

THEY RODE in companionable silence for another half hour while the temperature dropped noticeably and the snow fell in bigger and bigger flakes. Mrs. Flint was getting cold, and the team was balking. Rory figured anything else that had to be discussed could be seen to after they got to town.

Rory pulled the storm string down from his hat after tying a wooled scarf borrowed from Mrs. King around his ears and forehead. He then said, "Mrs. Flint. I'll take the lines. You swing over into the back and get under the blankets. We can talk more later."

Without a word, and thankfully, Mrs. Flint did as Rory had suggested, and he found himself alone with as much responsibility as he had ever had. There were probably ten or more miles yet to go. Not much when he said it that way. But with the snow falling harder by the minute, it seemed, he could hardly hold his eyes open without the windblown snow filling them. The team continued to balk. They had stopped dead twice, standing still with their heads turned away from the wind, when a particularly hard gust seemingly came out of nowhere.

The worst of it was, he had no landmarks. He had no sight line. And he could see little or nothing on the horizon. Although the land was reasonably flat, there were still dry swales, small valleys in the land that meant an easier few yards for the team on the downward side but a difficult pull up the other side. The team was tiring. He could feel it in the way they pulled and their willingness to stop.

He felt, rather than knew, which way was west, the direction he needed. He turned around a couple of times in the seat to take his direction from the tracks in the snow. To see if he was leaving a straight line behind him. But there were no tracks. The wind and falling snow blocked them out almost as quickly as the wagon wheels created them. He wasn't yet worried about being lost. That may come, but it wasn't yet. He knew if he had eased to the left, southward, he would butt up against the treed and hilly north rim of the small river that made its way east from the high-up hills. So, he couldn't go far off the track in that direction. But what about north? There was nothing to the north that would warn him of misdirection. Not for many miles.

Still, what worried him was the reluctance of the horses to keep pulling. To move forward.

He decided he would do better to mount the gelding and lead the team. It took a few precious minutes to rig up a lead. They had brought no rope with them. All he had to work with were the long bridle lines. He tied two lines off at the front of the wagon to keep them from falling and tangling in the horses' feet. One by one, he cut the other two lines off the horses' headstalls and retied them to the halter ring, thankful that he had decided to leave the halters in place while he was slipping on the bridles.

Mounting the gelding after brushing the snow off the saddle, he gathered the lines and wrapped them around the saddle horn. The team was reluctant to move, but a steady pull from the gelding had them stepping out. Their movements were slow and out of sync until they had moved forty or fifty yards, but they finally settled into a steady rhythmic pull.

They made perhaps another mile before the gelding stopped. Rory dismounted and moved to the horse's head. The poor beast had snow piled up on his forehead, draping downward toward his nose. His eyes were almost totally covered. Rory cleaned the snow away and then went to the team, where he found the same situation. Knowing the snow would only pile up again, and he would be stepping out of the saddle to repeat the cleaning, Rory decided to walk and save the strength of the big gelding. The snow was building up on the ground to the point where the wagon wheels would have a bit more resistance in their travel. Even the taller bunchgrass was now covered, except where the never-ending wind was able to lift it off and carry it into the far distance.

Tying the long reins more securely to the saddle horn, Rory stepped forward, grasped the gelding's reins, and moved out. With something to point on, which in this case was Rory, the gelding stepped up and followed. The team had little choice. The tug from the long leathers was steady and unrelenting. And so, the strange caravan moved, hopefully in the direction of Stevensville.

He wasn't without his doubts, but not knowing any good reason to change direction, Rory kept the small parade of horses, wagon, and people moving. The wind was quartering off his left shoulder when they moved out from the ranch. Hoping, but not at all positive that the wind was holding its direction, he kept his relationship to the wind steady.

He had hoped to see a light from the ranch he had visited that morning, but no such a thing happened.

If there had been options, he could have been tempted to consider one, but there were no options. He was tiring and the horses were nearing the last of their stamina. A trip to town that could have been taken at an easy trot in the summer had turned into a test of endurance for all involved.

He had no idea what was happening in the wagon, under the canvas sheet and the blankets. He hadn't heard a sound in a couple of hours.

That the progress was painfully slow troubled Rory. Ambrose King needed medical help. Even more so after the rough treatment from Rory, getting the man into the wagon. He shuddered to think what additional damage he might have caused. He fussed over the idea that there may be new bleeding where the bone was protruding from his upper arm. But what choice did he have? He had to carry the injured man no matter what additional damage he was doing. And he had to keep walking. Leave Ambrose to the care of the women. There were no other choices.

Rory decided it had to be well past midnight when he felt a difference under foot. He had just risen over a slight, sharp hump in the land and what he stepped on wasn't grass. Could it be the trail? He scuffed snow aside and bent low to feel the ground, to figure it out. His hands were so cold they were beyond true feeling, but he could at least sense the difference between the town road and the prairie grass.

He was sure, but just to double-check, he stepped the width of normal wagon tracks and scuffed snow again. Yes. It was there. Two tracks. He had found the trail. But where on the trail?

There wasn't much on that two-track road north of the Double J. If he had already ventured too far north, and kept going, he could cover many miles and still find no help. If somehow, he had swung to the south of town, the same problem presented itself. Wrapped up in that question, even with the short distance involved, could be life or death for the injured man. And perhaps for them all if the storm held. He couldn't afford that mistake. Rather, Ambrose King couldn't afford for Rory to make that mistake. Ambrose or the women or the two little children either. He had to get it right the first time.

The gelding answered the question for him. Rory was standing there trying to find a reason to turn one way or the other, and getting nowhere that gave him confidence, when the gelding, his saddle horse, started tugging to move to the right. That would be north. He knew the horse would have better sense of location than he had himself. Or, perhaps, more truly, a better sense of home. The gelding wanted to go to the right, to his warm, familiar stall in the barn on the Double J. Just how the horse knew that was beyond Rory's understanding, but he placed his faith in the animal's nature. But returning to the Double J wouldn't do Ambrose any good. If the Double J was to the right, town would be to the left. The decision was made.

Rory cleaned the horse's faces once more and moved off to the south. It took a bit of a pull for the team to lift the wagon up the grade, with their feet slipping and their energy and stamina about used up. But they were soon stepping out, looking for a light that would indicate the town. He came close to leading the gelding off the trail a couple of times, but finally, he saw the light, after a half hour of walking on the firmer surface.

Rory knew the lantern would be on at the livery. Tippet always had a lantern lit. He suspended it from an iron bracket he had formed that would hold it from smashing against the side of the building during a wind. Tippet had talked one time of being lost, and how desperately he had wished for a light to guide him. Ever since, he had provided that light for others.

Entering the town, Rory led the team past the first block of darkened businesses and turned down the side street. The doctor's office was the white-painted house on the corner, surrounded by a white picket fence. There was no light and no sign of movement.

He called the horses to a stop in front of the house and walked to the back of the wagon. Not too loudly, so as not to wake the children, he said, "We're here, ladies. But stay where you are until I get the doctor up."

He rapped solidly on the door three separate times before a light showed itself in the back room. Leading waving shadows before him as he walked, from the lit lamp he carried, the doctor was soon opening the door. Saying nothing, he waited.

"Sorry about all this, Doc. I've got a man in serious need of help."

"Well, bring him in while I get dressed."

"I'll wait while you get dressed. I may need help carrying him."

When the doctor returned, Rory led him out to the wagon, pulled back the covers, and said, "Alright ladies, I'm going to try to carry Mr. King, like I did before. I'm not happy about this snow underfoot, but it is what it is. I'll need one of you to hold the gate open and one to walk alongside me to hold my balance. The doctor will hold the other side. Please be careful with your feet so that you don't trip me."

Rory shook King's shoulder a bit and asked, "Are you awake, Mr. King?"

A slight nod of his head was visible in the light from the lamp the doctor held above him.

"We're at the doctor's, Mr. King. I'm going to have to carry you again. It's going to hurt. Scream if you must, but don't fight me. Are you alright with that?"

Receiving another nod of his head Rory slid the injured man toward the back of the wagon by pulling on the blanket he lay on. He spoke to the doctor, "Doc, he has a badly injured left leg. If you could steady it while I get a grip on him, we might get this done."

Without a word, Rory and the doctor worked together. The scream of pain, ebbing into troubled sobs, was every bit as shocking as it had been back at the ranch. Rory was sure the scream of intense pain would awaken the neighbors.

With King again slung over his shoulder, Rory turned to the path. The doctor let the injured leg dangle freely while he grasped one of Rory's arms. Mrs. Flint the other.

Mrs. King shooed the half-awake kids into the house and held the spring-closed gate open. When Rory managed to get that far, she let the gate go and rushed to hold the house door. By this time, the doctor's wife was ushering the kids into another room and out of the way. Rory's feet were slippery on the linoleum flooring, but together, the bunch made it into the examination room and lay Mr. King onto the doctor's raised workstation. The doctor immediately turned to the patient. Rory, still being balanced by Mrs. Flint, took two wobbly steps back and sunk onto a chair.

Mrs. King insisted on staying beside her husband, but Mrs. Flint gathered up the kids, not knowing what her next step should be. They had some friends in town, but to barge in on them in the middle of the night didn't quite seem appropriate.

Rory solved the matter when he said, "Come on, kids. Into the wagon. You too, Mrs. Flint. We're going to the hotel."

"I don't have money for the hotel, Mr. Jamison. I believe I told you that."

"You don't need money this night. What you need is to get on that wagon before I fall asleep."

At the hotel, Rory walked in before Mrs. Flint and her grandchildren. The night clerk was dozing in a big, overstuffed chair in the lobby. Rory shook him on the shoulder, "Come on, Tig, customers for you. We need two rooms. One for me. One for Mrs. Flint and the children. You look after Mrs. Flint. I'll be back after I see to the horses."

22

Still leading the gelding, Rory made a wide turn in the street and headed back toward the livery. Not waiting for permission, or bothering to awaken Tippet, Rory slid the big doors open on their tracks. Using the same method as he had the past several hours, he led the team and wagon into the barn. Tippet showed up at about the time Rory was lifting his hat and unwinding the breath-soaked scarf from his face.

"What's happening, young man?"

"Just hauled a family in from out east. A wild horse that didn't care for the idea of being tamed smashed the rancher up pretty bad. Brought him over to the doctor's just now. Woman and kids in the hotel, which is where I hope to go just as soon as I get these animals stalled and cared for."

"You go git yerself some rest, son. Leave me ta ma job. I'm up 'n awake an' it cain't be all that fer till morn'n. Might jes as well be work'n."

"Thanks, Tippet. I'll leave the most of it for you, but I'll show a bit of care to the gelding, at least."

With that, he slipped the bridle off the gelding and then the saddle. The fatigued animal didn't move. Before leading the horse into a stall, Rory wiped the snow from his face and then wrapped his arms around his neck, resting his own face against the horse's.

"Horse, I don't imagine you understand even a single word of anything I say, but I'm hoping you'll know you done good this night. Probably saved us all. I appreciate it."

With that, Rory stroked the animal's neck a few times and then repeated his actions with each of the team. Tippet had them unharnessed and was about to lead them into a stall when Rory approached. Tippet stepped back and watched, half in wonder and half in amusement.

"Well, Rory, they maybe don't understand the words, but they'll gather the intent. Now you git yerself out a here 'n into bed."

As DAWN HAD BEEN NEARING by the time Rory settled into the hotel bed, he slept guilt-free well past his normal waking time. He opened his eyes just once, to take a look at the big pocket watch he had inherited from his father. There was enough light seeping past the flimsy window blind to show him the time was easing past. He rolled over and slept for another hour. At nine, he walked into the dining room, hoping there was still a chance for a feed of eggs and whatever meat Ma had on hand. From the choices offered by Sonia, he selected sausages. With that behind his belt along with a liberal quantity of black coffee, he ventured out and into his plan for the day.

The first stop, as he had laid it out in his mind as he

dozed away the last few minutes of his morning laziness, was to arrest the town marshal. He figured it was the authority of Mike Wasson, as slim as it was, and the big .44 that hung on his hip, that the judge was hiding behind. Rory would pin on the badge he had kept carefully hidden and walk over to the marshal's office. From there, he would see what kind of a sheriff he really was.

Sonia's startled eyes had focused on the badge as he was standing beside the breakfast table, pulling on his coat. To the question she started to ask, Rory said, "Later." and went to the door. He didn't see or know, but Ma and Sonia stood in the window of the empty dining room, watching him as he crossed the street and walked the one short block to the marshal's office.

Without knocking, Rory pushed open the door and entered. There was no one there. There was a scattering of papers on the desk and floor. Opening the inner door to the sleeping room, he found a rumpled bed and not much else. No clothing hanging from the pegs driven into the wall. No spare boots. No saddle or miscellaneous items. No satchel such as a traveling man might hold in reserve. Nothing at all to show any recent occupancy. Hating to do it but figuring it might give him a hint, Rory touched his hand to the rough mattress, down low, where the covers had remained in place. Warm. There was still body warmth in the mattress cover. Wasson hadn't been gone long, but clearly, he was no longer in the marshal's office and, in all likelihood, no longer in Stevensville.

Rory closed the door as he left the office and turned back toward the hotel and general mercantile store. There, just two buildings down from the mercantile, cut out from the farm and ranch supply store, Ronald Thrasher, the pretend judge, held out in a small office fronting the boardwalk. The rented space was divided into two rooms. One he used for an office. The second, he used as a sleeping and living space.

Fighting against the urge to run, Rory walked as fast as his long strides would carry him to the judge's office. Again, without knocking, he shoved into the small space. The scene was similar to what he had found at the marshal's office. The difference, although it was slight, was that there were more papers strewn about, and an open filing cabinet drawer, holding still more paper.

After a careful look at the sleeping room, where the mattress again proved to be holding body heat, and a cursory glance at a few of the stranded papers, Rory sank onto the broken-down office chair and knew defeat.

Idly, he fingered the deputy sheriff badge pinned to his shirt. He half convinced himself that he should remove it, package it in some kind of a small box, and mail it back to the office in Denver. He had failed. While he slept lazy and warm in the hotel bed, his quarry had gotten away. Perhaps the news of his appointment as a lawman had also gotten out. It was obvious that word of the arrival in town of the King family and Mrs. Flint, and that it was Rory who had brought them in, had reached the ears of either the marshal or the judge. From there, it would have taken the two embezzlers only minutes to throw their personal gear into satchels, saddle their horses, and get gone.

He was sure the judge would have abandoned his buggy. There would be little chance of getting away burdened by anything preventing a cross-country run.

As he thought through everything he had planned and promised, he sank into as low a spot as he had been in since the day of his father's murder. He had failed.

There was no way to soften that truth. Yes, the wagon trip through the storm with the injured Ambrose King and his family was long and tiring. Considering his actions like a city dude might, he could even justify putting himself and his comforts first and taking to the hotel bed. But the truth of the situation was that the judge acted with more determination than Rory gave him credit for.

Rory had convinced himself that the judge would at least attempt to brazen it out. But he had done no such thing. And now Rory had nothing. Clearly, theft, the rustling of an entire herd had been done, and it was Rory's responsibility to deal with it. He had a responsibility to the King and Flint ranch and to the two mystery ranches that he had yet to locate. And, perhaps as important as the other matters, he had a responsibility to himself and the badge he wore.

Sitting in the judge's chair and studying a new fall of light snow that was overtaking the town, Rory tried to tie the pieces together. He knew, without even really thinking about it, that he was not going to quit. Forget the momentary thought of mailing the badge back. Jamisons don't quit. He had his father's firm word on that. And, after the murder, he had his own experience. It was no easy thing to recover from his own near-death and get his feet back under himself. It was no easy thing to secrete his gold cache and get it to the Boise bank. It was no easy thing to ride across most of Idaho and skirting the worst the Rockies, ride to Pierre, Montana, tracking the killers. And it was certainly no easy thing for a man not out of his teen years to face three assassins. No, he was not a quitter. And he wouldn't quit now. But where to start? Or rather, where to restart. His first start had come to an abrupt stop.

He sat for another several minutes thinking of the surrounding country, the towns, the villages, the distances, the one big city. Where could the fugitives go? Where would they go? There were long distances and sparse populations in every direction. And who had warned them? Who might have been awake during the most miserable part of the night to see him lead the wagon to the doctor's office? There was someone in town working on the rustlers' side. Who? And why? Profit. There could be no other reasonable explanation.

What was the possibility of hiding in the city? It was only after all his mental reviewing of the situation and the possibilities that the bank came to his mind. The bank. He had to get to the bank. Jesse Ambrewster had made no clear promise. But what if the man had done his own thinking and taken the action Rory had suggested? That could save the day. Financially, at least. That would leave the matter of justice to be dealt with, but it may save three ranchers from poverty and failure.

There was probably no real rush in getting to the bank. What was going to happen had almost certainly already happened, but still, he'd best get to his feet and to his job.

He entered the bank, feeling almost foolish to be at his final hope on the first task trusted to him as a deputy sheriff. He was barely in the door when Ambrewster hollered from his office. "I've been expecting you. Looked for you all last evening and again this morning. Thought you might even come to the house. Well, take a seat. Let's talk."

Rory, feeling a distant hope rising in his breast, walked into the inner office and sank into the big leather-covered chair. He sat silently as Ambrewster grinned at him and turned from side to side in his swivel chair, as if something was really tickling the man's fancy. After allowing Rory to suffer for a half minute, the banker took the pencil he had been chewing on from his mouth and pointed it at the newly badged sheriff.

"It's probably a good thing I like you, young man. Like all the Jamisons, as far as that goes. Can't think of another single thing that would make me break an unspoken banking law. Or it might even be written down somewhere, I really wouldn't know. Do you want to know what that law is, Rory?"

"Why do I have a feeling you're going to tell me, no matter what I say?"

"Yes, you might be correct in that. Well, here it is, spoken in layman's terms, with all the whereases and wherefores removed. As a banker, I am to remember at all times that the money put into my trust is not, in fact, mine. It belongs to the depositor. And must be available to the depositor whenever he asks for it."

Rory, feeling a bit lighter than he had sitting in the judge's worn-out office chair, half grinned and responded, "I'm hoping you are going to tell me you voluntarily broke that unwritten, or perhaps it is a written, law. And that the embezzling judge left town, a disappointed man."

"The embezzling judge, as you called him, was at my home door this morning early, very early, demanding that I open the bank immediately. His flunky, the embezzling marshal, was there with him, making a show of fingering that .44 he loves to carry around. But what so many of these young people choose not to remember or understand, is that when us older men were their age, there was a war going on. A war that grabbed mostly all of us and put us in a uniform of one color or another and put a gun in our hands. It was a lesson to me. It wasn't all that long ago either, really, and the lessons learned there will never be forgotten."

Rory's grin was getting wider as he listened. Now he asked a simple question, "So how did that lesson apply this morning, sir?"

"The lesson, young man, left me determined to never be without my own equalizer. I'm hoping it doesn't show, but I am armed at this moment. I haven't been without protection since I found myself being shot at, with me being out of powder and lead myself. That was a worrisome situation, I can assure you. Worrisome enough that I kind of took it to heart. So, when I answered the door wearing my big, wool night-robe this morning, my pocket-sized .32 was tucked safely away, out of sight but available. I opened the door with my right hand in my pocket. I listened for just a few seconds while I watched that fool marshal finger that Colt. The judge was demanding that I come immediately and open the bank. He needed his money. And all the time, the marshal was grinning like a cat with a mouse trapped in a corner.

"Now, I am sorry to say, I have a hole in my robe. Just a small hole, about the size of a .32 slug, but a hole just the same. And the marshal, coward that he is, running as hard as he could, with blood running down his hand, made good time away from my yard. The judge, seeing the error of his ways, at least walked with some dignity as he left. But he did most assuredly leave."

Rory was wearying of the dragged-out tale.

It's possible the banker recognized that he had garnered all he was going to get out of his delightful story. In any case, he said, "None of the ranchers can make a withdrawal until we sort out a couple of things, but the money is here and safe. That's where it will stay until you bring me some evidence to change my mind and satisfy the bank inspectors. Although I must confess, I've never seen nor met a bank inspector, but I hear they're around somewhere."

With sincere thanks and a handshake, Rory left the bank, heading to the doctor's office.

23

"Good morning, Mr. King. It's good to see you awake. Is that a sign that the doctor got you put back together?"

Walking in from the adjacent room, the doctor said, "That's a bit optimistic, but I will say he is in better shape now than he was when you brought him in. His leg will heal just fine, with time. The verdict will be a while yet on the arm and shoulder."

Rory looked back at Ambrose King. He hesitated before saying, "Mr. King. You're a heavy man. I apologize for the rough treatment yesterday. I well knew I was probably hurting you more than you already were, but I was without a choice. And it was a long, cold ride to town. That couldn't have helped you either.

"But I have some good news. I went to arrest the two culprits that got off with your herd but found they had pulled out early this morning. They must have somehow heard you were in town and that I had been deputized. I'm sure they sensed that their foolish plan was doomed and thought to grab their deposit out of the bank and get gone. Both their offices are empty. There's no sign of them in town.

"I'll look for them, of course, but this is a big country with a thousand places to hide in every day's ride.

"Now, here's the good news. Before I left to ride to your ranch, I had a talk with the banker. What was done to the King and Flint ranch was apparently done to two others. I don't know much about those two, but I'll stay with it. But the thing is, I asked the banker to put a lock on the funds from the sale of the herds. He made me no guarantee, but when those two were running this morning, they demanded the banker let go of the funds. The banker refused. In fact, he reversed the situation, putting the run on them. So, your money, along with the other funds, is safely in the bank. The banker wants some clear evidence of how this all came down before he will release any money, but eventually, it will be set right. Or at least as right as possible. It will be one of my jobs to provide that evidence.

"But just so you know, all is not lost. You'll get at least most of the value of your herd back. Now, do you have any idea who the herd was sold to? Did you hear any names mentioned while the crew was rounding them up?"

Ambrose and Katie King looked at each other, trying to recall. Mrs. Flint was still at the hotel with the children.

Shaking her head, Mrs. King said, "I was in the house part of the time, but while I was out with Mother and Ambrose, I heard nothing about selling. Either of us would sure help if we could. Sorry."

Rory left the doctor's small home and office and walked to the livery.

"Tippet, I'm sure you've heard by now that the

marshal and the judge pulled their freight early this morning. Did you hear or see anything? Even their direction of travel would be a help. With this snow covering the land, there's no use trying to find tracks. The snow should be gone by tomorrow morning, but there'll be nothing left of the tracks. I'm not all that good at tracking anyway. Never had any reason to learn."

Tippet answered, "Wasson kep' the judge's buggy and both the horses in the barn behind the marshal's place. They done no business with me, neither one a 'em.

"No, I talked to neither, but I did hear some excited shout'n. I taken a look out the door in time ta see the marshal a-whopping down the road, riding that gray a his and lead'n the buggy horse, carry'n a saddle. He look ta be in pretty much of a hurry. I saw him favor'n one arm, or hand, and shak'n it, as if to get something off. I walked out ta where he left the tracks. Seen blood drops outlin'n the path. Been hurt somehow; I'm guess'n on his hand."

"He had been shot alright. That's what got him into such an all-fired hurry."

"You shoot him?"

"No, sir. It was Ambrewster that did that little favor for me."

"Ambrewster? The banker?"

"Now, Tippet, do you know any other Ambrewster in this town?"

Tippet stared silently as Rory waited, hoping for more information. But Rory had dug out all the hostler had to give, and he wasn't feeling like giving any more himself.

24

Knowing it was hopeless, the deputy rode out anyway, making a wide circle of the town. He had to do something. He couldn't simply sit, waiting for a revelation or some brilliant insight that would set his sights in the correct direction. The trails north and south, the only established roads, were a maze of tracks, all blurred as the snow melted, even while a new, light snow was falling. No help there.

Circling wide to the west, right out to where the near hills sloped upwards and the forest began blocking, or at least limiting, easy travel, to end eventually in the snow-capped Southern Rockies. There were tracks aplenty from wild game, but none left by the fleeing rustlers. The wide, slow ride to the east of town provided nothing usable either. There would be little purpose for entering into the wide, sparsely settled eastern half of Colorado. Reconciling himself to the situation, and needing time to think, as well as a bath and change of clothing, he turned to the Double J and rode home.

He was met by his welcoming family and enough

questions from the girls to make his head buzz. Ignoring everyone and everything, he rode to the stable. There, his uncle George waited by the door to greet him.

"Welcome home, sheriff. Good to see you all in one piece. Now, both you and that gelding look as if you could do with some rest and a cleaning up. I'll do for the gelding. You'll have to care for your own self."

"Thanks, George, but I feel responsible for the animal. It was me that rode him nearly to death through that storm last night. It had better be me that cleans him up by way of apology."

"As you like, Rory. But leave him for now. You can get back to him soon enough. We'll go to the house for coffee. Dinner will be in a couple of hours."

They made a slow, silent walk across the ranch yard in the melting snow. The boys were with the herd, but the girls were waiting anxiously for news. Hannah, with Eliza's help, had made a small batch of donuts. Rory reached for two of them, placing them on the edge of his saucer. Eliza, figuring there would soon be none left, quickly placed four on a plate, covered them with a cloth, and laid them aside on the counter for when the boys came in. Nancy gave Rory enough time to enjoy one donut along with a half cup of coffee before she said, "So tell us."

Teasing his cousins, he answered, "It's confidential law business. To be shared only with trustworthy folks who know how to hold a secret."

Nancy laughed and said, "Nice try, Cousin, but I'm not buying it. You and I both know that everyone in town has heard the story, whatever it is, several times by now, and each time was a bit different from the last, and none of them were the absolute truth. I could get half the story at the millinery shop or the whole truth from you.

So should I saddle a horse and ride to town, or are you going to fess up?"

Rory finished his coffee before telling the brief outline of what had happened the day before and into the dark, cold night. The detail of the running fugitives took only a few moments to tell. He ended by saying, "There's no money in it, and I don't have the authority to even ask, but if you two ladies wanted to help out the law and the cause of justice, I could use your help tomorrow."

Hannah looked at Nancy and said, "Did you notice that only a couple of minutes ago we were unworthy of trust, and now that he needs us, we're ladies?"

"I noticed, but you'll have to admit that whatever it is, it will give us an excuse to ride to town. He might even buy us lunch at the dining room."

Rory answered, "I'll buy you lunch, but the government didn't give me an expense account, so it will have to be at Sonny's, not the hotel dining room."

Hannah, who was not yet familiar with all the small enterprises in the town, looked at her sister with an unasked question. Nancy responded with, "Sonny's is a low-end hash house fit only for cowboys and grub riders. I wouldn't dare walk into the place. I'd be the talk of the town for a month. I'll have to take a coin or two of my own for lunch or see if Ma would put the price of a meal on the sheriff's tab after we leave."

Rory didn't bother continuing that line of talk. Instead, he said, "The marshal and the judge both left in a kind of a hurry. I've locked up both spaces until we can get back in there. There're papers scattered about and some files in the judge's office. I need to know what information either one might have written down. And I need to find the other two ranches that had unfortunate interactions with the judge. If you ladies would read all those papers over, it could be a big help. We won't know anything until it's done, but you may find some evidence there that I can use. And I might even see if Ma has a bowl or two of mush leftover from breakfast that we can get at an affordable price."

Nancy grinned at her cousin before saying, "You go take care of that gelding you say you rode nearly half to death. Hannah and I will discuss the matter and decide on a reasonable fee and working conditions."

Rory wasn't long after dinner, heating bath water on the stove in the cabin. Henry and Thomas had both moved their cots into the cabin, but they gave Rory the privacy he needed to get himself cleaned up.

THE NEXT MORNING, Rory and his two cousins rode into town together. He took the girls first to the marshal's office and then gave them the key to the judge's rented quarters. They seemed to understand the task, so he left them there and rode to the doctor's office. After inquiring about Ambrose King and getting the doctor's standard answer, "Time will tell." Rory said, "Doc, did you by chance have a couple of men in here recently needing repair? One would have had an elbow needing fixing and possibly a stitch or two on his scalp. The other might have had a lump on his head."

"As a matter of fact, I did. Were you the one that treated them to such ministrations?"

"That sounds like the men, alright. And yes, I delivered a 'ministration' as you called it. There was cause enough. They, along with a couple of others, had taken to manhandling Cousin Nancy out at the Double J. That didn't quite sit well with me."

The doctor grinned and said, "Well, I'm sure it wasn't right either. Mind you, there are not many situations Nancy can't take care of for herself. I'm not quite sure how mean she could get if put upon. Don't know as that's ever been put to the test."

"She was holding a double twelve-gauge, Doc, loaded and ready, and she had fire in her eyes."

"Now that would be a sight. Those men don't know it, but a broken elbow and a few stitches might have saved them from much worse."

"The reason I ask, Doc, is because I need to find those men. Did either one leave a name with you?"

"I always get a name. I'm sure it's not always their right and true names, but I get something to hold in my records. Wrote them both down in my daybook. Just give me a minute here."

After flipping a couple of pages, the doctor said, "Right here. Page Newsom and Guy Fletcher."

"Any note of where they were from?"

"No idea, but they left town at a slow walk, each one with a grip on the saddle horn. I put the broken arm in a sling, but that would only reduce the throbbing pain, not eliminate it. And their headaches must have been fierce. They left to the south."

Knowing those names were his best chance of finding the judge, Rory thanked the doctor and began putting a plan together.

First, he would see what the girls had found. They must have finished in the marshal's office. It was locked and empty when he tried the door. He rode down to the judge's hangout and tied his horse. Walking in, he found the floor cleared of papers and the filing cabinet drawer empty. The strewn about papers were all neatly stacked in piles on the desk.

"Looks like you're making some headway. What did you find at the marshal's office?"

"A pigsty." answered Nancy.

"Yes, I saw that too. But I meant, beyond the filth."

Hannah answered, "There was nothing of importance. A few old wanted flyers and a couple of letters from some time before this current marshal. All in all, it was nothing. But there might be more here. We've just started sorting it out. The judge was one to keep notes. Maybe he had a poor memory. Give us another couple of hours and we'll know whatever is in here."

Silently, Rory sorted out the details in his mind. He had some riding to do. He would need his bedroll and some provisions.

"I'm making a quick ride back to the ranch. I need my bedroll."

"Are you going somewhere?" asked Nancy.

"I've got a couple of names to follow up on. And if you can find the names of those other ranches, I might be able to wrap this thing up, as far as the cattle are concerned anyway. Might never find the marshal or the judge. I'll be back shortly, and we'll get some lunch. Hopefully, you'll have something for me by then."

WHEN RORY RODE BACK, the girls were already seated in the dining room. Rory joined them. It was Hannah who answered his unspoken questions. She had the information written neatly on a sheet of paper.

"BL Ranch–Ben Lander. Half Anchor–Captain

Sperry. Both appear to be up in the high country to the west."

She slid the paper across to Rory. He fished around in his shirt pocket until he found the stub of pencil he carried with him, turned Hannah's paper so he could read it, and added the names of the riders treated by the doctor. As he was writing, he glanced up at Nancy and said, "The doctor figures I should have left you to handle those riders. Like an experiment, kind of. He figures I probably saved them a world of pain."

"A girl's got to look after herself."

Deciding that had been enough talk of judges and cattle thieves, Rory turned to study the menu that was chalked onto a wide, black-painted board and changed daily. Hannah noticed and said, "Don't bother. We already ordered for you."

Rory sank a little lower in his chair and tried for a defeated look, not quite making it. Both girls laughed in response.

After lunch, as they were ready to leave the dining room, Hannah said, "What's going to become of the marshal's job? Does the town even need a marshal?"

Rory answered, "That's not for me to say. But I'm figuring to try to find someone to clean the space out and make it livable. I'm going to ask Mr. Browning if I could use it as sleeping quarters when I'm in town. Until they get another marshal is what I mean."

Nancy looked at Hannah. Receiving a silent nod, she said, "Leave that with us. We'll go ask Mr. Browning. If he gives the okay, we'll clean it up. I'm getting a real tied-down feeling on the ranch. There's little to do out there. Even cleaning out a pigsty might be better than fighting boredom on the Double J."

"As you wish." was all Rory said in response.

"I've got some riding to do. I expect I'll be gone several days. Thanks for looking at those papers. If you would gather them together and take them out to the ranch for safekeeping, I'd appreciate it. And keep the keys to those two spaces. I may not be finished with either of them yet."

HIS FIRST GOAL was to locate Sheriff Anthony Clare. He rode south, hoping the man would be at his small office in town. It wasn't much of a town, no more than Rory's own Stevensville. But the townsfolk and the surrounding ranchers had somehow gathered themselves together enough to elect a county sheriff. Collecting enough tax money to pay him would be another matter altogether. Finding Clare at home would save Rory miles of riding.

As usual, knowing that few anywhere knew more about the happenings of the area than the liveryman, Rory rode that direction and spoke to the man sitting in a chair, enjoying the shade in the shadow of his own barn. With the sun shining and most of the snow melted away, it was a pleasant enough afternoon for sitting. His head was haloed with reeking tobacco smoke from a chewed and blackened pipe.

"I'm looking for Sheriff Clare. Can you point me in the right direction?"

Removing the pipe from his mouth and pointing over his shoulder, the man said, "Back Street. Behind the saloon."

Rory thanked the liveryman and looked around until he spotted the small saloon. He rode to the first corner and turned. One short block of riding, another left turn, and he was behind the saloon. An office, sharing space with a land surveyor, was the only building in the area. The rest of the block was empty, weed-choked land, waiting for someone to see value in it. Rory figured it might take a while.

He tied off his horse and walked to the door. The hand-painted sign nailed onto the vertical board-and-batten siding assured him he was at the correct location.

He rapped his knuckles on the door a couple of times and turned the knob. The door swung easily, and he stepped in. The grinning sheriff was seated behind a desk, obviously waiting for him.

"Saw you ride up. Figured you could open the door for yourself.

Have a seat. How's sheriffing?"

Rory tipped his hat back and walked to the desk. The two men shook hands before Rory sat.

"Sheriffing is going alright if you mean has anyone taken a shot at me yet. But it's not going so well when I have to admit I lost my first two serious suspects."

"Tell me about it."

The tale wasn't long in the telling. When he was finished, Rory said, "The doctor gave me a couple of names. Page Newsom and Guy Fletcher. They were both hurt some in the skirmish out at the Double J. Chances are one might be back to work, but the other has a broken elbow. Be a while before he's roping steers again.

"I expect they're rustlers on the loose. May have just been riding through when the judge put them to work. Or the judge may have had a regular thing going and kept them on the payroll. It would sure be helpful if I could find them."

Anthony Clare let the names soak into his mind for a few moments and then shook his head.

"I remember the men, of course, from that misbegotten ride out to your ranch. But the two you're looking for, and their friends, kind of held themselves off to the side. Didn't mix with the judge and the marshal. I'd recognize them if I saw them again. But I can almost guarantee they aren't from around here. If you feel like challenging the odds and you believe the chase is worth it, you might ride down to the city and weave your way through a few of the seedier saloons. I doubt those types will be found in the uptown hotels.

"Something to know and remember; the big-city police take a dim view of gun-wearing in town. I'd still not go without, if it were me."

"I already learned that lesson on my first visit."

"Good. Then I wish you well in your search. Mind you, as I'm sure you've already considered, it's a big country with few folks, spread thin on the ground. Your chance of riding for days and miles and accomplishing little are better than your chances of seeing the judge behind bars. And considering that the money from the sale of the herds is in the bank, you might take that as victory enough. Of course, you could get posters out and wait to hear from other jurisdictions."

"I could do that, but I think a ride to the city might be a better thing, for a start. If that doesn't bear fruit, I'll consider my options. Thanks for the information. Perhaps we'll see you again soon."

THE NEXT AFTERNOON, Rory rode into Denver. He checked into the same hotel he had been in before and put his gelding in the same livery. After a short talk with the livery hostler about nothing in particular, he carried his bedroll across the street and up to his hotel room. It was too early for dinner, and he had no purpose for being in town except to find his fugitives, so he went for a walk, to kind of size up the situation. He would come back after sundown if necessary.

There was nothing to distinguish one saloon from the other. For no particular reason, he walked past the first open door and entered the second. Every saloon he had ever been in looked and smelled the same, in his judgment. Long and narrow room. A rack of bottles fronting a big mirror behind the bar. Why the mirror, he had no idea. A few poorly rendered and unrealistic paintings of young women, that no right-thinking man would hang in his home. A pressed, decorative metal ceiling. A mismatched collection of lanterns hanging from hooks in the ceiling. Round tables with four half-round backed wooden chairs. Smoke hanging in a permanent cloud, shallow or deep, depending on the number of drinkers in the place and the time of day. And the collective stink of cigar smoke, stale beer, spittoon residue, vomit, and unwashed bodies.

Rory wasn't a drinking man, but he couldn't just walk around a saloon looking for his men. He placed a dime on the counter for a beer he didn't want, turned his back to the bar, and glanced over the drinkers and gamblers who half-filled the chairs and tables. Silently, without rising from his well-worn stool, the barman tipped a large glass stein under the spigot. He pulled the handle, waited for the foam to rise to the top and run down the sides, and slid the mug down the counter. Somehow, it stopped right in front of Rory.

A bedraggled rider a couple of feet away grinned at Rory and said, "Never misses. Never seen the like. Product of slinging suds in many a saloon across the

West, I'm guessing. I do believe Suds could slide a beer forty feet and stop it in front of your nose if the bar was long enough. But Suds, he ain't much on walking. He'd appreciate if you would slide that dime back down to him."

Hardly knowing how to respond, Rory looked at the man and then at the dime. A quick glance told him that Suds was waiting. Curling his pointing finger under the leading edge of his thumb, he flicked the dime down the bar. It got barely halfway before sliding to a stop in a sticky residue from another time and another beer. He stepped around the talkative drinker, moved three paces to his left and did it again. He watched Suds pick up the small piece of silver and said, "Sorry, Suds. I'll do better another time."

Suds saw no reason to respond.

Rory took the three steps back to where his beer stood untouched. The garrulous rider looked him over before saying, "Don't figure you for a rider. Clothes are a might too upscale for it. Course, you might have gone and wasted your pay on new duds. Special for a trip to the big city, maybe. But then, there are no scars on your hands either, although they're big enough and look strong enough. But you ain't handled a rope in a while."

Rory returned the fella's grin and made a point of studying him from head to foot. He needed a haircut and some new clothes himself. The boots were probably beyond repair. Holding his grin, he said, "I own a few head. Ride and work them when the need arises. But you now, you look like you just might be on lunch break from a job in a dry goods store."

The fella laughed and then started to cough and choke. He took down the last dregs of his beer and choked again on the foam. When he turned his face down and continued to cough, Rory dug out another dime and flicked it down the counter. It went all the way that time. When Suds looked up, Rory tipped his head at the choking rider. In a few seconds, a full mug came sliding and stopped directly in front of the man. The rider lifted his head and put a hand to the mug. With a single draught, he took down half. He then coughed again, this time into his hand, and looked at Rory.

"Buy one for you some time."

Rory, wondering what this man might know, asked, "You ranch close by?"

"Got no job at all right this very minute. Had a disagreement with a big-horned steer. Shot the steer to save my horse. That turned into a disagreement with the owner of the steer. That bit of talk progressed into one thing and then another. My memory isn't totally clear on the details. The offer to do more shooting might have entered into the discussion.

"Anyway, I may have to find another place to hang my hat. Somewhere further away. I have a feeling that story is going to follow me for a mile or two."

Rory gave the man enough time to get over his latest coughing spell before observing, "Been lucky myself. Of course, I haven't been at it as long as you, judging by age. I've broken no bones and done nothing worse than hitting the sod a time or two when I took on more horse than common sense would allow."

"Ain't a man worth his salt that doesn't push the boundaries a bit here and there. Been on the sod a few times myself."

Fishing for information, Rory said, "I suppose it's natural for a hurt man to come to town when there's nothing on the ranch to hold him."

The rider took down the last of the free beer, wiped his hand on his pantleg, and held it out to Rory.

"Bates. That's all I'm known by. Just Bates. You ask around ranches from the panhandle to Montana you'll find men who rode with me. Just mention Bates, and you'll hear some stories."

There were a lot of things Rory might have chosen to do other than shake Bates' filthy hand, but he swallowed his better judgment and returned a firm shake.

"Are you alone in the wounded group these days, Bates, or do you get company when the sun goes down?"

"There's always one or two in the dives further down the street. But up here, in the better places, there's just been me and two others that limped in from over east. Knew one of them from before, so I took notice. Page Newsom and Guy Fletcher. Guy, he could be working if that was his natural inclination. Had a small bump on the head is all. Pretty much gone now. Just plain lazy, I suspect. Always looking for the easier path. Page, he has him a sure enough broken elbow. Says he was thrown from a wild-caught stallion he wanted to break and geld. Don't you believe a word of it. That man never saw the day he could top off a wild stallion. More likely some sodbuster found him raiding the chicken coop and took a stick to him.

"Rode with him one time on a ranch down in New Mexico. A bit lazy and a coward to boot, but don't you be repeating that where he might be close by. He's handy enough with a gun if he can use it without risk to himself."

Rory could hardly breathe. Was almost afraid to speak in case he said the wrong thing. *It can't be that easy. It just can't be.*

Getting his wits about him, Rory said, "You say those

two ride together. So, they'll probably be here together come by and by."

"They came down with some coin from somewhere. I ain't heard of no banks being robbed, so it wasn't that. Course, robbing a little old lady of her grocery money would be more their style. Yes, they'll be sleeping off the day and waiting for the dark of night. You might know that the Bible says, "The people loved the darkness more than the light, for their actions were evil.""

Again, Rory studied this man. As was so common on the frontier, this man had more of a background than he let on.

"That's from John Chapter three, I believe."

"It is. But the same thing, or near enough, is said in other places. You'd have no trouble finding them. You'd think I'd take it all more to heart, wouldn't you? There was a time. And a lady... Well, that's a tale for another day and in better surroundings."

Rory slid his untouched beer over to his new friend and said, "I'm not doing you any favors by giving this to you. But you do what you want, and welcome. Perhaps we'll meet again. Another time. Another place."

Without looking up from the bartop, Bates said, "Be careful when you find them. They're lazy, but they're tough enough. And maybe change your shirt before you come back. Those pinholes say there's a badge in your pocket."

Startled into silence, Rory could do nothing but pat Bates on the back and walk out.

25

Rory, who now thought of himself as the newest, greenest, most unpromising deputy sheriff in the entire country, changed his shirt before going down for dinner. He picked up the shirt he had discarded onto the bed and fingered the two pinholes. *Pinholes. Just a couple of pinholes. They can chisel that on my tombstone. 'He forgot about the pinholes.'*

The sun had set behind the mountain peaks. Full dark would take over the city in a matter of minutes. Rory had used the mirror in the hotel lobby to assure himself that his guns were well concealed behind his buckskin jacket. With whatever was left of his self-confidence, he ventured out. The walk to the saloon row would take about twenty minutes.

He could only hope. Hope the men he needed to talk with would be there. Hope there would be no trouble. Hope his long ride would be proven to hold value. Aid him in his search.

He wove his way through the gathering throng of evening drinkers and the gathering crowd on the wooden boardwalk, careful to not make eye contact that could be taken as a challenge.

He pushed into the saloon he had been in that afternoon, glancing at the bar first. There was no sign of Bates. He then turned to the tables arranged along the wall and spilling out into the small space between wall and bar. He knew, as Bates had pointed out to him, that he stood out in the crowd. He wasn't quite as conspicuous as he would be wearing a tailored suit with a stiff-collared shirt. But even his simple clothing shouted that he didn't really fit in with the crowd.

At the furthest away table, a man sat with his back to the room. Rory couldn't see his face but could easily see the black cloth that had been twisted into a sling. A sling that held a well-bandaged, bent arm. It was the man's right arm. Everything fit. This had to be his man, or men if the other face he couldn't see turned out to be the man's partner. The man wearing the sling was one of four at the table. The two he could see held no familiarity. Slowly, so as not to draw attention to himself, Rory sauntered toward the group, brushing past a girl wearing not very much, trying to ignore her pleading eyes. As he neared his quarry, he eased himself into the space between the table and the wall. At first glance, he knew there could be no mistake. These were his men.

Holding his hands in plain sight so he wouldn't present any unmeant challenge, Rory said, just loudly enough to break into the conversation around the table, without being heard further away, "Evening, Page. Guy. Like to have a talk with you fellas. Maybe buy you a drink."

Guy, immediately believing the worst, jumped to his feet, reaching for his handgun that wasn't there. Page, who turned out to be the one with the broken elbow, just stared at Rory, saying nothing.

Rory held out his empty hands and said, "Just want to talk, fellas. Nothing more. If your two friends would give us a couple of minutes, I'd appreciate it."

Guy slowly retook his seat. Page nodded across the table and the other two stood. When the chairs were empty, Rory sat in one and placed his elbows on the table, his arms folded in front of him. He leaned forward just a bit, to bring the men almost into whispering range. There was complete silence around the table for a few seconds as the three men studied each other. Page finally spoke.

"What are you doing here? We done nothing to you. Leave us alone."

"I'm perfectly content to leave you alone, all things forgotten. I'm not guaranteeing that Nancy, the girl you were contesting for that shotgun, would feel the same way. You might be wise to avoid that area of the country. For a long while, at least. She's a girl with considerable determination.

"Anyway, I only need a couple of minutes from you. That, and a bit of information."

"We don't know nothing." responded Guy.

Rory smiled. He glanced from one man to the other before saying, "No one is out to cause you trouble. Either one of you. I'm taking it that you were just hired on for a job of work. Nothing more to it.

"But you must have wondered. Of course, the man that was paying you called himself a judge, and that holds some weight in this country. I can see how that might have set your minds at ease. That claim moves the matter from rustling to something else. A lawful impounding, perhaps. He's not a judge, though, or any such thing. He's a thief, an embezzler, and a rustler, and I need to find him. I also need to find the rancher that bought the stolen cattle. As far as I can discover, there were three herds taken before the attempt on the Double J. I'd appreciate any information you can give me, starting with, were you involved in driving off the other three herds? That would be a good place to start."

Page and Guy glanced quickly at each other and then turned their eyes down to the table. Page lifted his head and looked over his shoulder into the room, almost as if he hoped help was just a jump and a holler away. Finally, he looked at Rory, leaned back in his chair, and said, "Never got one nickel from the judge for that long ride to your place. I don't figure I owe him anything.

"Ya, we rode on those three jobs. There're a few good men I hire from time to time. Good with cattle and horses, is what I mean."

Yes, but not good men in the normal sense of the word. Even as Rory had the thought, he knew not to speak it aloud.

"Make enough on a few jobs like that to lay over for the winter. Once a fella's worked through a northern winter or two, he starts looking for an easier way. Froze pretty much every part of my body, one time or another. Thought I'd find toes froze off and lying loose in my boots a time or two. The judge, he paid well and didn't ask for much, and Denver's a nice place to winter.

"Rancher down in the panhandle. One of the first down there. Miles of grass. Buffalo about gone. Man wanted a herd fast. Wanted to grow his brand. Didn't seem much worried about the Comanche or the Apache, either one. Paid good cash money. Gold money. And there ain't nothing quite like gold to gather up a man's attention. Judge passed a double handful of that good money on to me and my crew. Fella's name was Webster Cunningham. Big C brand. If you were to ride down that way, likely you'd find all the old brands blotted out though."

Rory let that information settle into his memory for a half minute, studying the two men the entire time. When he felt the time was right, he said, "BL and Half Anchor. That's the names I have for the upcountry ranches. That square with your memories?"

"Those two and the K Slash out east a ways."

"Right. I've met with the folks from the K Slash. Now, if you could tell me how many head were driven off each of those spreads, I'll thank you, buy you a drink, and get on my way. I don't expect we'll ever see each other again."

Scratching their heads to dredge up their memories, the two men looked at each other. After a suggested series of numbers passed between them, they finally nodded in agreement. They were all small ranches. Small herds. Easy pickings in some folks' minds. It was clear that the judge wasn't about to go against one of the bigger spreads.

Rory wrote the numbers on the folded sheet of paper he pulled from his shirt pocket. And stood. As he was reaching into his jacket pocket for a coin, he casually said, "I don't suppose you have any idea where the judge calls home or where he might be found."

"He never once talked about himself. Him or that fool marshal, either one."

Rory dropped a ten-dollar coin on the table and said, "Men, I owe you. And don't worry that anyone will ever know about this little meeting. I've already forgotten that we ever met. I'd suggest that you might improve your chances if you were to find another way of life, but you probably wouldn't listen. Take care, men."

With that, he eased through the tables again on his slow way to the door. Outside, he walked far enough to get past the smoke and stench that was drifting out the door and stopped to take several deep breaths. He had his information. It had cost him personal money, but he'd live through that loss. With a bath and a change of clothing, followed by a night's sleep, he could ride back to Stevensville a satisfied man.

26

ON THE RETURN RIDE, HE STOPPED IN TO EXCHANGE THE news with Sheriff Anthony Clare. Together they wandered between the buildings and onto the main street, looking for lunch. A Mexican family had opened a small *casa de comidas*, an eating house, offering traditional spiced food at a reasonable cost. The taste was new to Rory, but he found himself enjoying it.

Anthony received the news from Denver gladly, shook Rory's hand for a job well done, and bid him further good hunting.

He rode directly to the Double J, finding no good reason to stop in town. As usual, the girls were the first to come from the house to welcome him. He simply waved his return greeting and went on to the barn. There was no sign of George or the boys. He expected they were out haying, a job Rory wanted no part of.

He cared for the gelding before making his way to his own cottage. After a thorough wash and a change of clothing, he strolled casually to the house. There was coffee ready and fresh bread just coming from the oven.

Not really knowing where the thought came from, he heard the silent words, *nothing smells more like home than bread, fresh from the oven.* For someone who had so few memories of a real family home, or freshly baked bread, the thought seemed foreign, yet satisfying.

After wiping his boots on the outdoor mat and hanging his hat on a peg beside the door, he greeted his aunt Eliza and the two girl cousins. Eliza welcomed him with a hug. She said, "Take a seat, young man. I expect you've covered some miles and taken some risks. It's good to see you home and in one piece.

"Hannah, that bread is probably too hot to slice proper, but see if you can get a piece or two off. And Nancy, you could lift down the butter and strawberry preserves from the cold pantry. I'm sure the sheriff could eat a piece of bread since dinner is a ways off yet. Might have a slice myself."

Hannah made a mess of the bread slicing, but Rory couldn't see that the crooked slices affected the taste any. Between himself and the three women, there wasn't much left of a loaf when their indulgences were satisfied.

At their insistence, the girls listened to Rory's shortened telling of his last few days. They then brought him up to date on the cleaning of the marshal's office and the current rumors that were entertaining the citizens of Stevensville, Colorado.

"The doctor shouted and stamped around his clinic a bit, saying it was too soon, but the Kings and Mrs. Flint harnessed up and drove out to the ranch anyway. They asked me to tell you that Mrs. Flint would come back in whenever the banker came to his senses and released their money."

Rory took all that in without comment.

❧

THE NEXT MORNING, he saddled up and prepared his bedroll and the two-bag set of panniers that would take the place of his leather saddlebags. The panniers held more than the leather bags, making his preparations for a long ride easier.

When he left for town, he had the keys to the two town offices in his pocket. He had things to consider. One was the possibility that the phony judge might have secreted something in his office that neither he nor the girls had found. The second was the possibility of using the marshal's office for sleeping quarters when he needed to stay close to town. He rode first to the judge's place.

Entering, he stopped after a single step and looked over every inch of the walls, wooden door and window casings, the ceiling, looking for loose or renailed boards, and lastly, at the floor. He found nothing until he pushed the old desk over against the wall and dragged the worn, tied-rag rug out of the way.

Running his hand over every inch of the floorboards, half of them warped and damaged, he finally felt a piece move. Not much movement, but enough to get his attention. It was a short piece, no more than two feet long. Looking carefully, he could see that there was scarring on one end, as if something, a knife perhaps, had carelessly been used as a pry in order to lift it out of place. He opened his own Barlow knife, a single-bladed affair that he had carried since he was a child, a gift from some occasion or other, he couldn't quite remember which one.

In a matter of seconds, he had the board loose, lifted out, and set aside. These built-in-a-rush buildings, the first in any small town, were built either over a small cellar or, more usually, directly on timbers or even trees flattened with an adze. This one was raised above the ground by several inches, enough to hold secrets, contraband or, unfortunately, snakes.

There was nothing visible from above, only dried-out earth. He could even see a few whisps of desiccated grass. Rory had never had anything close to a love affair with snakes. Not that he had ever been bitten, but the thought alone sent chills up his spine. Knowing he had it to do, he leaned back onto his heels and considered. A decision made, he stood, walked to the mercantile, and bought a pair of heavy leather gloves.

Back on his knees, determined, he pulled the gloves on, hesitated, and reached into the hole, up to his elbow. Nothing. The two-foot section of floorboard showed how far apart the supporting timbers were. He could only reach the two directions, between the timbers. With proof that he could find nothing in the first direction, he eased around on the floor until he could reach the other way. He heard no wriggling on the dirt and no rattling of an alarmed snake. With his mind somewhat stilled, he pushed in as far as his long arms would allow. Nothing. Again, he sat back on his heels.

If there had ever been anything there, it was now gone. Or, of course, it was also possible that the judge knew nothing about the loose board. But he had to try again. He'd feel guilty if he didn't.

Bending forward from his kneeling position, he extended his arm in again. Nothing. But as he was pulling his arm out, his shirt caught on something hanging from the underside of the floorboards. He turned his hand over and again felt into the hole, but this time, feeling upwards. A string. His shirt had

REG QUIST

snagged on a loosely hanging string. He looped one finger over the string and pulled his arm out. Feeling carefully, he found where the string was tied to a small nail. A couple of easy tugs shook the nail loose. It turned out to be a big-headed carpet tack. Slowly, so as not to lose whatever was on the other end, he pulled on the string. He had three feet of the grocer's twine lying in a heap in the bottom of the hole before his fingers touched whatever it was that was tied on the end. Another careful pull, and he had a canvas bag in his hands.

Standing, he waited a few seconds, waiting for his knees to feel limber enough to trust. He then laid the bag on the old desk and sat in the chair. He unwound the leather strip holding the top together and dumped the contents onto the desktop. The clinking of gold coins, including one much-tarnished ten-dollar piece, followed by a wad of folding money and a small, lined tablet, completed the loot.

Quickly formulating a plan, and needing a witness, he put everything back into the sack and stuffed it inside his shirt. The beaded leather jacket would disguise any bulge. He locked the door, stepped into the saddle, and rode to the bank. Entering, he walked straight into Jesse Ambrewster's office. Ambrewster, looking up at him and, saying nothing, waited. Rory pulled the sack out of his shirt, removed the leather tie and dumped the contents onto the banker's desk, and sat down, allowing time for questions to form.

Ambrewster hesitated, then said, "I'm sure you're going to tell me the story. Before either of us are much older, I hope. I actually do have other work to do, although I realize that most people think I sit in here all day running my fingers through their money."

228

"Found this under the floorboards in the office the judge was renting."

"Good work, sheriff, but why did you bring it here?"

"Because I wanted someone to count it with me and then put it in a safe place."

"Alright, I can understand that. But how can you be sure it belonged to the judge? Don't you think he would have taken it when he ran?"

"Logical to think that, Mr. Ambrewster. But you said yourself he left in an all-fired hurry that morning. Could be he planned to come back for it. That would seem logical. And there might be something in the notebook. I haven't looked yet."

"I'll count the money. You look at the book."

IN LESS THAN FIVE MINUTES, Ambrewster had a total written on a blank sheet of paper, and Rory was ecstatic with the information he found written in the little book.

"Can you put that money away safely? We'll add it to the total you already have on account from the sale of the rustled stock. I'm going to try to locate the other two ranches and see what they have to say for themselves. Then we'll see about sharing that money around."

Ambrewster just nodded before asking, "What did you find in the book?"

"Just about everything a stumbling lawman could hope for on his first case."

Which told the banker everything, and nothing at all. But he held any other questions he might have had. Rory thanked him and made his way back to his horse. He swung aboard with the intention of riding into the hills, but as he turned, the hotel and dining room came into view. Sometimes his private thoughts troubled him, but he accepted this one without question. *It's a bit early for lunch, but I don't expect I'm going to find another eating house up in those hills.*

It was a short ride across the street and down less than one hundred yards to the hitch-post in front of the hotel. He swung down, tied off, whipped some of the dust off his pants and shirt, and entered the dining room. Three tables had folks either eating or waiting for their food. Rory chose his favorite table, the one where he could see the doorway and glance out the window and, with a slight turn of his head, keep an eye on Sonia without being too obvious about it.

He feasted on a heaping plate of roasted beef, whole potatoes, and cabbage, with some grilled onion on the side. Every time he lifted his eyes from the dinner, he could see Sonia glancing his way. Once, when he looked up, Sonia indeed had her eye on him but what she didn't see was Ma standing in the kitchen doorway, looking at the two young people with a big grin on her face. Rory figured he had best finish up his meal and hit the saddle, or he just might still be there come sundown. He was uncomfortable with the thoughts running, unbidden, through his mind.

Sonia came to the table again, this time with a written-out tab for the cost of the lunch. As the cost never varied, the tab was hardly necessary, but Rory said, "Thank you." and reached into his pocket for a coin.

Sonia folded her hand over the coin, looking as if she had something else to say. When Rory hesitated, giving her the opportunity, she finally managed to find the words.

"It's about time for me to visit the folks again. Is there any chance you're riding up that way sometime soon?"

"I'm heading up into the high country right now, but to a different place than where your folks live. I shouldn't be gone too long. When I get back, we'll discuss it."

"Don't you forget, now."

"I'll remember."

27

RORY HAD SEEN NO MAP, SO HE HAD LITTLE TRUE IDEA OF the lay of the land. He knew that most of the mining towns lay to the south. He also knew from what others had told him that there were folds in the land, almost like low mountain ranges separated by grassed valleys. It was still early in ranching history. A lot of the land was yet unclaimed or unsettled. None of the ranches were more than four or five years on the grass, but there were enough of them prospering to prove the merit of the grassed areas. The Triple T, where Henry and Thomas had been working, lay on one of the plateaus. He would start his hunt for the BL and Half Anchor Ranches there.

By rights, he should have held over and begun his ride in the early morning. The day would be about done by the time he reached the Triple T. He wondered a bit at his own wisdom as he could almost hear his father say, *be thorough in all you do, but learn patience too.* His father had been a great teacher. Rory often found himself wishing he had listened more. Or listened better, to grasp the whole of what that good man had been saying.

He made better time than he had expected, riding onto the Triple T just as the iron triangle was calling the crew for dinner. Slim, the ranch foreman Rory had met when he was there looking for his cousins, hailed him with a wave.

"You're timing is spot-on, Rory. Turn that gelding into the corral and come. We'll get some grub behind your belt. Time enough after that to find out what brings you into the hills today."

A fine dinner, a visit with a couple of the men he had met before, and some vague directions that should guide him to the BL Ranch, followed by a few hours in a bunk, and he was ready to move on.

BY DAWDLING as he was preparing the gelding for the day's ride, while the ranch foreman detailed the men off to their work, he managed to get a couple of private minutes with Slim. He lifted the deputy sheriff badge from his vest pocket and held it out for the foreman to see. Slim needed but a quick glance to arrive at an understanding. His question was by way of a single raised eyebrow, and a single word question, "County?"

Rory responded with a shortened explanation of the one-year appointment, hoping the county would have arranged itself by that time, at least enough for an election, and then asked the foreman to hold the appointment confidential.

Slim let his mind work on all that for a moment and then said, "Thanks for telling me. It will go no further. And if I see or hear anything at all of the two you're looking for, I'll get word to you."

A handshake and a nod took the place of any further words.

Rory found the BL Ranch—a small, obviously struggling affair, tucked into a pretty little valley, an offshoot of a much larger high mountain grassed area.

The trail up from Stevensville wound among rocky uplifts, with several steep grades along its miles before it drew into the plateau where the Triple T held the grass. Following the natural terrain, the trail presented the traveler with almost as many downs as ups. Rory figured the ups and downs almost balanced each other out, and that the valley the BL lay in, just a few miles from the Triple T, was not really that much higher than his starting point.

A mixture of pine and cedar, among a scattering of poplars and aspens, outlined a good spread of grazing land. He saw no more than twenty or thirty cows on the grass, fewer than half of them with calves at foot. Three horses grazed along with the cattle.

Riding into the yard, he saw two more horses in a pole corral built off the side of a small log barn. There was a chicken coop and a shed of some kind, and beyond that, a small log house. Everything was laid out with care, attention to detail, and ease of movement.

A boy of about fourteen years watched his approach from the door of the barn. The boy was tall for his age, slim but strong-looking. He badly needed a haircut. He returned Rory's stare with a stern stare of his own, almost threatening a reckoning if trouble should present itself.

Glancing the other direction, Rory saw a woman standing on the covered porch near what he suspected was the kitchen door, judging by the nearby washstand

and the big laundry tub hanging on the outside, along with a few miscellaneous items.

He was not close enough for accurate judgment, but his initial glance told him this woman would be considered pretty and attractive by any man closer to her age. He was no judge of age, but if forced into it, he would guess she had seen somewhere near to thirty years come and go. Girls married young in the country. Having a fourteen-year-old son while being thirty herself was not unusual. She stood tall and slim and dignified, in possession of, and protection of her home.

The woman held a carbine in her right hand, draped over the crook of her left elbow. He saw no welcome in either the boy or the woman.

Rory stopped a good distance off, lifted his hat, holding it in his hands, and said, "Morn'n, ma'am." He turned his eyes toward the barn and said, "Morn'n, young fella."

"Ma'am, my name is Rory Jamison, Double J Ranch, from down in Stevensville. I'd appreciate if I could have a talk with Mr. Ben Lander. That is, if I'm at the right ranch. I apologize, I should have said right off, I'm looking for the BL Ranch."

He saw the woman's eyes flick toward the barn. Rory turned that way also, hoping to see Ben Lander coming his way. Instead, he saw the young man, now with a Colt tucked behind his belt and a shotgun in his hands, walking toward the house.

Rory replaced his hat and said, "Whoa down there, young man. There's no need for all the hardware. I mean you no harm. In fact, you walk over here, son, and I'll give you something to show your mother."

Slowly the boy approached, never taking his eyes off Rory. Rory said, "Now, son, I'm going to reach into my vest pocket. I'll do it slow so's you can see there's no harm meant."

Slowly he pushed his fingers into the little slash pocket and lifted out the badge. Holding it in the flat of his palm, he said, "I'm going to toss this to you, son. You catch it and take it to your mother."

The boy neither took his eyes off Rory nor lowered the shotgun as the badge flew across the ten feet separating them and fell at his feet. He scuffed it with his foot until the side with the writing on it was turned to the sky. With a quick glance, realization seemed to come to the young man. Rory could feel the lessening of the tension in the yard. The boy folded at the knees, keeping his eyes on Rory the entire time, picked up the badge, and sidled carefully toward the cabin. He held the badge out to his mother and waited.

"This for real?"

"Yes, ma'am. It's for real. I'm looking into the rustling of cattle from three ranches. The BL, the Half Anchor, and one from down below, out on the eastern flatlands, the K Slash."

Both the boy and his mother lowered their weapons but didn't put them down.

"You had better step down. It's a long ride up here. You had best water and care for your animal, and then come to the house."

Rory slow-walked the gelding to the corral and unsaddled it, balancing the saddle on the top rail of the corral. The water trough was inside the corral, so he simply opened the gate and turned the gelding in. When he turned around, the woman was no longer in sight, but her son still stood on the porch, and he still held the shotgun.

Lifting his hat from his head again, Rory stepped up

the three stairs onto the porch. The woman heard his heavy footfalls and called out, "Come in."

Rory gave his already clean boots a good wiping on the ragrug placed there for the purpose and, still carrying his hat, pulled open the screen door. The woman pointed to a chair at the table. His badge lay there, in front of a mug of steaming coffee. "Have a seat."

"Thank you, ma'am. May I take it that you are Mrs. Lander?"

"I am. And this is my son, Kenny."

"I'm pleased to meet you, ma'am, and you too, Kenny. Is Mr. Lander close by?"

"He is, in a sense. He's buried just behind the house."

Feeling foolish, knowing he should have suspected something of the sort, knowing how the judge operated, laying claim only on ranches where the man was no longer a threat, he stumbled through an apology. Fingering the badge before he finally slid it into the pocket, he tried to think of how to approach the purpose for his visit. He finally decided this woman could probably handle anything he had to say. That she was still there, on the small ranch, after the death of her husband and the theft of her cattle, spoke of strength and staying power.

"Mrs. Lander, that judge and the town marshal he rode with tried to pull off a steal on our Double J, covering it with paperwork and legal language they hoped no one would question. I had been away for near enough three years, and my father, who was the original owner of the Double J, had died during that time. The judge thought he saw an opportunity. He had no idea that I was still alive and would show up, speaking for myself. I arrived home in time to put a stop to the whole thing. But he managed to complete the steal on the K Slash, and I was told, on the Half Anchor and your own BL. Is that what happened up here, ma'am?"

"That is exactly what happened. There is only Kenny and me here now, and we were no match for a judge with legal papers and a crew who rounded up most of our herd and were gone within a few minutes. You can see that our land is easily defined between the hills, so the cattle are never far off.

"The judge insisted he had to lay his papers out on the table. Of course, that was just to get Kenny and me into the house so we couldn't see what the cowboys were doing. While we were inside listening to him explain the legal situation, the crew of thieves was outside gathering up most of our stock. By the time we came back into the yard, all we could see was the herd a good mile off and moving fast.

"There was nothing at all we could do. So here we live, just us and a few head of cattle, hoping we can hang on long enough for the herd to rebuild itself."

"There is some good news among all of that, ma'am."

"Please call me Patricia. Ma'am sounds so old."

"Alright, Patricia. And I, of course, am just Rory. I'm not spreading the word around about my appointment as county deputy. I figure I can work better without that news getting spread too far. I would ask you to hold it to yourselves until we're a bit further into this manhunt."

He then told them about the judge and marshal making their escape and about the funds in the bank. A look of relieved wonder crossed Patricia's face as she thought about the possibility of returned funds. He was tempted to ask about the number of cattle stolen, comparing it to what the cowboys he found in the saloon in Denver had told him. Further thought made him believe it might be better to hold that until they were all together at the bank.

"Patricia, I have to find the Half Anchor before we can start to wrap this thing up. So far, no one seems to know anything about it."

Patricia looked at her son and then asked, "Kenny. You went out to that school at the Burroughs' Slash B Slash Ranch for a couple of winters. Did you meet anyone there that ever mentioned a ranch by that name?"

Rory added to the question, "Or a family named Sperry?"

"There was a girl named Sperry. About my age. She told me about where their ranch is, but I ain't never been there."

"Can you remember what she told you, Kenny?"

Kenny remembered very well. It was about fifteen miles from the BL with the Burroughs Ranch, where school was held, about in the middle.

With everything he felt he needed now known, Rory bedded down in the barn loft after taking dinner with the widow and her son. Patricia sent him off the next morning after breakfast, with enough biscuit-wrapped bacon folded into an old newspaper to hold him over on his search for the Half Anchor.

HE RODE into the Half Anchor about midafternoon, after having to backtrack twice to retreat from dead-end valleys. The situation was completely different from what he had found on the BL and K Slash Ranches. There was a widow woman alright. That much held true to the pattern set by the judge. But, like Lavinia Flint,

Mrs. Sperry was older. Unlike Lavinia Flint, who was rail thin, with a strength that defied her image, Mrs. Sperry was heavier, not plump, as in a woman bearing excess weight, but in a woman born to some size, strengthening with time and toil.

Standing beside her, watching the sheriff approach, were two grown sons, armed and determined. Rory could see that much from a distance. It was near impossible to judge the age of a fully bearded man, as these two sons were, but as a guess, Rory decided there were some years between them. Perhaps thirty and early twenties would be an accurate guess. Big men, tall, hair flowing from beneath their hats. Strong, with the look of their mother to them.

He rode slowly into the yard with both his hands in plain sight. He didn't need a misunderstanding at this point of his search. He stopped where he would have to raise his voice a bit to be heard.

"Afternoon, folks. Rory Jamison here, Double J Ranch, down to Stevensville. Need to talk with you for a bit."

One of the men spoke with equal volume. "Come. Slowly as you been doing."

Rory approached within twenty feet and stopped. He had his sheriff badge in his hand. As he had done on the BL, he tossed it to the man who spoke.

That man snagged it out of the air and fingered it, turning it over and over, and then passing it to the second man and he, in turn, to the woman.

The woman spoke, asking, "You find this lying on the road?"

Rory laughed good-naturedly before saying, "No, ma'am. I got talked into the job. Don't wear the badge. Come near to being caught out down to Denver when I was trying to do some investigating. Two pinholes in my shirt. Two pinholes is all. Fella who didn't really have to get involved pointed them out to me. Added in that any man worth his salt would know those pinholes for a badge. Could have led to a serious misunderstanding, so I keep the badge in my pocket and don't wear shirts with pinholes in them.

"It's sheriffing business we have to talk about, folks, if you could spare the time."

The woman continued to speak for the family.

"Step down and tie off. Come up here. We'll sit in the shade. I'll get some lemonade."

Rory did as Mrs. Sperry had suggested, taking off his hat and climbing the stairs. Again, he introduced himself.

The two young men, both big, strong, with an ungroomed look to them, hesitated. Finally, the older of the two said, "Noah Sperry. My brother here is Alexander.

"Take a seat. We'll wait for Ma to come with the lemonade before we find out just why you're here."

Rory took a sip of the first lemonade he had tasted in several years and decided to open the conversation. His explanation didn't take more than five minutes, including sharing the news of the money in the bank waiting to be claimed and shared.

As he was speaking, a younger girl, about the age of the Lander boy, undoubtedly the one he knew from school, came into the kitchen from another room. She stood silently beside her mother's chair.

Noah was the first to respond when he said, "You're saying that Ben Lander is dead? I sure enough hadn't heard that. Mrs. Lander say how that came to be?"

"She didn't offer any information other than he was buried behind the house. I didn't ask. Didn't want to intrude. You sound as if you knew Lander. Mrs. Lander claimed she hadn't heard of you or your ranch. It was Kenny who remembered a girl from school carrying the name that got me on the right path to the Half Anchor."

"Met Lander just the once. Pa and I were riding down to the city after some supplies. Met him on the trail. Never met his wife or son. He probably didn't bother mentioning the meeting to his wife."

"Was that meeting recent?"

"No, Alexander and I have been away for some time. The Half Anchor is a small ranch. Dad's long-dreamed-of retirement project. He didn't really care if it made a lot or just a little money. He wanted to be away from the sea. Always said he never again wanted to smell salt water.

"There was no work for either Alexander or me on the Half Anchor. Result was that we went off the most of a year ago, heading down to the mining country. See if there really is gold under every rock you kicked over. There isn't. After one cold and starving winter, we put in a bit more time this summer and then decided we'd best come home. Rode onto the place just a few days ago. Found out Pa had died during the winter. Fool horse lost his footing on a short, snow-blanketed hillside. Ma found him the next day, his ribs caved in and blood on the saddle horn. She only saw that after she caught the horse."

Mrs. Sperry entered the story with, "Led that dumb beast home so's I wouldn't have to carry the saddle. Stripped the gear off him, tied a rope around his neck, and led him out into the wilderness. Shot him, reclaimed my rope, and rode home. I passed the word of my man's death on my next run for provisions. I was hoping somehow that word would get to where the boys were.

"Wasn't long before that judge and his sidekick marshal rode into the yard with papers and a gang of cowboys. Sounds about like what he done to those other two widows. Like to get my hands on that man. I'd give up on the cattle, or the money, either one, to get one good shot at each of those sneak thieves."

Noah picked up the story.

"Ma may be willing to give up on the cattle or the money but I'm not. I doubt as how Alexander is either. You'll note that Alexander, he don't say much. But there are few with more determination than my younger brother. Or the ability to see that determination to the end. We were discussing where we might find that judge when you rode into the yard."

Rory chose not to continue in that direction. Instead, he laid out his plan.

"What I'm hoping to be able to do is have you folks, along with Mrs. Lander, ride down to Stevensville with me. It wouldn't take long to get Mrs. Flint to town from her ranch and we could all meet up with the banker. Lay out your claim, add it up and sort out how much of the funds on deposit should go to each of you. It's not likely to cover all your losses.

"I found the cowboys that drove the animals off. They tell me they went to a rancher just starting up down in the Texas panhandle country. He was eager to grow his brand fast. Knew he was buying stolen animals. Judge apparently let them go for a serious discount from true value. Then, the judge held some coin back for his own expenses before he banked the rest. Divided three ways, it's not likely to come out as good as any of us wish, but whatever you get will be better than what you have now.

"With that rancher knowingly buying stolen, branded

cattle, I'm sure a claim could be made against him. I won't be pursuing that, though. I have enough to do here in the county. That's not to say you couldn't take a ride down that way.

"Mrs. Lander is making arrangements with a neighbor to care for her place while she's away. If you could do the same, we can ride for town just as soon as you're ready."

The Sperry family discussed that while Rory drank the last of his lemonade. They decided they needed two days. Rory nodded and said, "If you don't mind, I'd roll out my bedroll in the loft for tonight and head down country first light tomorrow. If one of you could ride to the BL and guide Mrs. Lander and Kenny safely to town, or even meet up and come as a group, that would relieve me of the need."

Mrs. Sperry, who was obviously familiar with command, with her life being spent mostly alone, while her man was out to sea, said, "We'll go one better than just that. We'll wagon up and do our half-yearly buying in Stevensville. Usually find enough things we need to make the trip to Denver worthwhile, but we'll hold that off till next spring."

With that decided, Alexander went immediately to the washbasin, soap and razor in hand. A half-hour later he had taken on a distinctly gentlemanly look. Strong and hard from a lifetime of work, but gentlemanly. A handsome man who needed a haircut. But men needing haircuts were a common sight on the frontier. He saddled a horse and rode out with a small bedroll tied behind the saddle. The brothers had agreed on a meeting place on the trail to Stevensville. Alexander was riding to ensure that Mrs. Lander arrived there safely.

28

After introducing himself to Mrs. Lander, and a lengthy explanation, Alexander was finally given a late dinner and permission to bed down in the loft. He was wishing he had brought Sis with him. The girl knew the Lander boy and could have eased the introduction. The next morning, taking directions from Patricia Lander, Alexander left to see if the neighbor, that had been a help to her before, could look after the place for a few days. After locating the middle-aged bachelor and explaining the situation, the two men rode back to the BL. The ride was silent, as neither man saw any purpose in idle chatter.

With everything in place and one more night in the loft, Alexander harnessed the team. The democrat wagon was loaded down with bedding, trail provisions, and a large, folded-over oiled canvas cover for use in the event of a fall rain. The snow was gone from the hills but, in places, the trail would still be muddy and a bit treacherous. It would take care to maneuver the team down the steep portions. With Kenny handling the reins, they drove across the grasslands of the BL Ranch. Three hours later the two groups met on the trail and that afternoon drove into Stevensville.

RORY RETURNED that evening with Mrs. Flint, handling her own wagon. She and Rory had reminisced a bit about the dreadful trip over the same trail just a few days before.

"That's our weather for you, spring and fall. You'd best be prepared for anything."

Rory agreed with a grim smile.

They all had dinner that evening in the hotel dining room. That was the first opportunity for everyone involved to meet each other and make plans for the morning and how they would proceed at the bank. When the conversation turned to the numbers of stolen cattle, Rory stopped the talk immediately.

"I figure we should give up those numbers only the once. I have some numbers given to me by the cowboys that drove your herds off. I'm hoping your numbers will come close to matching what they gave me. We don't need a disagreement at this stage of the deal."

THE RANCHERS WERE STANDING around the boardwalk after breakfast, waiting for the arrival of Jesse Ambrewster. Rory, the youngest of the bunch, except for Sis Sperry and Kenny Lander, was seen as the leader. Privately he chuckled at the thought. *Never before understood what a simple badge can do.*

The small crowd began easing across the dusty road

as Ambrewster was approaching on the other walkway. They met at the bank door. The anxiety of the ranchers was at a high pitch. Ambrewster laughed and said, "You're going to have to let me get to the door to unlock it, folks. Or we could have our meeting right here on the boardwalk."

The crowd divided, and they were soon in the bank. Ambrewster dragged two chairs from the front office into his private space. With them all gathered together, it was plain that the banker's private office would not be anywhere near big enough. He hesitated, and then said, "May I suggest that you ladies take the chairs. Men, you are welcome to gather around, of course, but I'm afraid you'll have to stand. Sheriff, I would like to have you in the office, as well."

No one disputed those directions, and within a half-minute, everyone was ready. The anxiety among the group had risen, even above its earlier presence. Mrs. Flint was the calmest of the group. She sat there, stalwart, determined and ready. Mrs. Sperry, after a lifetime as a sailor's wife, wouldn't hesitate to state her position, yet here calmness came near to rivaling that of Mrs. Flint. Mrs. Lander, on the other hand, was far more reliant on the return of the funds from her stolen cattle. She exhibited her nervousness with the slight tick in her eye and the wringing of her hands.

Noticing Mrs. Lander's unease, Alexander silently took Kenny by the shoulder, guided him past the doorway, and indicated that he should stand behind his mother. Then, for reasons he could not have adequately explained, Alexander himself joined the young man. His mother cast a questioning look his way, but his brother, Noah, noticing the action, stood where he was with a big grin on his face.

Ambrewster cleared his throat and needlessly adjusted the pen and paper on his desk. He finally worked up presence of mind enough to say, "Welcome, ladies and gentlemen. We haven't yet been formally introduced but with a crowd this large and with the matter at hand I believe we might be well advised to simply proceed as quickly as possible. Sheriff, by your presence, are you confirming that these are the owners of the three ranches involved in the case?"

"Yes. Mrs. Flint of the K Slash, Mrs. Lander of the BL, and Mrs. Sperry of the Half Anchor."

The banker nodded, yet hesitated, as he glanced from one to the other.

"Ladies, this is an unfortunate and, I am sure, a difficult matter for you and your families. I understand that each of you has recently been left a widow. And, adding to that, having a large portion of your herds pirated off by a scoundrel. Hopefully, we can set aside at least some of the distress this morning. Now, Sheriff, how do you propose we proceed?"

"I'm thinking the fairest way is for each lady to state her losses. If you could write them down, Mr. Ambrewster, we can compare those numbers with what the hired cowboys told me. We can then turn the agreed-upon numbers into a percentage of the whole and use those percentages for the dividing up of the funds. I'm hoping someone here is better at numbers than I am for doing the calculations. Does that sit alright with all of you?"

There was a general nodding around the table, so the banker dipped his pen in the inkwell and wrote the brand of each ranch on the paper, one above the other, leaving space for calculations. It took only a few seconds for each woman to give Ambrewster a number to jot beside her brand. Rory then reached into his shirt pocket and withdrew the paper holding the numbers Page Newsom and Guy Fletcher had given him back in the saloon in Denver. Every number was an estimate, as none of the ranchers had done a roundup or a careful count of the cattle remaining to them. Newsom and Fletcher were going by memory only.

After Ambrewster had all the information down in orderly fashion, he exhaled a deep breath and turned the paper toward the others. It was a thoughtful, but needless action. Everyone in the room had the numbers firmly fixed in memory.

Without a word Ambrewster turned to Rory, waiting for a response. Rory glanced again at the numbers to confirm his memory, silently wondering what his father would do in the same position. After that second look, he said, "The numbers remembered by the rustler crew are a bit lower in each case. The gap is very close to equal for the K Slash and the BL. The Half Anchor is out by about twenty head. I'm going to suggest that the claim by the Half Anchor be reduced by those twenty head, and we call it a close thing."

It felt to Rory as if every eye in the room turned to Mrs. Sperry. She returned none of the gazes. Nor did she consult with her sons. Instead, she said, "Sheriff, you get me one clear shot at those thieves, and I'll give up on the entire claim. Failing that, I have no problem with the suggestion."

The banker turned the page back to himself and scratched out the original number, replacing it with the reduced claim. He then said, with a bit of a sad grin, "I recall learning fractions and percentages in school, but that's not something I ever have to do in the bank, so memory is faded. I'm sure I could do it if you folks wanted to go for a cup of coffee and come back in a while."

Mrs. Sperry simply said, "Sis. Git yourself in here. Mr. Banker, you give Sis your seat and let her work it out. Might get some use from all that schooling yet."

Sis self-consciously took the vacated chair and picked up the pen. With her forehead resting in her upturned left hand, and her eyes glued to the paper, she began. Her first touch of pen on paper left a big blot of ink. The nervous young lady looked at the pen nib as if to ask where all the ink came from. She knew the answer of course. She had been taught the use of the dreaded instrument during her time at Mrs. Burroughs' school. Her next effort left little more than a scratch mark, with the nib now lacking in ink. The banker came to her rescue. Without a word, he opened the top desk drawer and withdrew a sharpened pencil, laying it in front of Sis. She picked it up and nodded her thanks.

With the pencil doing an adequate job, she first made a column of the three numbers representing the lost cattle. She added those up and, using that number as the denominator, that is, the bottom number in the fraction, and the number from her own Half Anchor Ranch as the numerator, the top number, she divided the larger number into the smaller, giving her a number less than one, represented by a decimal point that she added at the front. She then moved the decimal point two spaces to the right, converting it into a percentage of the whole.

This was repeated for the other two ranches. By the time she was done, the page was a scramble of numbers, but she had three circled numbers representing the percentages each ranch could claim from the funds. The percentages, added together, came to one hundred percent.

Kenny had watched every move she made, without comment. Surprisingly, Sis looked up at him and asked, "Did I do it right, Kenny?"

"Right as rain. Mrs. Burroughs would give you a gold star."

As the two young people grinned at each other, the banker harrumphed and cleared his throat. What came next was more down his alley.

"Folks, the amount the judge left on deposit was increased some a few days ago when the sheriff found a hidden sack of money in the judge's vacated office."

He then said, "Young lady, you write down this number, do your percentages, and we can wrap this thing up."

With the cash on hand finally revealed, Sis lifted the pencil again and went to work. When the three numbers were laid out and circled, as she had done with the percentages, she again looked to Kenny for confirmation. He smiled and nodded but said nothing.

Now it was Ambrewster's turn.

"Ladies, if we are all in agreement, I'll take my chair back and write out a chit for each of you. You can either take the cash with you or leave it here on deposit in your own names. It's your choice. But I must advise you again, this action is highly unusual for a bank. A big-city bank would never do anything like this without a court order."

Jokingly, which was not a natural position for the banker, he said, "If I end up in prison, I hope you will remember me from time to time."

29

The sheriff, the three widows, and their various children gathered in the hotel dining room that evening. They had all spent the day sorting out their business. Mrs. Flint needed the shoes checked on her wagon team, as well as a load of supplies from the mercantile.

Mrs. Lander led Kenny to the clothing display, commenting to Mrs. Flint, who was standing there also, "I don't think this boy is ever going to quit growing. Seems we're looking over pants and shirts every time we get to town. Still, I'd rather buy them than make them. Spending the evenings with needle and thread has never been something I enjoy."

Mrs. Sperry used the time to instruct Sis on the niceties of shopping, watching every penny and looking for bargains. This wasn't the first lesson in shopping between mother and daughter and it wouldn't be the last, but Mrs. Sperry was on the "repeat it until they've got it" school.

Alexander and Noah found acceptable replacements

for the clothing they had worn almost to the last thread on their hunt for the illusive gold nuggets.

In addition to the smaller matters of shopping for clothing for growing kids and a few treats, Browning had the biggest day he had enjoyed in some time. By the end of the day, the two upcountry wagons were brimming with a winter's supply of necessities. Mrs. Flint, living closer to town, purchased her current needs only.

WHILE THE GROUP was visiting and getting to know one another over dinner, somehow, Alexander Sperry and Patricia Lander found themselves quietly talking, leaving the others out of their conversation. Kenny and Sis were also visiting privately, not really a part of the adult conversation, and content with the situation.

Rory, feeling he was no longer needed, was intent on heading out to the Double J for an evening with family and a night in his own bed. When he came into the dining room to say goodnight and wish each rancher well in the future, Mrs. Sperry asked, "How did those two men get our names and locations, sheriff? It's clear they only approached recent widows. Seems strange to me."

"It seems strange to me, too, Mrs. Sperry. I'm working on just that question, but I don't have much to go on. Yet. But if I pin it down, I'll let you know."

HE WAS EARLY in town the following morning. He had offered to ride along with Mrs. Flint, rather than her going it alone. The risk for a woman alone was not great, but nor was it zero. In a still unsettled land, there was little to prevent anyone from marauding the countryside, taking advantage of anyone weaker than themselves.

Since being appointed deputy sheriff of the unorganized county, Rory was becoming aware of the size of the land under his jurisdiction. To hope to prevent every criminal act, or to catch every criminal or bad actor was not realistic. But by riding along to the K Slash, the chance of Mrs. Flint arriving home safely was increased considerably.

The wagon was lightly loaded, causing it to rumble over the gravely soil and the bunch grass. Conversation was not easy. Still, Rory was able to ask Mrs. Flint what her intentions were now that she had the funds to restock her ranch.

"Living on the wide-open land was my husband's dream, not mine. He could visualize a steadily growing herd with grass everywhere and no fences to prevent their grazing the best parts. He well knew that as more ranchers moved in, there would be serious competition for that grass, but he hoped to get his herd built up to where few could challenge him. Who knows, he might have made it, given another five years. There's still not much competition for all that grass. But he's gone and his dream died with him.

"Ambrose and Katie were really only there to help the ranch grow. Now I doubt if they will want to stay, even if Ambrose recovers his strength. And I, for sure, won't stay. I was talking with the women from the Half Anchor and the BL. Their talk of well-watered grass, forests and hillsides outlining their holdings, caught my attention.

"I'm thinking we'll try to sell, but I doubt there will be many buyers when land is so plentiful. Still, I figure to spend the winter in town, and in the spring, take a ride around the higher country. Ambrose and Katie, I'm sure will come to town. Then we'll just have to see. See what happens. I hate to leave Mr. Flint in a grave that will probably be grazed over in the future and forgotten, but life has to be for the living."

Rory couldn't see that any of that called for a response, so they proceeded on with only the turning of the wagon wheels disturbing the silence of the morning.

When he returned to Stevensville late that afternoon, there was no sign of the Half Anchor or BL Ranchers.

30

Knowing he wouldn't be satisfied until he at least put some effort into running down the judge and the marshal, Rory thought of this as he rode toward town. And he thought of the family's ranch and his part in it. He, George, and the cousins had joined in a serious discussion the evening before about the future of the Double J Ranch. They had known from the beginning that it couldn't support everyone in its current situation. The discussions were to look for alternatives. There was still land available to the east and north if they decided to expand.

The newly purchased purebred bulls ended up becoming the center of conversation. George pushed that discussion forward with, "We won't see the results of that purchase for a year and some months yet. But there's no reason we shouldn't expect an improvement over the past. And, of course, that has me thinking of purebred cows. You mentioned once, Rory, that one of the farmers you met down east was selling bred heifers."

"I did. He was quoting a premium price for them too.

The market should be good for upgraded stock for years ahead, as the country grows and the market is demanding better beef. It only makes sense. A better grade of animal rather than more quantity of scrubs, or near scrubs. The purebreds don't eat any more grass than the scrubs, and they drop one calf each spring, same as the others.

"With a good price per bred yearling, if we decided to go that route, we could hold the herd down to manageable numbers and grow in size only when we were ready and only if we wanted to. And with the purebred calves packing on more beef, the market price should outstrip what we're enjoying now.

"If one of us boys should find a woman foolish enough to marry up, we would need an income to support a family. That might mean growing the Double J, or even starting a new brand. With a good herd of breeding animals, there would be the seed herd for expansion."

Henry said, "All this talk imagines that we can simply step out and do as we wish. Costs money, though. Purebreds do. Unless there's something I don't know about the operation, we're a long way from buying more than just a few upgrade cows. Take a long time to grow a herd that way."

The silence around the big kitchen table confirmed that the others had been thinking the same thing.

Thomas eased toward territory the Jamison family had been careful to avoid, after the initial start-up loan was paid off.

"The J has a good reputation and a steady cash income, year by year. I suspect Ambrewster might crack the vault open, just a little bit anyway, if we were to ask."

The comment was met with silence, and eyes cast toward the tabletop.

Since his return to the ranch, Rory had been reluctant to divulge the whole story of the hunt for gold. He didn't like being secretive with family but, at the same time, he saw no reason to lay it all out. After all, it was he and his father who had done the digging and the panning. By all rights, the gold was his. And he had not yet decided if his future lay on the Double J. He had seen no opportunities he thought might be better. But he was still young. His eyes might be opened in another direction, given time. No, he would hold some secrets. But he could hold the secrets against his own future while still laying out some of his banked funds to build up the ranch.

"When mother died, Mother and Peggy, none of you were here to see how their loss affected Father. My father was always a strong man, when strength to work and do and to stand up for what was right was the criteria. He was awful big on rights and wrongs. He was strong spiritually as well. And he was a teacher, forever showing Peggy and me the plants and the birds and local animals. He taught us from the Scriptures, and he helped mother with the teaching of our ABCs and the doing of numbers. He read constantly, trading books with anyone who had one he had yet to read. When I was a kid, I thought he hung the moon and that he knew about everything there is to know.

"I never saw one sign of weakness in Father until he lost two that were precious to him. He came near to coming apart at that. He could still lift about anything he could get his hands around, but it wasn't that kind of strength that let him down.

"At barely fourteen, I was too young to hold up more

than just some of the ranch work. The rest, as often as not, was left for another day. That's when he sent for you, George. You and the family. Waiting for your answer in a mail system that moves at a slow, walking pace, and then waiting for your arrival, not knowing for sure if you were coming or not, was a suffering time for Father."

The room was absolutely silent, every eye on Rory as he spoke.

"When he told me we were going to get away for a while, to camp out for a year or two, maybe look for some gold, or just fish and laze about, I hardly knew what to think. Of course, I knew nothing at all about camping out or searching for gold. And I had no idea that he did either. But it turns out that he had read a book. That was always his way.

"Riding all those hundreds of miles, camping out, hunting our meat, and fishing when the mood took us, allowed father to use those other strengths, while his mind sorted out his weaknesses.

"Father somehow had an eye for a streambed. We stopped at several before we pitched the tent and settled in for good. Father would dig around some, cut some brush to follow the old, curving streambed, pan a few shovels full, then load up and move on. When we finally did stop, the digging for nuggets and the panning out of the old streambed was profitable from the first day. Father had the knack that many a gold seeker spends his lifetime hoping for.

"We sacked up gold right from the start. Now, I say we, but, of course, it was all father's doing. I simply followed his lead and directions, putting in some bull-work, digging out the old streambed while he panned the slowly running water.

"Come that first freeze-up we dug out our canvas sacks that we had buried behind a small fall of rocks, and we shut down the tent, leaving it all there to hold the claim for spring. We rode out to Boise, just a small town to the south of the territory. There we turned the gold into cash dollars and deposited it in the bank. We repeated all that the second summer, and were working on the third when father was murdered and I was shot down. You know the story from that point to this.

"The whole reason for telling you this is so you will know the struggle we had, searching out a future, when father felt that so much of his future was buried behind this cabin. Dying so suddenly, from a thief's bullet, certainly wasn't the direction he saw his search going, but I would have to say the murderer's bullet brought it all, his search and his pain both, to an end.

"Now. I'm left with half ownership in a ranch I don't feel at home on, and a small deposit in Ambrewster's bank, plus a bigger deposit I split between two Denver banks.

"What I would like you to do, with no input from me, because I don't know if I will even be here, is figure out a plan. A plan for an upgrade, or perhaps purebred cows. Possibly more land. Figure out a good future for the Double J, one that includes all who wish to stay here.

"You know what we paid for the bulls. The same farm was offering pregnant heifers for less than the bulls. From that, you can figure what it would take to grow the brand. You lay out that plan and I'll see how much of it I feel I can cover."

31

THERE WAS NO PARTICULAR RUSH IN CREATING A PLAN FOR the Double J. A few days would make little difference. Rory convinced himself that a few days' delay in searching out whatever trail the judge had left behind, if any at all could be found, wouldn't change anything either. He rode to the hotel dining room with a bedroll behind his saddle to talk with Sonia.

When he took his usual seat beside the front window, the late breakfast takers were just enjoying their last cup of coffee and lighting cigars. Rory found the stink of the cigars nearly enough to justify leaving, waiting for a better time, but he stayed, hoping the men themselves, would soon leave. When Sonia came with a clean mug and the coffee pot he asked if she could sit for a minute. Her answer was to return the coffee pot to the big cast iron woodstove in the kitchen and return with a mug of coffee for herself. As had happened before, Ma stood in the doorway with a grin on her face.

Sonia took her seat, studied Rory for a long moment, and said, "You are older. Your face, it has become more serious. And you are tired. I can see it in your eyes and in how you walk."

That introduction to conversation took the sheriff by surprise, not having recognized any of those things for himself.

"Been doing a lot of riding the past while."

"Yes. And carrying a lot of responsibility. Everyone is talking about it. How a man so young can somehow do these things that you have been doing."

While Rory was inwardly pleased by her words and her attention to him personally, he knew men his age were expected to carry a man's load.

"Sonia, there are men my age owning and running ranches, working in mines, driving cattle herds. Fighting in wars. This is a young man's country. And a young woman's, when it comes to that."

"That may be so, but to have the future of others on your shoulders is what has put the tiredness in your eyes and the serious expression on your face."

Wanting no more of that talk, Rory said, "If I could change the subject for a moment, I am wondering when Ma is giving you time off to visit your family. I was thinking of taking a few days myself before I go looking for the judge. We could go together up the hill if the days worked together for that."

As if she could hear through walls or around corners and past doorways, Ma came from the kitchen.

"Sheriff, I see you've loaded that gelding down with a bedroll. That's just excess weight unless you have plans for traveling. If that travel was in the direction of the I-5 Ranch, perhaps you could see Sonia safely into her mother's arms. Of course, if she ended up in someone else's arms…"

She didn't finish the sentence, almost, but not quite, regretting that she had started it.

Sonia was blushing wonderfully while Rory nearly choked. He couldn't have hollered fire if the table was to suddenly burst into flame.

When he finally got his wits about him, he said, "I could spare that much time, but it would have to be soon. I have other work that needs doing."

Sonia looked pleadingly at her employer. "Could I go today, Ma? Now? Who would do the work?"

Acting like handling the restaurant was nothing at all, Ma brushed the question off with a sideways hand wave and, "Pshaw, get away with you. You don't do enough work in this small place to even be missed." She wasn't quite successful in holding back the smile as she said it.

Sonia leaped to her feet and hugged Ma, which caused the older woman to back away in surprise.

"You ride past the rooming house in fifteen minutes, Sheriff. I'll be ready. Or if you come a bit sooner you can saddle my horse for me."

With that, she passed her apron to Ma and dashed out the kitchen door, just a two-minute walk to her rooming house, or a half-minute run.

BY THE TIME the two young people rode into the yard of the I-5 Ranch, lunch had been served and the kitchen cleaned up. But the first thing Anelia Ivanov did, after nearly hugging her daughter to death and offering a much-reduced greeting to Rory, was to fire up the big stove again. Grigor, Sonia's father, politely shook Rory's hand and welcomed him with thanks for securing the safety of his daughter on her ride. Pavel, her older brother, followed his father's example, with a greeting and a handshake. Ivan, who showed nothing but disdain for his sister's friend the first time they had met, was with the cattle.

After a hurriedly prepared lunch, Sonia stayed at the house to visit with her mother, while her father and Pavel saddled up and rode across the I-5 Ranch, giving Rory a guided tour of their upland plateau.

As they rode, Sonia's father asked, "You will stay with us for some days? Wait to take Sonia back to town?"

"I am sorry. I cannot do that, sir. I must ride up into the hills. I seek two men who may be up there."

Pavel pulled his horse to a stop. "What do you mean? You're looking for two men? What two men, and why are you looking for them?"

Rory and Pavel's father also pulled rein and turned inward, toward each other.

Up to this point, he had hesitated to talk about being sheriff. But perhaps now was the time. He reached into the small slash pocket in his vest and fingered out the badge, holding it where both men could see.

After a questioning look from each man, Rory—who was managing to shorten the story with each telling—explained the hunt for the judge and the marshal.

"There is something I must tell you. Since I was last here the state people down in Denver appointed me deputy sheriff for this county. It is only for this one year. I don't wear the badge because I don't wish to draw attention to myself."

With as few words as possible, he explained about the judge and the three ranches that lost cattle. Neither Pavel nor Grigor had any response.

After a short pause, he continued with, "One of the cowboys from another ranch told me about a cabin. An old cabin. Back in the hills. He said he had been up that way a few days ago, looking for wandering cattle. There was smoke rising from the stone chimney. He had never seen that before. He stayed away. His only interest was finding the cows. He thought maybe I should take a look. Sonia was sure that one of you would ride down with her if I didn't get back in a few days."

His story was met with questioning silence. Finally, accepting the situation for what it was, they resumed their ride.

Pavel, who was proficient in English, while his father struggled for words at times, said, "Here you can see we have built a fence, to divide these few acres from the larger portion."

He said that while his father stepped down to open the gate. In the newly separated pasture, with the gate again firmly closed, the trio of riders rode toward a small gathering of white-faced cattle. Almost immediately, Rory spotted the three purebred bulls, standing off to themselves, as if looking over their collective harems. Grigor pointed with pride, "You see, we have chosen only the very best of our herd to be with your bulls. We will get fine calves, no?"

Rory smiled and agreed, "You will get fine calves, yes."

With a little more time spent with the cattle, Pavel finally said, "Rory, we must get back to the yard. There is much to do. First, and soon, we will have the frost, and then before long, the snow. We must be ready. You could come to the house, or you can ride over the remainder of the grass, whatever you need to do."

"I will be riding on, my friends. Sonia knows I may not be back in time to take her back down the hill. I'm sure one of you will see to it that she does not ride alone."

Grigor looked a question at Rory, while Pavel asked, "You are riding to somewhere? Somewhere you know? Or are you just riding, hoping to find this cabin?"

"I am riding and hoping. I can't say much more than that. I know the general location, is all."

As Rory turned his gelding, ready to move on into the surrounding hills, Pavel said, "You will find Ivan out there somewhere. He may show you a couple of the trails into the higher country if you ask. Or he may not. He rides much in those hills. He may even decide to ride with you. There is no telling with Ivan.

"Perhaps you can make friends with him. It would be good to be friends, but that is not easy either."

32

Ivan watched as Rory slowly approached. He was sitting on his black gelding, enjoying the shade, as the sun moved over and past a steep, tree-covered hillside. His suspicious eyes never moved away from the visitor. Rory, on the other hand, was in no particular hurry to confront the angry brother, a man of about his own age. He wound his way through the herd, taking care to notice brands, along with the general health and conditioning of the stock. It came as a relief to see only the I-5 brand. To have found other brands would raise suspicions, a situation he was eager to avoid.

No matter how long he held off, he couldn't escape the meeting with Ivan forever. Reconciled to whatever happened, he rode toward the shaded side of the pasture.

"Why are you here and why do you study our cattle?"

"Hello, Ivan. I am here because I rode the trail with Sonia. It is not good for a woman alone on the trails. It is not always safe."

"And she is safe with you?"

Rory looked directly at the questioner and smiled,

"Why, yes. As a matter of fact, Ivan, she is. Are you somehow thinking other thoughts?"

Ignoring that question, which in reality, was really an accusation, Ivan said, "And you look carefully at our animals. Do you wish to keep them safe also?"

Rory laughed out loud at that question.

"No. I think they are plenty safe where they are. With you and Pavel to care for them, and your father, too, I would say they are safe enough. No, I look to learn. There is much I don't know about cattle. I was raised on the ranch until three years ago and was learning from my father. Then he and I rode to another place for those three years. My uncle has been caring for the ranch. That time away took me from the cattle. Now I am back and would learn all I can."

"And what did you learn with looking at our animals?"

"I learned that they are doing very well on this grass, and that you and your family take good care of them."

That statement was followed by a time of silence as Ivan pulled a sack of tobacco and a fold of papers from his shirt pocket. He tucked a single paper carefully into the space between his first and second fingers of his left hand and tipped a trickle of tobacco into it. With his teeth, he pulled the string on the little sack, closing off the top, and then pushed it back into his pocket. He folded the paper over the tobacco, somewhat clumsily rolled it tight, licked the paper, and pressed the edge down, sealing the paper tube. Scratching a match with his thumbnail, he held the flame to the cigarette, and while the match continued to burn, took a deep drag and then blew smoke into the air. With a satisfied look on his face, he shook the flame from the matchstick, rubbed the heat off the end with his fingers, and flicked the now cold and safe match into the grass.

There was no offer to share—an insult in some cowboys' eyes—but Rory, who had never smoked, took no offense.

"And now that you have seen our cattle and brought my sister home, you will be riding back down?"

Reluctantly, and yet with a vague hope that Ivan may know something of the hills that would help in his search, he told the sheriff story once again, this time in an even shorter form. He briefly mentioned the part about locating the cowboys who drove off the herds, saying only that they had mentioned a hideout cabin in the hills above Stevensville. When he came to the bit about the lost cabin in the hills, Ivan's eyes lit up with interest. Rory noticed the change in the man's face and demeanor. Wishing to take advantage of any knowledge Ivan might possess, Rory said, "Perhaps you have seen this cabin."

Ivan chose to not answer that question. Instead, he put both feet back in the stirrups, squeezed the glowing end off the cigarette, and said, "Come. We will ride. Perhaps we will catch these thieves."

Rory had to kick his gelding into motion to keep up with the determined Ivan. When he caught up, he said, "Should you be letting the others know you are leaving? And you have no bedroll or fixings."

"The others will know where I am. I ride often into the hills. I have a friend. I can find food there."

Within one-quarter mile, the trail through the evergreens and the trailside aspens faded away, becoming a single track. There were horse tracks enough to confirm earlier travel, but no marks from the passage of cattle.

The short but steep entry to the trail was enough to discourage contented cattle from wandering.

Rory fell behind, trusting Ivan. He would continue to trust him, for a while. But trust had to be earned. If he felt Ivan was fooling with him, he would go his own way.

They rode in silence for longer than Rory was comfortable with, but he said nothing, sensing that Ivan would not appreciate conversation. The trail wound through the hills, only once opening into a clearing of perhaps fifty acres. The grass in the clearing was still green and lush, strange for the lateness of the season. Looking more closely, Rory could see a stream tumbling through the forest before it broke into several small watercourses, a few of them no more than a trickle, but enough to keep the entire area constantly watered.

Rory spoke for the first time since the two of them had set out.

"I'm sure you've scouted out a trail to this graze."

"One day, I-5 cows will be here."

"Only if you get here first."

Ivan ignored that comment.

There was no sign of settlement, just mile after mile of winding, sometimes hard to follow, trail, that left Rory turned around in his directions, leaving him with no idea where they were in relation to the town and ranches on the flat land below. No cattle, no cabins. No corrals. No human habitation. No prospect diggings leaving their ugly marks on the land. The mining activity was well to the south of where they rode.

The land was, except for the narrow trail, untouched. Rory figured the Utes, and probably other tribes, knew of this land and had ridden it for generations, perhaps centuries, but they had left no mark upon its face.

Where the trail divided, still riding in silence, Ivan

swung onto the right-hand fork. That narrow path through the forest turned almost ninety degrees, now edging toward the north. A half-hour ride brought them to the first sign of settlement Rory had seen. It wasn't a ranch. It was nothing more than a pole corral holding a single horse with his head hanging over the top rail of a small corral, attached to a lean-to shed built off the side of a well-constructed log barn. There was a chicken coop and a small, recently built log cabin that showed the marks of a craftsman. A small stream, little more than a trickle, ran past the cabin and through both the chicken yard and the corral.

Sitting on a hand-built captain's chair beside the cabin was a man of some years. Judging through the bush of his beard and the wrinkles, with his eyes covered by the turned-down rim of a much-worn hat, Rory couldn't even guess at how many years. Glancing all around, Rory could see no purpose in the man's presence. There was certainly no way to make any kind of a living in the forest, unless the man was hunting, trapping, and selling the skins. But there was little enough call for skins in the age of broadcloth, canvas, and denim. And winters, up this high, could be a serious matter, something to be considered.

"Hello, Ivan. You ride with a stranger, yet you bring him to my home. Who is this man?"

Only less than half of this introduction was spoken in English. Ivan answered in the same mix of tongues.

"Good day, Kiril. I ride with the new sheriff. He looks for two men. Perhaps you have seen these men."

"It is not good to be riding with the lawman. You cannot trust the law."

"You always say that for the old country, Kiril. I think here, in this new country it is different."

"It is not different. You cannot trust this man. I am not happy that you brought him here."

"Are you also not happy that I have come, Kiril?"

"We are friends. The old man with many memories and the young man who would learn. But this lawman, he will cause you trouble."

"Even so, Kiril, the day is nearly done. Would you not welcome us for the night? Maybe to share a piece of bread and the shelter of your roof? You have often told me of how no one was ever turned away from your home in the old country. Would it be different here, my friend?"

The old man stuffed his pipe as he thought, casting his eyes from Ivan to Rory and back again. Finally, swinging back to English, he said, "Turn your animals loose to graze. They will not leave this place. I have deer meat, how you call it, venison?"

"Yes, venison. My friend, the sheriff has coffee. You would drink with us?"

"I would drink. One cup only. You know where the pot is and how to light a fire."

It all sounded strange to Rory, this talking, half in English and half in a language strange to his ears. And for Ivan to refer to him as a friend left a question or two for another time. Yet, it sounded as if they would be welcome for the night, and that suited Rory. Whether he could trust this old man or not, was yet to be proven. Whatever else was true, Rory felt sure that this old man was the source of Ivan's beliefs in the relative positions men and women should hold in society.

The venison steaks, fried in bacon fat, were good. It was just the venison, nothing else, but there was plenty, and Rory made no complaint. After the meal was behind them, in the dimming light, Rory left the two friends to visit in their old language while he groomed his gelding. With that done, he turned to Ivan's horse and did the same. He then led them both to the corral, where he hoped they would be safe for the night.

After a final cup of coffee, this time in the flickering light of a wood fire the old man had lit in a stone firepit beside a log bench, Ivan moved into the cabin. Rory took his bedroll and walked to the trees, close to the corral. His horse would warn him of any intrusion.

BY MIDMORNING THE NEXT DAY, Rory and Ivan had resumed their silent ride, with Ivan again offering no information on their destination. Since Rory had no knowledge at all of the mountainside, he followed without comment. He studied every turn of the trail, every hillside where the trees separated, allowing visibility. He noted every stream. As they gained elevation, he studied the subtle differences in the undergrowth and the surrounding forest. He knew little of tree species, but he could see variations as they climbed.

He turned around often to look back over the trail, wanting a memory from that vantage point. He estimated the miles and the time in his mind. He tried to guess at their elevation since the trail wound steadily uphill.

When Ivan finally pulled off to the side, weaving his way into a small clearing in a circle of golden leafed quaking aspens, they were just short of the crest of a small rise. Ahead, looking along the trail, Rory could see little but blue sky, with the faded green of a higher mountain off in the far distance. If they kept following the trail, they were obviously going to break over the top of the rise and head back down. A thing they had done often. Ivan's move into the aspens put a temporary halt to their forward motion.

Ivan dismounted and flipped his reins over the strong stub of a broken pine branch. Without invitation, Rory did the same.

The two men stepped back onto the trail, but Ivan motioned for Rory to stay where he was, and with a finger across his lips, demanded silence. Ivan himself turned up the trail.

Ivan was often silent. He was silent now. Not only verbally silent, but silent as he made his way up the trail to the crest. Just before he gained the summit, he removed his hat, dropped to his knees, and then to his belly. How the man remained silent as he wiggled on folded elbows and slightly bent knees the last few feet, through dried-out fall leaves and loose gravel, Rory could only guess.

Intending to follow, Rory took one step only, which he himself could plainly hear. Without turning around Ivan waved him back. He stood there, quietly waiting.

After a slow five minutes passed into history, Ivan wiggled off the crest, rose to his knees, crawled backward some more, picking up his hat along the way, and then stood. Only then did he replace his hat. When Rory opened his mouth as if to speak, Ivan warned his questions off.

Ivan made his way back to the horses before speaking. Even then, he spoke in a near whisper.

"The cabin is just over that crest. The trail comes down behind it. I come up here time to time to hunt or fish. Sometimes just to be here. To be alone. I didn't know anyone else ever came here. There have been no signs of others. But there are two men there now. Horses in the corral. Fading smoke from the chimney, as if their breakfast fire is dying down.

"Now, seems to me we have two choices since we don't know who these men are. We could simply ride over the crest and down to the cabin. We might receive a friendly welcome, or we might be shot out of our saddles. Or we could leave the horses here and squirm down through the trees, hoping to get a look at these men before they hear us or see us.

"Or, if you thought you could do it quietly enough, you could crawl up there and take a look for yourself. I warn you, though. We're close. Any noise and the horses will hear. If it's the men you are looking for, we could end up losing them. Or in a gunfight."

Rory's answer was simple and quick.

"I'll take a look."

He hung his hat on the saddle horn and removed his heavy gun belt, draping it, unbuckled, over the saddle seat. He then removed his boots, and on stocking feet, entered the trail. He wasn't quite as silent as Ivan had been, but anyone any distance away would have heard nothing. He dropped to his knees, and then his elbows and belly at about the same spots that Ivan had. Even Ivan didn't hear him covering the last three feet. Cautiously he lifted his head, just to eye level.

At first, he saw nothing. Then a man came from the house speaking to someone. He could clearly hear the voice, but not the individual words. The way the speaker positioned himself, it seemed logical that the second man was seated in front of the cabin, out of sight. That detail didn't matter. The speaker was unquestionably Mike Wasson, the phony marshal.

Rory had seen enough. He reversed his crawl and made his way back to Ivan.

"Those're my men. No doubt about it. I first believed they would be miles away. They face serious jail time if they go to court. Unless they were hoping to somehow get the money they left in the Stevensville Bank, I don't know what would be keeping them here. And they can't do much, way up here in the forest. It's a mystery to me."

Ivan asked, "Why don't we go ask them?"

Rory chuckled, liking the simplicity of the plan. He whispered, "I'm not so sure it would be all that easy. Anyway, it's my job. There is no reason for you to take any risks. When I let them pin this badge on me, I took on the responsibility. Now I have it to do."

"We will go. I do not like that you are spending time with Sofia. But I like that you are the sheriff. Sofia, she should not be gone from the home. A woman's place is with her family until her father finds a good husband for her."

Rory felt it was not the time to discuss the beliefs and practices of Old Europe. He let the conversation fade, choosing instead to say simply, "I will lead. We leave the horses here. Perhaps we can get to the cabin without being heard. With the horses crashing through the bush there would be no chance."

Rory eased toward the ridge, slowly and carefully picking his way through the forest. Away from the established trail, it took several minutes to reach the crest. Staying behind the last of the treed shelter, he carefully parted some branches to gain a look at the path they would have to follow. Ivan stood beside him after a short delay. They hadn't been heard, but the effort was all in vain in any case.

Their first unobstructed view of the small corral showed Wasson saddling his horse. Clearly believing they were alone, or at least out of voice range of anyone, he hollered, "Best git up and at it there, Thrasher. Your time of pretending to be a judge is about over. And a good thing it is too. We've got miles to travel. No sense hanging around here any longer. Ambrewster ain't ever going to turn that money loose. He never was going to. Just one more of your foolish schemes. Don't know why I ever listened to you in the first place. Don't know who's dumber, me or you. You for thinking up these fool ideas, or me for going along with it all. So, you read a book one time, and now you call yourself a judge. You ain't no more judge than this jug-headed gelding. Dumb as fence posts, both you and me, but to you, it comes natural. Me, now, I have to work at it, to act dumb enough to pretend I'm a lawman and to follow you. Now get yourself up here, or sit right there for the rest of your life, it makes no never mind to me.

"Money or no money, I don't want to be caught up here with winter coming on. You get yourself up or I'm leaving out of here without you. May leave off riding with you anyway. Mostly I could do better following another man's cattle for thirty a month and found."

Another half-minute wait showed the judge sauntering toward the corral, apparently in no rush. He had a blanket roll and trail pack slung over his shoulder. His anger at the cutting words caused him to shout back at Mike Wasson, the pretend marshal, at the equal or louder volume as that directed at him.

"Don't get your tail in a twist. There's time enough and not a soul anywhere around."

Rory judged the distance to the corral to be around two hundred yards, split about equally between horizontal and vertical. He was a good shot, seldom missing his target with either handgun or carbine, but he knew how tricky shooting up or downhill could be. Tempted as he was to end it with a few ounces of lead, eliminating the need for a long chase that may not end with the desired results, he decided to hold his fire.

It was way too late to worry about silence. Rory simply said, "The horses."

Both men turned away from the crest of the hill and ran for their mounts. There was no doubt they were making noise, but even that noise would be as nothing compared to what they would make crashing and slipping and sliding down the half-bushed-in trail below the crest.

With a simple gathering of reins and a foot lifted to the stirrup, Rory was in the saddle. Ivan matched him move for move.

When Rory topped the hill and urged his gelding onto the downward path, both fugitives turned their eyes that way. With a shout of warning, Mike Wasson swung into the saddle, lifted his carbine from the scabbard, and fired off three, rushed, ineffective shots. Rory, knowing he was well out of range for the handguns he handled with such great efficiency, pulled his own carbine. He one-handed three return shots, knowing they came nowhere close to the fugitive. They probably missed the corral, for that matter. But sometimes the sound alone is enough to light a fire under a man. Especially a man facing serious jail time.

The combination of threats was enough for the marshal. The judge was only a breath behind. Whatever fighting spirit they imagined themselves to have, vanished like the powder smoke from Rory's carbine. There would be no shootout. That might come later, but at the moment, the fugitives thought only of escape. They came close to running over each other in their haste to get away.

The two riders were one behind the other coming from the corral. Before long they were side by side and then, as they put distance behind them, the judge pulled ahead, although the marshal was urging his mount forward with spurred heels and the ends of the long leather reins. It was clear that the judge had the better and faster horse.

Rory heard Wasson shout, "It's that Jamison kid that was appointed sheriff. Him and some other dude. That kid's shot through and through with luck. How else did he find that cabin and corral, and us with it? With anyone but a weak-kneed excuse for a judge as partner, we might stand them off."

The recklessness of Rory's descent caused him some unease later, when he got to thinking of it. But at the moment, the chase was all that mattered. He hit the level ground with the gelding running full-out. Ivan was only a few seconds behind. He had little doubt about catching Wasson. The man's horse just wasn't up to the challenge. The judge, steadily pulling away, was another matter.

Rory knew none of the trails in this high country. It seemed that neither fugitive did either, as there was no attempt to leave the only visible path through the forest. Thrasher was outpacing Wasson by a good margin. Wasson, frantic, was in danger of driving his animal to its knees with the spurring and whipping. As much as he had an eye mostly for gathering in the old judge and marshal, Rory's heart went out to the abused horse. Any rider should know that he would soon be afoot if he kept on the way Wasson was going.

The race for Wasson ended within one crooked, up-and-down, brush-crowded mile when, as Rory predicted, his horse went down. Perhaps the phony marshal felt him going, giving just a second or two of warning. In any event, the rider proved to be more adept than Rory was giving him credit for. As the horse started to fall, Wasson grabbed his carbine, pulled his feet from the stirrups, swung one leg over the saddle horn, and dropped trailside, scrambling into the bush.

Rory pulled his gelding down to a slow run before he also dropped to the ground. Ivan raced on, following Judge Thrasher.

As Rory's feet dropped into the long grass beside the trail, a bullet nicked a branch above his head, throwing leaves into the air and gaining Rory's full attention. He dove further into the forest and rolled behind a rock, part of a moss-covered jumble of granite that would hide him from the shooter.

With Ivan's hoofbeats fading into the distance, Rory shouted out, "Let it go, Wasson! You're never getting off this hillside alive unless you throw out your gun and come out yourself."

"You fool, kid. You think because someone was dumb enough to pin a badge on your shirt, you suddenly become a real lawman? Come and get me then, lawman. Or are you too scared to move?"

Wasson waited for an answer, but Rory was already moving. The voice gave him a target, the forest was dense, and the rocks were plentiful. And he was nowhere near the spot where he had dropped off his horse. He remembered Anthony Clare, the sheriff from the adjoining county, saying, "Unless you're dealing with a hardened criminal, it's amazing what a bit of hot lead does to the attitude of the man you've cornered."

Wasson wasn't exactly cornered, but he was afoot. Rory knew pretty well where he was, although he, too, may have moved. In the silence of the hillside, it was as if the two men were out-waiting each other. The difference was that Rory had all the time he needed, while Wasson was in a panic for escape. Rory hoped that urge to be away and off the mountainside would be Wasson's undoing. He remained behind his rocky barrier, but he slowly crawled a bit closer to where the voice had come from.

A slow quarter-hour ticked past. Rory had listened very carefully the whole while and had heard no movement. Easing a bit more to his right, where his rocky sanctuary hung close to the steep mountainside of rock behind it, he removed his hat and, using a small bush for shelter, carefully raised his head to eye level. All around the area, there were spots similar to his own. Rocks had tumbled down from above, settling along the base of the hill eons ago. The rocks were moss and lichen covered. Trees had grown tall and strong, some of them growing out of cracks in the hillside. Outside the rocky cirque, there was a small area of grass somehow surviving beneath the covering of low-growing bush. Looking all around, Rory saw nothing at all of the fugitive. And then he did. He saw a small bush move, just a bit, but it was movement, without a doubt.

Studying the area with care, Rory could find no safe way to approach Wasson. He thought again of the words of Anthony Clare and wondered how to apply them. With further care, he considered his situation. He didn't really want to shoot or kill anyone. And he most certainly had no desire to be shot himself. Of the two options, the choice was clear. It would be better if he was to be doing the shooting.

Behind where he had seen the movement, there was a rock wall similar to what was behind his own redoubt. He would have to stand to be at a level where shooting into the rock backdrop would be effective for ricochets.

There was risk in standing, of course, but there was risk in doing nothing at all too. Wasson might be crawling to where he could get a shot at the sheriff, or he may be escaping into the forest. He could lose his prey and have to begin all over again.

He checked the loads in his carbine, took a steadying breath, rose quickly to his feet, and squeezed the trigger. The lead cleared the rocky barrier by only inches before whanging into the rocky backdrop. Rory could hear the awful, whining sounds of a ricochet. Yes, it was awful, he admitted that, but it was also effective, and what he had been hoping for. He levered the carbine and squeezed off shot after shot, scattering lead all through the space where he believed Wasson had taken shelter.

After seven or eight deadly lead pills had been freed from their confinement, sending them at startling speed into the area, Wasson screamed in fear, frustration, and anger, and leaped to his feet. He had his carbine pointed toward Rory but before he got a shot off, Rory had swung his sights that way and squeezed the trigger. Wasson's dropped gun clattered off the rocks and landed outside the shelter. Wasson folded at the waist, with his arms wrapped around his middle. Giving him no time to recover himself, if that was even possible, Rory leaped over his rock shelter and ran the few yards to where Wasson had fallen.

He picked up the dropped carbine, threw it behind him, further from the fallen fugitive, and carefully looked over the rocks. It was possible Wasson would be lying there holding a handgun. Even dying, a man could do that. He wasn't.

33

Rory bent over the wounded man, whose eyes were tightly shut in pain. He had blood seeping from under his shirt and welling up between his fingers. Rory had no clear idea how much blood a man could lose without giving up the fight for life, but what Rory saw was not, in his mind, a serious matter. There was no doubt about the pain. How serious the wound was would have to be decided by others. Of course, there were no others on the mountainside so that would have to wait. If Wasson died in the meantime, it would save the doctor and the courts considerable trouble. Rory didn't really feel callous about the matter, but this man had stolen cattle from women and children. He had run from the law and taken several shots at Rory himself. And it was doubtful if those were his first activities outside the law. Sometimes a man had to pay for his actions.

After relieving the injured man of his Colt, he forced Wasson's hand away from the wounded area and ripped open the shirt, scattering buttons in several directions.

He pulled his belt knife, using it to cut the filthy union suit away from the wound. Wasson finally opened his eyes, staring at the sheriff. Through gritted teeth, he said, "How bad is it?"

"Well, now. You know I'm not a doctor. But I would say with the bullet going right through and out the back, this far to the side, you just might live to spend years in prison. Or, if there is any justice left in this country, perhaps you'll be hung."

"You're a hard man for someone so young, Jamison."

"There might be different opinions on that, but right now I'm hard enough to tell you to get on your feet. You have some walking to do unless that horse you were beating half to death somehow found his second wind. Now, get up. And no whining. And don't bother looking for your hideout gun. I have your weapons, including the derringer from your pocket and the .32 from your boot. And your knife, of course."

Folding both carbines under one arm, with the extra handgun stuffed behind his belt and the derringer and .32, along with the knife, pushed into pockets, Rory stood well back, watching every slow, painful move Wasson made. When he was on his feet, with his hands again pressed against the bullet wound, he carefully stepped over the rock that had sheltered him. Rory indicated with a swing of the carbines, both acting in unison, that Wasson should head back out to the trail. He stumbled a bit and didn't move fast, but eventually, they broke into the sunlight of the narrow path. Both horses were there with their faces buried in the growth of grass along the trail.

"Looks as if you're in luck this day, Wasson. You stand right where you are while I sort out these animals.

You move even an inch, and you'll have another hole in you, one that won't need doctoring."

With that, he caught up his own gelding and replaced the carbine in its scabbard. He then opened the flap on one saddlebag, placed Wasson's hand weapons inside, and then re-tied the flap. He unloaded the second carbine and dropped it into the scabbard on Wasson's horse.

While he had been putting Wasson's weapons in his saddlebag, Rory had retrieved some light line he had brought along for stringing up his canvas shelter in case of rain. He held it in his hand now.

He wrapped the abused gelding's reins around his fist and took a firm grip. He then turned to Wasson and said, "Get yourself up on this animal. Take a hold with both hands on the horn. Hang steady while I tie you down."

Wasson griped and moaned about pain and claimed he was about to bleed to death, but Rory held back any response he might have. With the man's hands firmly tied to the saddle horn, Rory stood back.

"Start off. Stay on the trail. Hold to an easy trot. I think you already know what will happen if you kick that animal into a run."

They had been riding for almost a half hour when a faint shot, indicating some distance, broke the stillness of the early afternoon. Both their heads came up, but Wasson was the only one who spoke.

"Did you hear that?"

Thinking the question didn't demand an answer, Rory said nothing.

The distance indicated by the barely audible shot told Rory that whatever was going to happen had probably already taken place. They would hold to their mile-eating trot.

Something like five minutes passed before they rode around a bend in the bush trail and saw a horse lying crumpled on the trailside. It was Thrasher's animal, and it was clearly dead. Rory pulled to a stop, telling Wasson to do the same. Stepping to the ground, Rory led his animal into a small space between a grove of aspens, tying him firmly with his halter lead, allowing him enough length to nibble at the sparse growth of grass.

Doing the same with Wasson's animal, he then untied the marshal's hands and pulled him off the horse, dropping him onto his back beside his horse. Wasson screamed in pain. Through whimpers, he said, "That's pretty rough, kid. I ever get my hands free and on you, it ain't going to be a happy day for you."

"You had best hope that day never comes, Marshal. You never saw the day you could stand with me, fist or bullet, either one. Now shut up and be happy I don't simply shoot you."

Rory picked Wasson up with a firm grip on the back of his shirt collar and thrust him toward a large aspen. With the man's arms wrapped around the tree, he lay one arm atop the other so that Wasson was holding each elbow with his opposite hands. Rory then carefully tied the man's arms together. Again, he silently thanked his father for teaching him something of knots.

"You sit tight and silent. You make any noise, I'll come back and put a silencing on you. And don't you doubt that."

Having seen no sign of Ivan or his gelding, Rory wasn't sure where to start. But the bush was too dense to creep through, either silently or quickly, so he stepped back onto the trail.

He lifted his handguns, one at a time, and cleared any accumulated leaves or twigs from them. After checking the loads, he replaced them loosely into their holsters. He then thoroughly checked his carbine. Contented that he was as prepared as he was ever going to be, he started out in a slow jog. He was in no sense a tracker, but he didn't have to be to follow the tracks of Ivan's big black. The first hundred yards of tracks showed scuffed marks with deeper indentations at the front and dirt and small pebbles scattered at the back. The horse must have been running. Perhaps Ivan had sighted the fleeing Ronald Thrasher. But before long, the tracks changed as if the animal was now in a slow walk. He hadn't noticed at first, but now he saw boot prints, unclear but certainly there. They, like the hoof prints, indicated a running man, undoubtedly the judge.

Neither the hoof prints nor those of the running man went far down the trail. After about the equivalent of two town blocks, winding along the crooked trail, Ivan's black stood alone, grazing loosely. And only a few yards beyond the horse, the shattered limbs of several aspens indicated that both men had broken into the forest. Cautiously, Rory stepped to the ground and followed.

He moved in about one hundred yards, following the trampled grass and brushed-aside limbs, and then stopped. He could hear nothing at all except the natural sounds of the forest, mostly the wind-rustled golden leaves of the quaking aspens. The trail continued, so Rory continued also. Fearing he would be greeted with a bullet, he paused often, listening and looking before proceeding. He considered calling out to Ivan but hesitated, not wishing to give his position away.

The trail before him dipped down into a hollow in the rocks. There was shelter there for anyone anticipating a gunfight. Surrounding the hollow was a clearing of perhaps two acres where the growth was no higher than three feet. The tracks led that way, but still, Rory hesitated. It looked too simple. Too tempting.

And then there was movement. Just the slight flutter of some small growth. The situation was similar to what Rory faced with Wasson. A cirque of moss-covered rocks protected one man. Was it Ivan or the fleeing Thrasher?

Rory eased closer, staying low as he duckwalked through the brush. He held his eyes on where he had seen the movement, still wondering if the man behind the parapet was friend or foe. His answer came in the form of a bullet that raked the outside of his right shoulder, tearing his jacket, shirt, and enough skin to sting like a thousand bees had attacked him at once. He sank to a sitting position before rolling behind a rock that, in truth, only provided partial coverage. He took several deep breaths to hold back a cry of pain.

As he was recovering from his pain and surprise, he held his eyes firmly on the rocks ahead of him. He was unable to see anything at all. The fugitive must have either popped up to get his shot off or he had found a peephole between two rocks. Either possibility gave Rory more reason for caution.

Where the rocks Wasson had hidden behind had a granite backdrop, making his ricocheted shots effective, and potentially deadly, these rocks were lying on the forest floor with only a sloping hillside behind them.

Unless he was to sit there until hunger or thirst drove Thrasher into making a foolish and dangerous break for freedom, the situation appeared to call for a frontal attack. And he still had no idea if Ivan was somewhere close by or if he was alone.

The answer came in two ways, one when Ivan hollered, "It is good of you to join our little party, Sheriff.

Unfortunately, the party has been getting a bit dull. But I have something here for the judge to play with."

The voice was coming from the opposite side of the rocks from where Rory squatted.

Only a moment after Ivan finished speaking, his arm flashed up, holding a forked stick. The stick moved backward just a bit and then forward. There was something dangling from the fork. The movements were too sudden and too quick for Rory to see clearly what it was. Then it became obvious. Sailing through the air, wiggling and squirming, was a snake. Few rattlesnakes were seen at that elevation, but they weren't unknown either. Rory knew little about snakes, except that he hated every single one of them. But he hoped this one was a rattler and that the judge feared the creatures as much as he did himself.

With Thrasher's eyes firmly glued to where Rory had fallen, he failed to see the snake flying his way. He turned as he heard Ivan say, "Here, Judge. Something to play with."

The snake landed several feet from Thrasher, but it was close enough to startle the man. In instant fright he scrambled backward, firing several shots at the creature that was now on the ground, and then, he foolishly stood up, backing further from the crawling menace.

With Thrasher standing at full height and facing away from Rory, there was never going to be a better opportunity to take the man down. But instead of simply firing, Rory hollered, "Give it up, Thrasher. We've got you. No use in dying over it."

What all moved Thrasher to take the action he did would never be known. Perhaps he feared jail to an unreasonable extent, or perhaps there were other things in his background that would call for hanging. In any event, he turned suddenly, lifting the carbine toward Rory. He never got the shot off.

Rory fired immediately and jacked another shell into place, ready. The first shot turned the judge and caused him to hunch over in pain. At the same time, a shot from Ivan, followed closely by a second shot from the rancher, put an end to the life of Ronald Thrasher—thief, cattle rustler, abuser of women and children, and fake judge. It was over. He was now facing an eternal judge.

For Mike Wasson, he would have the opportunity to face a real judge, if Rory could get him off the mountain and to medical help quickly enough.

Slowly, Ivan rose from his hiding spot and stepped over the sheltering rocks. With his carbine unnecessarily held on the dead judge, he walked toward the crumpled form on the grass. Rory met him, coming from the other side. They both took a long look at the dead man and then lifted their eyes to each other. Their eyes held solemn looks, as if they recognized that the happenings of the day had just taken a serious turn. That much had now changed. A chase that had started out somewhat undefined had been completed in a most dramatic fashion. And a man was dead at their feet.

Rory had shot before, and his adversaries were weeks in their graves. For Ivan, it was a totally new experience. There was nothing to say. So they remained silent.

Foolishly, perhaps, Ivan looked back down at the crumpled form of the judge. Time seemed to stand still as he contemplated this now dead human form. His lips were constructing words that did not become audible. With a lost look on his face, he seemed to recognize the gravity of the situation, and that it was his two shots that had finalized the life of Ronald Thrasher. As if his body had suddenly lost all strength, his carbine slipped from his fingers. With a pleading look at Rory, as if seeking forgiveness, understanding, perhaps permission for his actions, he suddenly turned and quickly walked a few feet away. Leaning heavily against the trunk of an aspen tree, he bent over and retched up whatever was in his stomach. He managed a couple of gasping breaths and then retched again. Finally, getting some control over himself, he wiped his mouth with the back of his hand and stood up straight.

When he turned back toward Rory, he was somehow a different man. The cocksure Ivan, the young man who knew it all, who wanted to live in the old ways, to control the lives of others, women especially, the young man who had listened to the tales of the old man in the hills, seemed far away. The stories he'd been told of riding into battle with banners flying now seemed doubtful. In any case, they had lost their glory. It was hard to see the glory with your mind fixed on death. Death, blood, and eyes that had shown dreadful fear moment the lead smashed them from this earth.

Perhaps it was time for him to become his own man, to see the belligerent and controlling past for what it was, foolishness. The judge had wanted to live. Every man did. And Ivan wanted no less for himself. But the judge was dead, and Ivan had been the one who killed him. It was a sobering thought, something that would cost him hours of sleep.

After a short interval, Rory bent to the ground and began to go through Thrasher's pockets. When he bent down, Ivan was able to see the torn fabric on Rory's jacket and the bit of blood that had soaked through the shirt beneath.

"You have been shot."

"Just a bit. Hurts like I would never have believed, but

it's not serious. Now, let's see what secrets the judge was carrying on himself."

In his pockets, Rory found the normal collection of things a traveling man would carry, but when he ran his hands over the body, looking for other weapons or whatever the clothing hid, he was startled to feel a bulk under the shirt. He ripped the garment open and sat back, looking up to Ivan.

"He's carrying a money belt."

"I can see that, although I am not enjoying looking at this."

Rory glanced up at him. Ivan again looked sick, as if he just might heave up even more of the venison breakfast they had enjoyed hours earlier.

"Alright, leave me to do this. If you will walk back up the trail you will find Wasson and the horses. He's wounded, but not bad, I'm thinking. If you'll get him mounted and tied to the saddle horn, and bring both animals back here, I'll have this dealt with by that time. And thanks. For this and all."

Making no response, Ivan wound his way from the bush and out to the trail. Rory stripped the money belt off, went through the clothing again, and stood. There was nothing to gain by toting a dead man all the way down the mountain when they were already short one horse. He glanced around the cirque, looking for ideas. They had no digging tool, and the boulders Thrasher had hidden behind were far too heavy to move around or stack over a body. He kicked through the grass, hoping to find enough smaller rocks to cover the body, without finding the snake that had been so unceremoniously thrown that way.

Closer to the rise of the hillside, there were a lot of smaller rocks. Fist size to the size of a head. It was almost as if they had fallen from above with the large boulders but had lacked the weight to carry them further. In less than ten minutes, the body was under enough rocks to keep the scavengers from it. That would have to be good enough.

34

By the time Ivan returned, astride Rory's big bay gelding, Rory was standing in the trail holding the reins to Ivan's black. Mike Wasson was looking sick, bent over the pommel, with his hands firmly tied to the horn. He seemed unaware of his surroundings. Rory tried to find some sympathy for him but finally gave it up.

With Rory and Ivan back on their own horses, and with Ivan asking no questions about what Rory had done with the body, the two men sat there looking at each other. Rory finally spoke.

"We have to get out of these hills. I'm totally lost, but I'm guessing this trail must go somewhere. It's a long way back to your friend's shack and I'm not too sure he's even your friend anymore. I know he's not mine."

Before Rory could say more, Ivan turned his horse and led off. Not having any better option, Rory followed, holding Wasson's reins. This mountain trail was no place to be having a horse race if the man decided to make a break for it. He would just go ahead and lead the animal.

There was little talk after Rory asked the question that had been troubling him.

"You always play with snakes, Ivan?"

He didn't receive a direct answer, only, "The snake, he was close enough. I was not happy to have him close. I saw the stick with the small fork. I picked up the snake. I didn't want him, so I gave him to the judge."

They rode for less than one-half-hour when Ivan swung onto a side trail. Rory was left wondering who had bothered to make all these trails that seemed to go nowhere. But without discussion, he turned and followed. Almost immediately the trail became steep, causing the horses to dig in and scramble on the rocky terrain. They climbed a short few hundred yards and then broke onto a level area. Ivan never spoke nor stopped. He kept pushing ahead until they came to another small clearing, one that ran right to the edge of the plateau. Ivan stopped and turned to Rory. He took that as an invitation to join him. Rory stepped his horse the few feet and stopped, glancing down. There before him was an open, high mountain plateau such as what many folks preferred to call high mountain valleys. It was a green and lovely sight. The few cattle in sight grazed, scattered at will across the grass. At the upper end of the plateau, he could see a log cabin, a barn, and a couple of corrals, as well as a few small outbuildings.

He studied the layout and then, grinning, turned to Ivan.

"That's the BL Ranch. The Lander outfit. I've met Mrs. Lander, she prefers to be called Patricia, and Kenny, her young son. Is there any way off this rise of land to…"

Rory was speaking to a man who was no longer there. Ivan was already heading down a narrow trail and moving rapidly. Within a few yards, the trail became almost too steep for safe riding, and within another few yards, ended on a moraine of slide-rock.

There was not the slightest possibility that Rory would have tackled the slope if Ivan had not led the way. Even then, he had hesitated before finally moving forward, still gripping the reins to the other horse.

Together they rode down. When the trail moved onto the moraine, Mike Wasson could finally see the slope and the dust cloud that enveloped Ivan's sliding horse. He shrunk back, staring at his captor.

"You're crazy. You and that Russian, or whatever he is, the both of you. I'd rather you just shoot me than force this horse over that ledge."

"Now that's a temptation I just might give in to."

Rory pushed his gelding over the steepest portion of the narrow trail. The led animal had no choice but to follow. Wasson screamed in terror, but Rory had no sympathy. He dropped the reins of the led horse and concentrated on his own ride, leaving Wasson to the mercies of the trail and the loose animal. There was no way of turning back, so Rory knew they would meet at the bottom.

The horses spent at least half their time with their front feet extended, and their tails dragging on the ground, their haunches stirring up the rocks and dust. Once started, there was no stopping. In less than one minute, the horses were standing, shivering in fear and fatigue, on the grass of the pasture. Rory looked at Ivan and simply said, "I don't want to do that again."

Ivan said nothing and Mike Wasson, locked in fear and dread, couldn't or wouldn't talk.

It was no distance at all to the cabin. They rode in that direction. Of course, they had been seen and heard. They had raised enough dust to warn of their coming, even if the rattle of bouncing rocks and sliding gravel hadn't awakened anyone. From a distance, Rory could see Patricia Lander standing on the cabin porch, shading her eyes. Her son, Kenny, was running from the barn to join her. He was carrying something. Rory figured it would be the shotgun he had seen the young man carrying during his first visit to the BL.

Rory turned to Ivan and asked, "Have you been here before? Did you ride that slope?"

"I have only been to the top. Maybe there is an easier way down. I didn't look."

They pulled up before the cabin and removed their hats.

"Good day, Mrs. Lander. Kenny. I hope you don't mind this intrusion. We needed a way out of the hills and my friend here, Ivan Ivanov, of the I-5 Ranch, knew of that path. Although I am now questioning his sanity, I have to admit, it did get the job done.

"We have a wounded man. I'm hoping that Kenny might show Ivan where he can care for the horses while I see to the wound. Perhaps you will allow us to lay him out in the shade somewhere. I could probably use some hot water and a clean rag, if that is not too much trouble."

Patricia Lander said, "Kenny, you help this man with the horses. But first, Sheriff, if you and your friend would bring the wounded man into the house, we will settle him in a cot in the back room. You can work on him there."

"Thank you, Patricia, but I need to tell you first. This is one of the men responsible for the theft of your cattle."

"And where is the second one, Sheriff? Did you catch him too?"

"We caught him. We left him up on the mountain. He will not be coming down."

"Oh, I see. Well, no matter, bring this man in. I won't turn him away when he's in need."

Between Ivan and Rory, with Kenny assisting where he could, Mike Wasson was soon laid out on the cot. Rory said, "Thank you all. Now I wouldn't ask any of you to get involved in this. I'll handle it. Do what I can. Then we'll head for town and the doctor."

Patricia laughed a little before saying, "I'm sure you will do just fine, Sheriff, but may I suggest you wash those filthy hands before you start? And wait until the water is heated?"

Rory rolled his hands in front of him, studying both back and front.

"You really think I need a wash?"

"I really think that, yes."

They were both smiling by the end of that brief discussion.

As HE HAD SUSPECTED, after the initial look in the forest, the bullet had passed right through. There were a couple of small strands of cloth from Mike's shirt and his union suit sticking out of the bullet hole. The edges of the wound were red and puffed, inflamed to a startling degree. Rory carefully pulled the cloth out and washed all around the wound, both back and front. Wasson was unconscious, following the initial burst of pain as Rory pulled the shirt loose from the dried blood. After he poured a couple of ounces of some kind of disinfectant that Patricia found in her cupboard directly into the wound, the patient awoke, and that brought on a scream of pain and enough curse words to hold anyone sensitive to such matters for a long time.

Still finding no sympathy, Rory lightly slapped the man on the cheek, as he might do to a child who was foisting a tantrum onto his parents.

"That's enough of that. Enough noise and certainly enough talk. Now you pipe down. As soon as Ivan has the horses cared for and ready, we'll load you up and get you to town. It would be easier if you simply died along the way, but you probably won't. You're not hurt all that bad. Now take some rest. We'll soon be back in the saddle."

35

IVAN SEEMED TO KNOW EVERY TRAIL THROUGH THE HILLS, no matter how remote or faint on the ground. An hour after leaving the BL Ranch, he led off back to the east, into a dim opening through the aspens. Rory asked no questions, having learned to trust this man. For several miles, as the sun swung to the west, with the warning that they were not going to be anywhere close to Stevensville when darkness descended, they rose over small rocky upthrusts, down steep slides, and around one small, lovely lake. No one had attempted conversation, concentrating wholly on their mission.

To Rory's surprise, after riding down a half mile of a well-forested slope where the trail followed a small stream, they rode again into the upper end of the I-5 Ranch grassland. There was just enough light left in the sky to see the outline of the hills and the cattle spread around the grass. In the distance was a single lighted window, showing the way to the cabin, and another, that Ivan explained was left burning every night, outlining the big doors to the barn.

Within minutes, they pulled up at the hitch-post outside the cabin.

Pavel came from the house, followed by Sonia. Through the open door, Rory could see Mrs. Ivanov working at the big iron kitchen range. There was no sign of the father.

Pavel grinned and asked, "Did you just return for a visit, brother, or do you intend to stay for a while?"

"For a visit only if there is food, and perhaps a fresh horse for each of us. Otherwise, we will keep on to town."

Sonia spoke for the first time, replying, "And when has there not been food? And is it not late to be taking the trail to town?"

"It is late but necessary, Sister. This cattle thief we have caught needs a doctor. Unless you have now become a doctor, we will keep riding."

Pavel said, "Step down, all of you. Go to the house for food. I will move your saddles."

A HALF-HOUR LATER, they were fed and back in the saddle, picking their way down the darkening, but much wider and familiar path. When Rory had suggested he would be back in a couple of days for his horse, Ivan surprised everyone when he said, "Perhaps you can take Sonia down with you at that time. To keep her safe."

The evening was far gone when Rory knocked on the doctor's door. He opened it with a question, "Is this to become a pattern, Sheriff, where you only bring patients to me in the dead of night?"

Rory was too tired to pick up on whatever humor

was in the question. He simply said, "Prisoner needs a bullet hole treated, Doc."

Ivan somehow found the strength and the will to ride back up the trail to the I-5. Rory secured a room at the hotel and then went back to the doctor's office. The first thing he did was check the bindings where Wasson's hands were tied to the metal frame of the gurney. The doctor was just cleaning up after stitching the wound, both back and front.

"He'll live, Sheriff. And he'll be here in the morning. I've called in a friend to watch over him tonight. I can't have fugitives running loose in my home or office. Go to bed. Come back in the morning."

THE FOLLOWING MORNING, seeing that all was well with Wasson, he led the man across the street and into the single cell in the marshal's office. The same retired neighbor the doctor had recruited the night before volunteered to guard the prisoner. Rory promised him a wage for the couple of days and rode out to the ranch.

After a bath, a shave, and another sound night's sleep, he rode up the trail to the I-5. He would deliver Wasson to the authorities in Denver, but he wanted his own horse for the ride.

There was a smiling welcome at the Ivanov home, and an early lunch of homemade smoked sausage and boiled potatoes. He saddled his own horse and rode to the cabin to say goodbye. To his surprise, Pavel had saddled a horse for Sonia, and at the same time, Ivan was moving his saddle from his morning ride to a fresh animal. With no words to ease into the statement, Ivan said, "You will need help to get the prisoner to this Denver place. I will come with you."

Feeling he now knew Ivan well enough to tease him just a bit, Rory said, "I'm not sure that's a good idea, Ivan. Denver is a big city. A lot of people. Men wearing business suits and beautiful women everywhere. A hill-country boy might feel out of place."

Ivan swung onto his saddle saying, "Are you coming or not? We haven't got all day."

Rory and Pavel laughed. Sonia smiled behind her spread fingers.

IVAN RODE WITH SONIA, caring for her horse in the small stable while she again settled into the boardinghouse. She then walked back to the dining room and tied on her apron. Rory unlocked the cell door and led Wasson out.

Rory and Ivan drank coffee while the prisoner ate a big lunch Ma served up for him. Within a half hour, they were on the road to Denver, arriving late the second afternoon, after an overnight stop in a small hotel. Wasson had suggested it would be easier for all of them if they took the stage. Rory's response was, "If you do something that causes me to have to shoot you, I wouldn't want others in the line of fire. We're better off out in the open."

RORY SAW to Wasson's imprisonment at the local lockup and then reported to his superior, filing a written explanation of the crimes, the ranches involved, the chase, and the death of the judge. He left the choice of charges to the lawyers, not knowing enough of the law to sort that part out himself.

Oscar Cator, from the state office, watched over the proceedings. When the lawyer asked his last question of Rory and thanked him for the work done, Oscar shook Rory's hand and simply said, "Well done, Sheriff. We'll let you know when court will be held and if we need the ranchers here as witnesses. Until then leave it with us."

Over dinner, Ivan asked if the lawyers had asked about the money. Rory grinned, "Not directly. I simply said it had all been dealt with fairly."

Privately, he agreed with Ambrewster, the less said of that, the better.

"What about that money belt?"

"There was only a few hundred dollars in it. I'll return it in shares to the three ranches when next I see them. That's after I pay for our expenses for this long ride."

Ivan nodded and stared at Rory, stacking that information up, along with the other things he was learning about the world outside the hills. They were just completing their dinners, waiting for the fulfillment of the promise of apple pie, when a female voice gaily said, "Why look who's back in town. It's that handsome Mr. Jamison. With a friend who could also pass as handsome, if he hadn't stood so far from his razor."

Both men looked up at the voice, startled that a lady would speak so openly in a public dining room. From where he was seated, Ivan was looking directly at the unfamiliar woman. Rory, recognizing the voice immediately, didn't even have to turn or look over his shoulder to know who the speaker was. When he did turn, she was walking across the floor toward their table. As the woman behind the voice came nearer, he stood and smiled, "Why, Miss Strombeck, a man could come to think you spend more time in town than you do on the ranch. It's good to see you again."

"And it's good to see you. Father had to come on business, as usual. And as usual, we tagged along."

As she said this, her sister joined her.

"Ladies, I would like to introduce a friend from down home. This is Ivan Ivanov. He and his family have the I-5 Ranch up in the hills above Stevensville. Ivan has been assisting me with some work.

"Ivan, this is Allie and Polly Strombeck."

Ivan stood, joining Rory in that courtesy, but clearly, he had no idea what to do next. This was a world totally unfamiliar to him. Idly he wondered what old Kiril would think of these bold women. He wasn't sure whether to offer to shake hands or just what to do. He had no desire to shake hands or otherwise touch these women. In fact, he was quite frightened. He hoped it didn't show.

One by one the ladies said, "Hello, Ivan. It's good to meet you." There was no offer of a handshake.

"We were just finishing up here, ladies, but would you join us?"

At Rory's invitation, Allie, with a single step was beside Ivan. Polly stepped close to Rory, who pulled out a chair and held it while she sat down. Ivan was totally frozen. He couldn't have duplicated Rory's actions even if he had tried. Finally, Allie adjusted her own chair and sat down.

For the remainder of the evening, through the pie for the men and the entire dinner for the women, the girls carried the conversation. Ivan said fewer than a dozen words the entire time.

To the query from the girls of, "So what's been

happening in your lives since we first met you a few weeks ago?"

Rory got by with, "Oh, you know, ranch work. Dull and boring."

Ivan, true to form, said nothing.

The evening ended with Rory saying, "If you ladies will excuse us, we have a long day tomorrow and an early start. Greet your father for me, please. Perhaps we'll meet again if I ever get back down this way."

Polly responded, "Or perhaps could make a point of it."

Not liking where that comment might lead, Rory said good night and excused himself. Ivan found enough courage to duplicate Rory's good night.

THE MEN RODE BACK into Stevensville two days later. The town looked the same. To Rory, it was home, or close enough to the Double J to pass as such.

To Ivan, nothing was the same. It was as if he had fallen into a funnel and been squeezed out the other end, a different man. He had run through miles of forest trails, chasing fugitives, and found them. One man was in jail, the other dead by Ivan's hand. He had visited the ranch of a widow and her son. He had seen the big city, slept in a hotel, and eaten several meals in dining rooms, all new experiences to him. Perhaps most seriously, he had met two beautiful ranch girls, girls as much at home in the city as they would be on their own ranch. That girls who could ride, rope, and work with the men, while still coming to the big city feeling comfortable in such beautiful clothes, was a revelation to him. He hardly knew how to think about it.

At his single mention of the Strombeck sisters on their ride home, Rory had answered, "They're a bit more outspoken than most, but they're still lovely girls. Ranch raised. Ride and work cattle along with the men. Carry Colt .44s everywhere they go. Good girls. And they will choose their own husbands. They are not the kind of girls your friend Kiril would approve of."

After a moment of contemplation, Ivan said, "I am not so sure that Kiril is really a friend."

Not wishing to push Ivan on that topic, but wanting to know more about the old hermit, Rory asked, "What's with the old fella? Living up there in the bush alone. I can't make heads nor tails of it."

"Kiril is just Kiril. He came there because of my family. He knew no one else from the old country. When he met my father in another town one day by accident, father invited him to the ranch. My mother ran him off without even feeding him. Still, he wanted to be near someone from home, so he moved into the hills and built that cabin. He has enough money to buy what he needs, and there he sits, waiting for someone to come speak the old language with him."

Although the Ivanov family had spent little time in Stevensville, still it was at least a semblance of home to Ivan. It represented relative security, second to the ranch, of course, but much safer and less challenging than the big city.

The men shook hands as they parted, both heading back to their homes.

"Ivan. Alone, I could not have done what we accomplished together. Thank you. It was a good piece of work. I'd be happy to ride with you anytime, except for that slide onto the BL Ranch. I'm not doing that again. God bless, my friend. We'll see you again soon."

"Yes, soon. It is finished now? This matter with these two men?"

"It is mostly finished. At least, my part is finished. I still wonder how the judge found those three widows, but I can't think of that right now. Now I need a few days' rest and time to think, and I wish to stay around town for a while. I need to talk with the town fathers."

Ivan nodded at that and turned his horse toward the uphill trail. "Perhaps you will ride with Sonia when next she wishes to visit home."

"Perhaps. Yes, indeed, perhaps."

Ivan nudged his horse into action. Rory turned for the dining room. He didn't need any more coffee, although he would probably have one. But he had a question. When Sonia set his coffee in front of him, he said quietly so only she could hear, "Tippet, over at the livery, he has a fringe top buggy he rents out. If I rented it, would you like to go for a ride after church on Sunday?"

Sonia's smile could light up the night, or at least Rory's eyes. "I would like that. It is getting cold. We would need a lap robe. And a lunch. I can bring a lunch."

"And I'll bring a lap robe."

They grinned at each other as Rory stood.

"Sunday, then."

"Sunday."

FUGITIVES FROM JUSTICE

A SNEAK PEEK AT BOOK TWO

Historical and action-packed, award-winning author Reg Quist delivers book two in a series that details the adventures that define and stretch a young lawman.

At the request of the state administrator, Rory Jamison is assigned with putting together a census of the county—in preparation for the organizational vote that will determine Rory's future as County Sheriff.

But as a vicious gang passes through in an attempt to reach the railway and holds up a local bank, Rory gets tangled up in a hostage situation that sees a ranch family thrown into despair as their lives are put on the line.

With determination—and the voice of his dead father reminding him of his duty—Rory dives headfirst into a perilous situation with an unforeseen outcome.

Full of deception, frontier action, and desolate pursuits, Rory is on a steadfast mission to end his county's violence once and for all...while protecting the innocent lives of those caught in the crossfire.

1

"HELLO, RANCH. LOOK'N FOR SHERIFF JAMISON. WE'RE need'n the sheriff in town. Sheriff. Sheriff, you here about somewhere?"

The voice was loud, carrying from the ranch roadway to the house and further, taking in the barn and the neat little cabin that sat between those two structures. The rider was just easing his horse to a slower pace, not sure if he should race on toward the barn or call again at the house or cabin.

Key Wardle had ridden, with obvious excitement, into the yard of the Double J Ranch. His excitement had twin sources. The first, and most troubling, was the fact that the Double J was home to the very beautiful Jamison sisters. That alone was enough to make a young fellow kick his toe in the dust of the roadway and whip his hat off in reverence.

Key was new to town, having arrived just weeks before from a ranch in the mountainous section of Wyoming, off to the northwest of Laramie. He hadn't met either girl, but Dusty Macklin, owner of the Roundup Ranch Supplies store had pointed them out.

The second reason for his excitement was that the bank had been robbed, but somehow that seemed like a dull matter compared to the other.

He had just made the decision to carry on to the barn, or perhaps even into the grazing pasture where the men might be working, when, glancing around, he saw two doors open almost simultaneously. The first to open was the house door. And there, as if she had just floated in from a special, dreamy part of the universe, stood Nancy, the younger of the two girls. He pulled his gelding to such a sudden halt that he jerked forward in the saddle, his face almost touching the animal's neck, a most unhorseman-like action for a ranch-raised man, someone who had been riding since before he could walk.

Neither of the young people spoke, although they both had questions ready. The questions were halted by the opening of the cabin door. Sheriff Jamison stepped out and asked, "What's all the hollering about?"

Pulling his hand away from the hat he was about to lift in deference to the girl he had been longing to meet, he turned his head toward the sheriff.

"Been a bank robbery, Sheriff. Folks in town are pretty wrought up about it. Dusty Macklin, who I work for down at the Roundup Ranch Supplies, sent me out. Said to bring you in. So here I am."

"Yes. I can easily see that you're here all right. Tell me more about the robbery. Was Jesse Ambrewster hurt?"

"Banged up pretty bad, but not yet dead. Leastwise not so's I know about it. Still alive last I heard. When he refused to open the big safe, those boys thought to beat him till he changed his mind, but he done no such a thing."

"What about his clerk?"

"Robbers took him."

"What do you mean, the robbers took him?"

"Seems like pretty clear use of the language, Sheriff. Took. Like they held their guns on the banker while they hustled the clerk out and threw him on a saddled horse that was tied there. Wasn't no way their horse, neither. Anyway, they took the clerk and scampered out of town just as fast as their mounts would carry them. One was bleeding pretty bad. Shot in the shoulder or arm. There wasn't time to sort all that out. Anyway, there was blood dripping all down his arm and leaving a trail off the ends of his fingers. I seen that much from clear across on the opposite boardwalk. He might have been look'n a bit sick too. Like I said, there wasn't a lot of time to fit all the details in."

"Who shot him?"

"Him? Why the banker. That's who. Wasn't no one else there, sept'n Ma and the clerk, and neither one was tot'n a firearm. How he managed to do what he done while they were a whopping on him with fists and feet I don't know, but that's what Ma Gamble, her from the dining room, said. She was there. Making a deposit I'm guessing. Anyway, it was her that carried the story to the town. Seems like the banker, he refused to open the safe. Told the men to get out before he got angry. Who'd have ever thought that of an old man like the banker? That just made the robbers more angry. Ma, she backed into a corner and told the clerk to get down on the floor. The robbers, they went to whopping on the banker, like I just said. Then, that old man, he pulls a small handgun from his jacket pocket and shoots one of them fellas.

"The banker, he was pretty stove-up, what with the punching and the kicking and the whack on the head with the butt of a gun. Still, he somehow got off that shot. Ma says the robbers, they kicked him a couple more times, cleaned out the cash drawer, and then dragged the clerk out. They told Ma to tell you that if you follow, they'll kill the clerk. Anyway, you had best come to town."

Rory turned back into the cabin and was out in a few seconds with his already tied bedroll and some trail provisions he kept at the ready. Key, just starting to relax and get his wits about him, made the mistake of looking around the yard. Now, adding greatly to his unsettled mind, there were two Jamison girls listening. Only they were no longer on the porch, they were right beside him. Right there beside his horse. Why, he could have reached down and touched either one of them, a thought that both thrilled and terrified him.

When the sheriff started walking toward the stable, Key nudged his animal into movement and followed. He hoped there was safety in gaining some distance from the girls.

Within a few minutes, the two men were riding out of the JJ Ranch yard, heading to town. When Key said something, using the title sheriff, Rory corrected him.

"The name's Rory. I'm guessing you have a name. Mind sharing it?"

"No, of course not. Key. That's what they call me."

ABOUT THE AUTHOR

Reg Quist's pioneer heritage includes sod shacks, prairie fires, home births, and children's graves under the prairie sod, all working together in the lives of people creating their own space in a new land.

Out of that early generation came farmers, ranchers, business men and women, builders, military graves in faraway lands, Sunday Schools that grew to become churches, plus story tellers, musicians, and much more.

Hard work and self-reliance were the hallmark of those previous great generations, attributes that were absorbed by the following generation.

Quist's career choice took him into the construction world. From heavy industrial work, to construction camps in the remote northern bush, the author emulated his grandfathers, who were both builders, as well as pioneer farmers and ranchers.

It is with deep thankfulness that Quist says, "I am a part of the first generation to truly enjoy the benefits of the labors of the pioneers. My parents and their parents worked incredibly hard, and it is well for us to remember".